3800 18

KT-151-607

HIGH LIFE HIGHLAND

THE
RIVAL

Charlotte Duckworth has spent the past fifteen years working as an interiors and lifestyle journalist, writing for a wide range of consumer magazines and websites. She lives in Surrey with her partner and their young daughter. You can find out more on her website: charlotteduckworth.com.

THE
RIVAL

CHARLOTTE DUCKWORTH

HIGH LIFE HIGHLAND LIBRARIES	
38001800365060	
BERTRAMS	04/09/2018
THR	£14.99
AF	

Quercus

First published in Great Britain in 2018 by

Quercus Editions Ltd
Carmelite House
50 Victoria Embankment
London EC4Y 0DZ

An Hachette UK company

Copyright © 2018 Charlotte Duckworth

The moral right of Charlotte Duckworth to be
identified as the author of this work has been
asserted in accordance with the Copyright,
Designs and Patents Act, 1988.

All rights reserved. No part of this publication
may be reproduced or transmitted in any form
or by any means, electronic or mechanical,
including photocopy, recording, or any
information storage and retrieval system,
without permission in writing from the publisher.

A CIP catalogue record for this book is available
from the British Library

HB ISBN 978 1 78747 093 4
TPB ISBN 978 1 78747 094 1
EBOOK ISBN 978 1 78747 096 5

This book is a work of fiction. Names, characters,
businesses, organizations, places and events are
either the product of the author's imagination
or used fictitiously. Any resemblance to
actual persons, living or dead, events or
locales is entirely coincidental.

10 9 8 7 6 5 4 3 2 1

Typeset by CC Book Production

Printed and bound in Great Britain by Clays Ltd, Elcograf S.p.A.

Every mother is a working mother.

ANON

One mouthful at a time. That's it. You can do it.

The smell of my own milk in my nostrils, and something else in my ears: a voice. Gentle, infuriating, insistent. A hint of desperation.

Please.

The cold press of metal against my lips.

Feeding me like a baby. Like a *baby*. I grab his arm, tell him how funny it is. Everything is back to front, mixed up. Everyone swapping places. Musical chairs!

Eat, drink, sleep. That's what the nurse keeps telling me.

But the texture is wrong. Too lumpy. Something's not right. It's sticking to the roof of my mouth, clinging to the cracked skin on my lips. I spit it out, let it run down my chin. It's obvious now. He's trying to poison me. He's on her side. Of course he is.

She always gets what she wants. People like her always do.

Ashley, a voice says. Funny, it sounds like mine.

He shakes his head, pushes the food into my mouth once more.

No. The spoon catches my teeth, sending a spike of pain shooting through my gums.

It's just us in here.

PART ONE

NOW

SEVEN MONTHS LATER

Helena

It's Tuesday. Again.

The Tuesdays of my previous existence slipped by unnoticed. None of the loaded expectation of a Monday, the bitter-sweet bliss of a Sunday, nor the joyful anticipation of a Thursday. Instead, they simply vanished into the working week, absorbed by the busyness of life, eaten up by meetings and emails and Things To Attend To.

Tuesdays are somewhat different now.

There's a poster in my therapist's office. It's hidden behind the door, as though she's not quite sure if it's in good taste. Colourful calligraphy reminds me *It's good to talk!* every time the door is closed, barring my escape. Good for her, yes. Even now, I still drive the four and a half miles to her practice, once a week. I pay my six pieces of silver (ten-pound notes) and sit on her sofa (I am still a little disappointed by this – I had pictured a Le Corbusier for that money, at the very least) and I cry like a bereaved mother is supposed to. I cry so much that I hate myself. I cry until blood

5

vessels burst under my eyelids, until I'm so full of self-loathing that I want to scrub myself out and start all over again. And at the end of my forty-five minutes I wipe my face, blow my nose and go home like a good girl.

Tuesdays.

Jack is waiting for my return, his face a backlit smudge hovering at the living-room window as I pull up in my car. He's hoping desperately for a breakthrough, for a sign that I've made some progress. But I have nothing to give him. Instead, I step into the hallway, put my bag down on the floor and silently wrap my arms around him. He doesn't ask me how the session has gone.

Tonight, as usual, there's something warm in the oven, waiting: comfort food – even though he knows I'll only pick at it. We make small talk over dinner and then, despite the fact it makes me drowsy with the medication I'm on, I drink red wine in front of the fireplace.

It's not so much a fireplace as a brick-built fire *area*, complete with enormous tiled hearth, wood-burning stove and old rusty nails, left over from the previous owners' collection of horse brasses. This is what you get for escaping to the country. An acre of land that leads down to a sad excuse for a river, with five bedrooms, two bathrooms, outbuildings to house your husband's new carpentry business, and no neighbours for three-quarters of a mile.

The perfect family home. Except for the people dying on my doorstep on a regular basis, that is.

As we do every evening, we sit in front of this fireplace, in what people always describe as a companionable silence, but which is more often merely indifferent. Jack is reading. I know he wants to be watching TV really, a political drama on Netflix, something like that would *do nicely*, but he's trying to be supportive, by providing the space for me to 'open up'. Instead of talking to him, however, I am guiltily staring into that space, as I always do, counting the rusted horse-brass nails in the bricks, from top to bottom. There are eighteen, but I always count them carefully, in case I've missed one.

Today I'm thinking how, in a previous life, I would have used these nails for something decorative. To hang pictures, perhaps? Me, Jack and our adorable brood. No, that would have looked too messy. What else, then? At Christmas, you could use them to hang a wreath from. Not a wreath, that's the wrong word. Wreaths are for front doors and graves. A garland. A beautiful winding garland, with holly and snowberries – it would twist all around the arched opening to the fire, creating a 'centrepiece'.

The week is stretching ahead of us, empty and cold. We haven't lit the fire yet this year and my toes are chilly underneath my blanket. October is such an empty month. I wonder what we can do with a cold, dull weekend at the end of a cold, dull week, just the two of us here at home. A few weeks ago, my father made noises about coming to visit us this Sunday but, as usual, he hasn't confirmed. I phoned his PA yesterday. She had no record of his planned visit in her diary.

I swallow a large gulp of wine.

Suddenly, Jack puts down his book. My eyes rest on the spine. It's a biography of a racing car driver, Senna. I am vaguely aware that he died young but that he died doing what he loved. People were devastated at his death, lamenting it as a terrible waste, but I envy him. That's the way to go. We all have to go at some point, so why not go like that? And after all, death is only sad for the people you leave behind.

Jack is looking at me.

'What are you thinking about?' he says. In the dull light, his face looks more drawn than I remember it, and I give myself an inward kick for not noticing him more, the toll it's taken on him too.

'Senna,' I say, because it's true. I nod towards the book laid down on the arm of his chair. 'I was thinking how much I envied him.'

Jack shakes his head. He doesn't know how to deal with this. In the old days when I was given to moments of self-pity he would write me off as being melodramatic, but I'm untouchable now.

'Darling—' he says, and I know he's about to ask me how my therapy session went, but he thinks better of it and so he stops.

'It's fine,' I say, giving a lopsided smile. 'Sorry. I was being stupid.' I adopt a sing-song voice, all feigned nonchalance. I pick up my wine glass, holding it aloft. 'Don't worry. Not going to top myself. Not this week when there's still Malbec left in the cellar!'

A flicker of disapproval passes across his face; his lips are set in a line. He knows the drinking makes my depression worse. I hate what I am doing to him.

'I was only going to say that you had a phone call while you were out,' he says. 'But you looked so serious . . .'

A phone call. The way he's said it makes me think that finally, finally, she's got in touch. There's been an epiphany and she's penitent, devastated, she wants to beg for my forgiveness. She wants to make it right, somehow, even though she knows she never can.

But this is the Ash of my fantasies. She doesn't exist, because she isn't a real person. This isn't how Ash is. This is someone far removed from reality, someone I imagined into existence when I met her, someone I credited with more than she could ever deserve.

Suddenly, the wine tastes acrid and I put my glass down on the coffee table, watching as one dark red drip travels back down the inside of the glass.

'Who was it?' I ask. In the few seconds before he replies, I try to guess. Kate, perhaps? My father? Not my mother . . .

And then, just as he tells me, I realize I already know. Of course it was him, he's been trying to track me down for weeks. I don't answer my mobile any more. Most of the time, in fact, it's switched off. But I have seen the missed calls gathering, and I have listened to his breezy message.

Jack lets out a great sigh. And I wonder if he knows, or if he's just tired of dredging up the past, never knowing how I'll react.

'David,' he says, and the name is somehow comforting; proof that my powers of deduction, if nothing else, aren't as sodden as the rest of me. 'He wants you to ring him.'

THEN

Ash

I take a seat in the furthest corner of the reception area and pull out my notebook and pen. Today is a triumph and it isn't yet 8.30 a.m. I begin to write.

It's your attitude not your aptitude that determines your altitude.

It's a secret, this notebook. Not even Gary knows about it. A few years ago I heard someone talk about morning pages. At first, I misinterpreted: *mourning* pages – thinking it was something you wrote to lament all you'd loved and lost. Self-indulgent. But then I read an article about them online – how they'd transformed people's lives and mental health – and I decided, why not? Any excuse for new stationery.

So I started. Just one page per day of rambling thoughts. Notes on the weather, my fitness, the condition of my skin, how Gran is. But lately I've become a little, I'll admit it, obsessed with aphorisms. I have an app, and every morning at 6 a.m. when my alarm goes off, one flashes across my screen. A focus for the day.

And today's seems apt.

I bring the pen back to the page as the running commentary begins in my head.

Drum roll, please!

The Life of Ashley Thompson: A Biopic

An unwanted child. Brought up by her grandparents, she grew up in a home where a game of Cluedo was considered an intellectual pursuit. Where the only thing to read was **Woman's Weekly,** *and where crosswords were ignored but word searches were agonized over. But she rose above such challenges, secured her place at the London School of Economics (editor's note: not Oxford, but that was clearly a case of prejudice – the interviewer heard her accent and wrote her off immediately), studied Business, gained a first with her dissertation on 'Women Who Smashed the Glass Ceiling', spent two years interning and working in a clothes shop to pay the bills, and now, here she is, the newest recruit for one of the biggest tech start-ups of the past five years. In a brand-new office. On the fifteenth floor, with floor-to-ceiling windows overlooking Granary Square.*

Kids, learn from Ashley: you can achieve anything, if you try hard enough.

It's your <u>attitude</u> not your <u>aptitude</u> that determines your <u>altitude</u>!

I draw a border around it, the corners spinning off into elaborate curls. My handwriting, one of the few things that frustrate me, is not neat and ordered like my mind. It has too many flicks and twists, which is why I always write in capitals if I think anyone will see. It might look aggressive, but it's better than the alternative.

What else?

Today is the first day of my new job. Before work I ran 10km and got a personal best, if you can trust the app I'm using, which I'm not entirely sure you can, as it seemed to lose me briefly somewhere between Colliers Wood and Tooting. I arrived at 8.15 a.m., but my manager isn't actually in yet. So I'm waiting in the lobby to be collected. I need to get a photo pass to allow me in and out of the building. The woman on reception said the machine was broken at the moment but that an engineer was coming to fix it this afternoon, so hopefully I'll have one before the end of the day.

I pause, and cross the last two sentences out. Snore, snore.

On the way in, I had two double espressos, which I now slightly regret. My hands are quite shaky. We shall see how the day pans out. I've already made great plans for—

I'm interrupted mid-sentence by the sound of a chair scraping. I look up. A girl with stringy orange hair and uneven freckles has decided to sit opposite me, despite the other four tables in the waiting area being empty.

She dumps her handbag on the table right in front of me. It's a Mulberry, but it's old, battered, almost an embarrassment.

'Hi,' she says, smiling. 'Your first day, too?'

Fake it till you feel it.

I give her my broadest grin, closing my notebook.

'Hello!' *A little too high-pitched there, Ashley, sort yourself out.* 'Yes. Exciting, isn't it?'

'I'll say. I cannot believe I've got a job here – I keep having to pinch myself!' She gives a small, almost apologetic laugh. 'My little sister is such a fan of KAMU, she spends hours poring over all the product reviews and is obsessed with their editorials. I think she's more excited than I am. Did you know they have a ping-pong table in one of the meeting rooms?'

I wonder what I can add to this, but am saved from further conversation by Helena's approach. Today she is in skinny jeans, pumps and a Breton top, and I am disappointed. Somehow, the UK Creative Director of a Silicon Valley import shouldn't be wearing jeans. And the Breton top? Does she think she's Kate Middleton?

She looks a bit like her, in fact. Not quite as thin, but with deep-set almond eyes. But blonde, of course. Her hair is long and curly and volumized. I suspect a weekly blow-dry in a Chelsea salon. I've seen the sort of places, watched the sort of women, on my many window-shopping trips down the King's Road.

'Ashley!' she calls, hurrying towards me.

What would her running commentary say? I know her story almost as well as my own; I did my research before my first interview.

Helena Brenton (née Cawston), only child. Oxbridge with an MBA. Clever, then, but upper middle class, brought up in the Home Counties and educated at boarding school. Thirty-four. Recently married to a supremely eligible, supremely clichéd banker. Her father owns a chain of department stores, while her mother had a brief career as a model before Helena was born.

I look up and smile at her, wondering whether to stand now or wait for her to reach me. Opposite me, Freckles grabs her phone and starts fiddling with it, downcast, as though she's last to be picked for the netball team.

'Helena, hello!' That screechy voice again. But Helena doesn't notice my voice, or my concern. Of course she doesn't. Women like her don't notice anything.

'Sorry to keep you,' she says, slightly breathless herself, but only because she's rushed here. I'm an inconvenient chore, something she's remembered at the last minute. 'Our app crashed so I've been having crisis talks with our tech team. Shall we get a coffee before we go up? I'm desperate for one.'

I search for an excuse. Another coffee would send me over the edge; into what Gary calls my 'manic mode'. It's not even two seconds before the escape forms on my lips.

'Oh, I don't drink it,' I say, confidently, as I stand up, the lie suddenly not a lie as the idea plants itself in my mind. 'I don't drink any form of caffeine. It dehydrates and ages you. But I'll have some sparkling water.'

Helena's eyebrows twitch, ever so slightly. She strides towards the coffee bar at one corner of the reception, all neon lights and dark-stained wood, then looks back over her shoulder.

'I'm not sure you'll last five minutes at Kiss and Make Up without caffeine but I admire your . . .' She tails off.

She doesn't admire me yet, I think. But she will.

NOW

Helena

It's late. Or early, depending on how you look at it. 2.34 a.m., to be precise. Like most new mothers, it's not unusual that I'm awake at this time. But of course, I'm not like most new mothers.

I look over at Jack. He's sleeping. How he sleeps through the accidents is beyond me. I know he wears earplugs – he has done since the noise of his Fulham Palace Road days – but he complains they fall out. I stroke his back before I climb out of bed, pushing my feet into my slippers and tucking my phone into my pyjama waistband. I tiptoe down the stairs and across the flagstoned hall.

Tonight I heard the car coming – I was awake, anyway. There was a split second before impact when I thought the driver might make it. Might be lucky, might just miss. But it wasn't to be.

Outside, I can see the car sticking up above the wall. It's twisted slightly, leaning on its side, but it hasn't flipped over completely. I leave our driveway and walk towards the wreckage. It's a silver Corsa this time, an old model. Unlike the car, the driver behind the smashed windscreen is young – and not drunk, I don't think. I steady myself, breathing deeply and squinting the tears away as I open the passenger door and lean into the car. After checking he's still breathing, I call an ambulance. His wallet is lying on the front seat beside him and I find his driving licence inside. Born in 1994.

Aaron. His address is on the licence, too – he lives in the next village. He was probably coming back from the pub after lock-in. But if he's a local, he ought to have known what he was taking on, really. Ought to have been prepared.

I remember the piggy-eyed estate agent reassuring us that the unbelievable price of our house had nothing to do with the road. That of course it wasn't dangerous, that the spate of accidents last year happened before the farmer who owns the field opposite had taken down the cobblestone wall, replaced it with wire fencing. That it was perfectly safe now. *A wonderful spot to raise a family*, he'd said, one eyebrow arching at Jack.

As I am thinking of him and his lies, the boy regains consciousness, his eyelids fluttering open like a baby waking from a nap.

'Stay still,' I say, leaning across the passenger seat to squeeze his hand. 'It's going to be OK.'

'I want my mum,' he says, beginning to cry. He starts to jerk about, to try to climb from the car.

'Stay still,' I say, a little more strictly. 'You'll do yourself more damage if you keep moving.'

'Mum . . . please . . . my mum.'

His mum. I can picture her: plump, cheeks mottled with broken thread veins, bushy eyebrows and a full smile. Proud of her son. He probably has a brother, or perhaps a younger sister. She's still at school. Aaron. He's her big brother, her hero. And now he's lying here, helpless and spotty with shaving rash, a line of blood running down his cheek from underneath his baseball cap. I can't see what's under it, what the damage is. His breath is coming fast and shallow now, almost as though he's sobbing. Like a fish removed from water, desperate for air.

'My mum . . . I want . . . my mum,' he says, twisting his head to stare at me with eyes that seem both right here and far away at the same time. I shush him, squeeze his hand, tell him to hold on and that the ambulance will be here shortly. I tell him not to worry, say again that he's going to be OK.

But how do I know whether he'll be OK? The last year has shown me how deceptive your health can be. How one minute you can be absolutely fine, and the next . . .

The ambulance takes longer to come than it should have done. I am timing it on my phone: twelve minutes exactly. A good five minutes over the average response time. I know that Saturday nights are incredibly busy, so I'm not too surprised. But still, it's not good enough, is it? Imagine how much blood you can lose in twelve minutes.

They thank me, as they always do. Sometimes I recognize the paramedics, but not tonight. They always look at me with sympathy and confusion. I know what they're thinking – why does she live here? Why doesn't she move? Who is she? What's her story? I wonder if they can tell that I'm younger than I look, that underneath the eye bags there's 'something of a beauty, like her mother', as I once overheard someone say at one of my father's parties.

They strap him up, and put him on a stretcher. They don't remove his baseball cap, so I'll never know what was going on underneath it. I hear them muttering something about his leg. I hadn't noticed his leg; I was too taken with the blood running down his cheek. I wait while they load him into the ambulance, squeezing his hand one last time as they take him away. The police are busy making notes; I tell them what I know. It's cold and I'm only wearing a thin hoodie, grabbed from the rack by the door. I want to get back inside.

As I turn to leave, one of the policewomen asks me if I'm all right. I tell her I'm fine. Because I am. Because, upsetting though it always is, nothing will ever be as upsetting as when I lost her.

I'm back in my office now.

It's called my office, but I don't do any work in here, so really it's just a sanctuary; a place to hide from the world. Jack decorated it for me, as a surprise, filling it with mid-century furniture – a rosewood desk, an original Arne Jacobsen chair, an Anglepoise, String shelving. The walls are lined in a deep brown grasscloth, the carpet a sludge green, thick pile. At the window hang slatted vertical blinds, the kind that gather dust in NHS dentists' waiting rooms and that most people rip out, nowadays. But the scheme works. It hangs together.

When I'm tucked away in here, Jack will sometimes pop his head round the door unexpectedly and catch me, poring over a spreadsheet. He'll wink, smile with forced cheeriness and say something like, 'I knew it, world domination – Round Two – not far off, then!' and I'll grin and nod back and wish he'd disappear.

Jack.

What can I say about Jack? We haven't slept together for more than a year. He's more interested in the rugby, now, than in sex. He has no idea how to help me. He's kind. He liked me better when I was working.

None of it is his fault. I can tell I'm an inconvenience now: like an ageing relative he must take care of, someone he views with nostalgic affection but at the same time wishes would hurry up and die. I've thought about it, a bit. Dying, I mean. But I'm a coward. Maybe if they could find a totally painless way to do it, maybe then I'd consider it. But deep down, there's still that flame, flickering in my heart. Just a tiny amount of hope. That things will get better. That things *can* get better. That's the most torturous thing of all.

I don't do any work in here, but I do keep track of things. Someone has to, and seeing as I'm closest to it . . . Something has to be done about the road, and I'm determined to force the Council into action. There's a calendar pinned on the back of my door. Each day there's an accident I mark the calendar with an A. In red if there's been a fatality.

I won't have long before Jack comes to find me, so I make tonight's notes in my file. Aaron Turner. He's the first for three weeks. It's been a peaceful three weeks. October has crept in with a gentle sweep, rather than a dramatic downturn. It's still mild during the day, and the only chill is first thing in the morning – a pleasing, crisp bite that makes the air feel fresher. The winter will be worse. There'll be more to come in the following weeks.

From my desk I can see where Aaron's life changed forever. I make a note of his words to me, his expression, what he was wearing, all the little pieces of his story.

And then, pricked by shame, I take out my sketchbook and begin to draw. It's the only way; by tomorrow, I will have forgotten the details. Those eyes, asking for his mum. I want to remember them.

THEN

Ash

I'm aware that it's not the done thing, when you're new, to interrupt your manager in full flow. But still. When someone is so
wrong, what are you supposed to do?

'I think,' I say, my voice louder than intended as it cuts across
the discussion, 'you'll find that Instagram works much better
when it's more off the cuff.'

Helena looks at me, her eyes hardening, but not unkindly –
more with surprise.

'Sorry?'

'Instagram,' I reply, swallowing back my nerves. 'Scheduling it
will look flat, lifeless. It's more important that it seems sponta-
neous, natural. And technically, you can't schedule posts, anyway
– they don't let you. It's nothing like Twitter.' I've warmed up
now. 'And you certainly can't try to ram a corporate message into
each caption. A sure-fire way to fail. People don't engage with
that, they slag it off.'

There's a pause. The digital bigwigs – I haven't quite worked
out yet what they are about but they are certainly more senior
than I am, and they have flown over from the US for a week of

'onboarding' of the new staff – stare at me as though I have interrupted them on the toilet. They've never even seen Instagram, let alone used it. Why the hell are they in this meeting, anyway?

'Well,' Helena replies, noting the bigwigs' response. 'I think, you'll find there's not a great deal of point in having a corporate Instagram account if we don't use it to some extent to promote the core values—'

'Core values?' I interrupt.

'I appreciate your input . . .' Helena begins.

'Listen, I don't want to seem rude but, well, you've hired me for my social media expertise, right? I know what I'm talking about. I've curated a personal account of more than three thousand followers with barely any money, glamour or excitement in my life. Not that I don't find my life exciting but . . . what I'm saying is: trust me. I know what I'm talking about. This is make-up. We don't want just boring conventional pack shots borrowed from our suppliers. We need something fun, something inspirational – something about the brand, behind the scenes . . .'

I'm in full flow, what Gran describes as 'on a mission', and nothing and nobody is going to stop me.

'Jesus, this is London! This is the glamour capital of the world.' I've never been to Paris, so it's probably true. I stand up. I read somewhere that standing gives your message gravitas, and I gesture towards the floor-to-ceiling windows, sweeping my arm across the view. 'Look at this place! It's *so* . . . *cool*. People think we're cool. We're the coolest website for cool people and our followers are cool. We need to reflect that by being cool ourselves. You know, shots of the roof terrace with our staff drinking champagne before a night out . . .'

The bigwigs raise their eyebrows but I ignore them.

'Shots inside our own personal make-up bags . . . competitions . . . oh, you *know* the sort of thing . . . boyfriend does my make-up, that stuff!'

'Boyfriend does my make-up?'

'Yes, it's when you get your boyfriend to do your make-up for you. And you film the results. It's huge with YouTubers.'

'Yes,' says Helena, her voice tight. 'Thanks, Ashley, for your input. It's appreciated, and I do see your point.' Her tone is clear: it's your first day, shut up and sit down.

I cross my arms and sit, sulkily, back in my chair. I don't care that this isn't the 'done thing'. What does it matter what the done thing is, if it's so bloody wrong?

There's a silence that seems to stretch and stretch until it finally snaps, with Helena and one of the bigwigs both speaking at the same time.

'Well, this has been . . .' he says.

'I think, perhaps . . .' Helena says.

The bigwig tails off.

'I think, perhaps,' Helena repeats, 'Ashley has a point. We did, indeed, hire her for her knowledge of this sector – of our core audience. I'd like to put together some proposals for you.' There's a pause and she glances across at me, then back at the suits. They're not wearing suits, of course, but they might as well be. Dinosaurs. 'If I may. Some mock-ups of the sort of thing that I think Ashley is referring to. We can work on them together, OK, Ashley? I'll send them over first thing in the morning, for you to see. If you think we're on to something, we can take it from there?'

One of the VIPs starts fiddling with his BlackBerry. A BlackBerry, for fuck's sake. Just shows how out of touch he is. He looks up when Helena finishes.

'Yes, OK, sounds great,' he says, his voice monotone.

'Excellent,' Helena replies.

Stalemate.

The tension is relieved by the sound of the glass door creaking open. We all look up as a man walks in. He's somewhere in his early forties, with perfectly preened black hair, and the kind of deep tan you get from years of holidaying in the Caribbean. Even if I didn't know who he was already, I'd be able to tell that he is important from his perfectly white teeth, his perfectly rolled-up shirtsleeves revealing a big-faced watch, and the way Helena and the other men look at him.

'David!' Helena says, and there's something in her voice, not nerves exactly, but excitement. From the flash of trepidation in her eyes, she clearly thinks a lot of him. 'Thanks for popping by!'

She turns to me.

'Ashley, I'd like you to meet David. He's the CEO for KAMU UK.'

David walks towards me with an outstretched hand and I stand up and shake it. The skin on his palm is smooth and his grip the perfect strength. But I see something else glinting on his other hand. Something my Google searches didn't tell me. Of course he's taken. I imagine his wife, always waiting for him at home as he toils at the digital coalface. Spending a life surrounded by Jo Malone candles. She's probably called Claudia, her defining features being her long blonde hair and fabulous friends. And, of course, there'll be two children dressed head to toe in Boden, all loose ponytails and wide toothy grins.

'Great to meet you,' he says, and he sounds like he means it. 'Helena was very pleased to have you on board, says you're quite the trailblazer. We're all very excited to see what you can bring to the company.'

'I'm very excited to see what the company can bring to me,' I say, and they all laugh, as though I've made a really clever joke.

He turns to the bigwigs. 'Listen, guys, I'm pleased I caught you. We've had some feedback from the developers . . . coffee?'

And in that moment, his charm dissipates. Helena and I no longer exist. We have been dismissed and it's time to disappear.

Helena pushes her chair back, stands up and closes her notebook. She clears her throat loudly and makes a big show of checking her iPhone.

'Sorry, sorry,' David says. 'How rude of me. Had you finished?' He gives her a full smile, his eyes sweeping over her face in a manner that could almost be seen as loving, but she's having none of it. He thinks he's nurtured her, I realize. Taken her under his wing, made her what she is today.

'Yes, just about,' she says, her voice just a tiny bit too loud, just a tiny bit *rude*, summoning everyone's attention again. 'We'll get off and get on with that, then. Pick this up again tomorrow.'

So much power play in one tiny meeting. But I'm pleased that Helena has put them all in their place – surprised but pleased. Perhaps I've underestimated her.

'Ashley?' Helena says, glancing sideways at me.

'Sure. Let's head,' I reply, and I don't know where this alien business jargon has come from. It's certainly not something I've ever said before, but it slips out so easily and I want to smile with self-satisfaction.

We leave the meeting room without saying goodbye. It's a small thing – perhaps no one even notices – but it feels rude and it feels defiant and it feels good.

You have to visualize a goal to achieve it. It's 9.30 p.m. I waited until everyone had left before going home for the day. Even David left before me, coming out of his glass cube and waving at me from across the empty desks as he whistled his way towards the lift. He'll remember that I was still there, he'll appreciate my working late on my first day. But what he won't know is that my reluctance to leave wasn't just to impress him.

I double-check the maths on the train home. My new salary will cover the rent; it'll be tight, but I can do it, and Maria has already said I can continue doing shifts at the shop on Saturdays, which will give me an extra £300 or so per month. My feet are heavy as they take me closer to the inevitable conversation and its inevitable messy ending.

Gary.

I always get myself into these situations, I only have myself to blame. It's such a *shame*. And Gran will be so upset; the fallout will last for weeks. I run through all the possible methods of getting it done, but, like ripping off a plaster, there's no easy or painless way to do it. I steel myself, remembering last Saturday when he rolled in at 3 a.m. and vomited all over the side of the bath, then bought me a box of Quality Street from the off-licence as some kind of apology. I deserve better.

Any woman deserves better. Gran will understand. Eventually.

'Listen. There's no easy way to say this but . . . it's not working,' I say, once I've pulled off my coat and dumped it on the arm of the sofa. Gary is sitting, as usual, in his pyjama bottoms in front of the TV. 'I think one of us should move out.'

'You're funny,' he says.

I sit next to him, resting my hands on my knees, and lean towards him. I adopt my most sympathetic voice – imagining that I am telling him his puppy needs to be put down.

'Let's be honest here,' I say, softly. 'We're drifting apart. We're not making each other happy.'

'What are you going on about?' he says, slumping back on the sofa. 'It's 10.30 p.m., where have you been, anyway? It was your first day at work – I've been waiting for you to come home. I even got us Domino's. Ham and pineapple, no cheese.' He gestures for me to turn round. 'They'll be cold now.' He actually sounds upset about that.

My eyes flick towards the corner of our living space – a square box with no discernible decoration or focal point. The 'kitchen' – comprising a four-cupboard-wide run of units – sits along one wall. I can see the pizza boxes stacked on the side, grease seeping through the cardboard.

'I thought you said you were going to cook?' I say, irritated. Does he seriously think that this is impressive, that this is what every woman wants to come home to after their first day in a new job? Is he really that stupid? How have I been that stupid, not to have realized it before? I am suddenly overcome with an almost allergic reaction to his presence. I want him out, now, with his greasy cardboard pizza boxes and his questionably stained pyjama bottoms. My brain fizzes with excitement as I imagine having the studio to myself – what I could do with the place. For a start, I'll paint the wall behind the sofa – something dramatic, a deep purple. And fill the place with plants. And some proper artwork, take down these hackneyed film posters.

Gary's shape swims into my vision, lumpen and unmoving on the sofa. His eyes are red and puffy, and the reason why is clear and unsurprising: a small tin left open on the coffee table, minuscule crumbs of illegal herb scattered next to it. His fingers are stained, his gingery hair slightly too long. Long enough to look lazy. He does not fit in with this picture.

'I don't make you happy,' I say, and I know I sound cold, but now I know he's stoned I'm not sure he'll care. I'm actually doing him a favour. It's a liberation, of sorts. 'Look at you. You're miserable. You're wasting your life. What happened to the guy I first met? The one with ambition, the one that moved off his bum in the evenings? Seriously. What about my special cooked dinner?'

'You know why I stopped cooking for you,' he says. 'Keeping up with all your faddy diets is exhausting.' His eyes redden further, and with dread I realize he is about to cry. Oh, please don't cry, I think. I really don't have the energy for this.

'Yes, well,' I say. 'Like I said, we've drifted apart. I'm not happy. I don't think you're happy. I'm only twenty-five. I don't want to continue in a relationship that doesn't work. I'm sorry. It's not my responsibility to make you happy. That's just the way it is.'

'Why are you being like this?' Gary says, sniffing a little. Thank God he knows not to break down in front of me.

I turn away from him and rummage for my phone in my handbag.

'Well, fuck you, then!' he says and I am momentarily impressed by this show of fire. He stands up then, pushing past me and sniffing heavily. He walks towards the bathroom, then stops and turns back. 'I've got nowhere to go! For Christ's sake, it's nearly 11 p.m. on a Monday!'

'I'm sure Jamie will put you up,' I say. I sit down with my phone, to see if I have any emails. I have to learn to stop trying to fix people. Gary is a grown-up, and I've tried my best. I really have. He is twenty-seven years old, he has a good job at an accountancy firm, and if he wasn't so lazy he could have made his first million before thirty. He's brainy enough – that was what attracted me to him in the first place. Brainy, not too arrogant. A bit tight-fisted, but frugality is never a bad thing. But the lack of ambition. Why doesn't he understand? There's nothing attractive, and there never will be, about someone who doesn't use everything they have, everything they've been given, to try to better themselves. He's just coasting along – working his way up at a snail's pace, passed over for promotion by the likes of Jamie. Mental note, Ashley: no more falling in love with job titles. They mean nothing.

I've got to start putting myself first. Behave like a man.

Gary reappears in the doorway with a rucksack flung over one shoulder. He's put some jeans on, thank God.

'I don't understand,' he says, pathetically. 'Is it the pot? I was just bored waiting for you . . .'

'No, it's not the pot . . . not just that, anyway.' I'm tired now, and the dull ache of a migraine hovers around my temples, trying to find the right place to take hold. My stupid fib to Helena. I've had no caffeine since first thing this morning. How am I going to keep that up tomorrow? I look over at the kitchen, see the tin of Earl Grey waiting for me, calling me. But it's no good. The decision has been made. No more caffeine. I stand and walk towards the tin, almost forgetting that Gary is still there, looking at me, eyes wide and pleading for an explanation.

'Have you got your period?' he asks, and I almost burst out laughing.

That's another problem. We've only been dating for eight months and our sex life has fizzled out and become the odd fumbled quickie before work, or a token Sunday morning session during a 'lie in'.

'Is there someone at the new job? Is that it? Someone you like the look of?'

Not exactly, but it will do. I breathe deeply. *Cruel to be kind.*

'Yes. That's it,' I say. 'I'm sorry. I didn't want to upset you, but you've sussed it out. I guess you've always known me . . . always been able to read me like a book. You're a wonderful man, Gary. Sure to make someone very happy one day. Just not me.' I look down, contrite, then meet his eyes again.

He gasps, his mouth making an unattractive fish-like shape. But finally, it's done. The mention of another man is enough of a blow to unleash that small fragment of male pride he has left.

As he turns to leave, I feel a curious but not unpleasant cocktail of emotions: relief, excitement and contempt all at once.

NOW

Helena

Ash and I used to run together. Not often, because she was always faster than me, and although at the start I thought it was a good thing – to let her beat me, to let her feel superior in some way – after a while, I just got tired of struggling to keep up. Of watching her smirk slightly as I panted along behind her. She was always determined to push herself, push herself, to be seen as super-human, and it sucked the enjoyment out of things. But still, a few times in those early months, we'd pull our leggings and trainers on at lunchtime and set off along the Regent's Canal. She knew all the routes, had all the gear. *All the gear and no idea!* She'd laughed at me as I fiddled with my Fitbit, trying to work the damn thing out.

I no longer have the Fitbit. But the motivation to run is stronger than ever. It's the perfect morning for it, anyway – clear and crisp but not so cold that the air feels as though it's setting fire to your lungs with each breath. I used to run for fitness, for weight loss. But now I've got no weight to lose, so I run for me. For headspace. Because I have to fill the day, somehow, and everyone keeps telling me how good exercise is for your mental health.

Jack is on the phone in the kitchen as I come downstairs,

dressed head to toe in black Lycra, like a woman in a very unique sort of mourning. I linger on the bottom step. There's no point in denying what I'm doing as I strain to hear him. The old me would be horrified at the thought of it. But is it so wrong to eavesdrop, in a marriage? You could say that it was a way of trying to feel close to someone, that if you didn't eavesdrop, then you didn't care, and surely that was worse?

'We've tried,' he is saying. 'It's the only way. Nothing else is working.'

He is frustrated but polite – whoever he is speaking to has the upper hand, but at the same time he doesn't respect them, he thinks they are in the wrong. I have been his partner for nearly twelve years, I know everything about him; the subtle cadences in his voice tell me more than the words ever could.

'It's changed since then! You must realize that. It's been years since . . . it's much more effective now. I understand. Of course, of course I do. But . . .' He gives a sharp sigh. 'Yes, OK. Well, I'll talk to her again. OK. I'll speak to you later. Bye.'

These last words leave his mouth as he turns from the kitchen and walks into the hall. He sees me, standing on the bottom step, a black ghost with sweatbands, and there's a second where we both feel as guilty as each other.

'Darling,' he says, pushing his phone into his pocket. 'How long have you been up?'

'Long enough.'

'It's . . . that was . . .' he begins, but he's a terrible liar, and so he stops.

He knows I won't ask him who he was speaking to. I don't want the confrontation any more than he does.

31

'Are you going for a run?' he says, instead. Back to the comfortable, the familiar, the mundane.

'Thought I'd make the most of the weather,' I say.

He's wearing smart trousers and a shirt, for once, no overalls. He'd usually be in the workshop by now.

'What are you up to today?'

He pretends to look at his watch but it's deliberate, he knows the time. City habits die hard.

'I'm going to have a look at a potential shop later,' he says. 'Didn't seem much point getting covered in sawdust beforehand. And I was going to pop out and get some groceries . . . I was worried when you didn't come back to bed last night. I came to find you in the office but you were asleep on the sofa. I wanted to wait until you woke up, to make sure you were OK.'

'There was another accident. He was so young . . .' I say. He gives a sympathetic sigh, but I can tell he's exhausted by my angst. The kind, compassionate, eager-to-help man I fell in love with has gone, absorbed in his new-found obsession with antique hand planes. The old Jack would have been campaigning alongside me, leafleting the local area, drumming up support. But this year has changed him, just as much as it has changed me. He doesn't care about other people's lives being ruined when his own is no longer up to scratch.

Charity begins at home. Her voice, again, always there with another pithy piece of advice.

'It's the third this month,' I add. 'I'm going to phone the Council again today.'

'OK,' he says, after a pause. 'If it will make you feel better. But

you know I think you should leave it, focus on yourself until . . .
Listen, I ought to . . . run. Ha!'

There's a genuine smile, a second of normality, of the old life,
the good life. He walks towards me and kisses me on the cheek.

'Look after yourself,' he says, without meeting my eyes, and
then he is gone.

I wait a few minutes, watching through the bubbled glass in the
front door as his car reverses slowly out of our driveway. He's always
careful now – he might pretend not to care about the accidents, but
they've affected him too, in his own way. Once I'm sure he's gone,
I pick up my iPod, strap it to my arm, and set off. I don't track my
progress, because how can I make any progress any more, when
my entire life is just running around in circles, looking for answers
I'll never find, like a hamster on a plastic wheel? Most of the time,
I just run down to the stream at the bottom of our land, cross it
with a jump, and head out into the woods. Where no one can see
me and where the only thing that can hurt me is myself.

Today, for some reason, as I run I think of one of the last times I
saw her. Me, squeezed into an office chair, heavily pregnant, my
stomach like an overstretched balloon filled with sand, heavy and
misshapen. Her, radiant with joy, suddenly taller and slimmer,
getting what she wanted. A vampire in a cream silk blouse and
navy trousers. That jet-black hair, her strangely thick skin, as
though it was made of silicone, not human at all. Pale, always so
pale. Those blood-red lips mouthing platitudes, telling David she
could handle it, when all I wanted to do was stand up and scream
to the world that she couldn't be trusted. But I didn't. Because I
wasn't myself; I was a greasy, bloated, sweaty version of myself

who hadn't slept properly for a month. *Sleep as much as you can now or you'll regret it when the baby comes*, everyone says. But I couldn't sleep at all, and their advice only worsened the insomnia.

I pause to lean against a tree, my heart pounding with exertion as I think of her words to me that day, as she watched me push my chair back and leave her there.

'Don't worry, Helena.'

The smile that came after it was a smile of nothingness. A smile that might just as well have been a blank stare, for all the emotion it conveyed.

And then the final words, the final slap, as I walked away, knowing I was leaving it all behind: my life, my work, my ambition, my everything.

'You just focus on your baby.'

It's only in the last few weeks that Jack has felt able to leave me alone for a whole day like this, and even though it's better than before, when someone was always there, watching over me, I'm not used to the silence.

I miss him when he's not here, and wish he wasn't here when he is. What does that say about me?

It's 6 p.m., and too early even for me to go to bed. I've cleaned all the bathrooms (what people don't tell you about having more than one bathroom is that you will spend your life transferring toilet rolls around), put two loads of washing on, made a chicken pie that I froze instead of eating, and tried to distract myself in front of the television. But try as I might, I can't get the thought of David out of my head. How did he get our number here? Who could have given it to him?

For the first time in three days, I log into my email account. I used to have a work email, of course, and it was used for everything, for my entire life. It was brimming, overfull, constantly telling me to *delete, delete, delete* to make space for all the people who wanted to talk to me. But I had to hand it over. So now I only have the Yahoo account that I set up as a teenager – a sad remnant of my youth, with its ridiculous address.

HelenaSparkles@livemail.com. No she bloody doesn't. Not any more.

No one I care about has the address, so I rarely bother to check it, these days.

But as I log in, I feel sure I will see his name at the top of my Inbox, and there he is, buried between offers from fashionable clothes stores I used to shop in, and organic food delivery companies (for people who think that a potato is somehow better if it comes in a dirty crate and costs twice as much as in the supermarket). He has found me. Or rather, he has found Helena Sparkles, RIP.

Once upon a time, seeing that name in my Inbox filled me with excitement. The brightest person I'd ever met; the person I was so desperate to impress: *David Marlow*.

As the subject line, he's chosen a word that might as well have been Fuck You: *Opportunity*.

I hesitate for several seconds. Is the best course of action to simply delete it unread?

The cursor hovers over the tiny trash icon next to his name. It's so tempting. To bin him. To throw him away, both literally and metaphorically. But I don't. Of course I don't.

Instead, I do what any sane person would do and open the email, and I read it, even though I know what the email is going to say. Because this is David, and David doesn't do small talk, or time-wasting, or surprises.

From: DavidM@kamu.com
Subject: Opportunity

Helena
How are you? Other than hard to track down. I understand it's been a tough year, but I might have something that you'd be interested in – that, more importantly, you'd enjoy. Can we talk? Or meet? Give me a ring when you can – number's the same as before.
    Cheers
    David

I shut his email. So far, so predictable. As I am pondering my response, I idly go through the motions. The same series of webpages every day, over and over and over. It has become something like second nature – an autopilot task, like brushing my teeth or putting my knickers on. I click, and click again, my eyes scanning, flicking back and forth, finding nothing of interest. The main company page is so corporate now; no mention of the management team. But I still look, every day, just in case. And today I'm lucky. There it is, the hit I am looking for, the satisfactory reward for my stalking. A small two-sentence teaser post on the company's LinkedIn page. Cryptic, giving everything and nothing away all at once.

Typical of her.

36

Some exciting news coming up at KAMU! Watch this space!

Rage boils inside me at the arrogance of it, thinking people give a shit.

Although, of course, here I am, doing exactly that.

THEN

Ash

Helena leaves the office every evening at 6.30 p.m. It's taken me two weeks to get a proper grasp of her routine: in at 8 a.m., coffee break at 10.30 (an Americano, black, no sugar), lunch at 12 (usually soup or a wrap at her desk), more coffee at 3 p.m. Sometimes she has a cigarette, most usually on days when she has a presentation with the Americans – she thinks no one notices, but I've seen her sneak a lighter and a tab under the cuffs of her sleeves, like you might hide a tampon. I've no idea where she goes to smoke – she certainly doesn't hang around with the twenty-a-day developer team in their wolf-like pack. I've joined them a couple of times now, trying to assess whether there's anyone of interest there; but there's only one, and his T-shirts smell of soap powder, so he's probably got a girlfriend.

It's an open-plan office, and we're all grouped in teams of four, facing each other in a kind of starfish shape. Everyone except Helena, who has her own double desk in the corner by the windows. On the face of it, she's flawlessly tidy – just her laptop, some hand cream and a perfectly organized in-tray on display. But I've seen inside her desk drawers, and they tell a different story. She's a hoarder; all salt and pepper sachets, dried-out highlighters, hairbands and odd coins gathering dust. If you called her on it, she'd give an embarrassed laugh and tell you she just *never* has time to go through it all.

From my desk – annoyingly, Freckles sits right next to me, even though she's on the sales team (she's on the Dukan Diet, and every morning I have to smell her eating two boiled eggs) – I face her directly, and so I get a perfect view of what she's up to all day. Today has been like clockwork, so far, but it's 6.33 p.m. now and she still hasn't packed up her stuff. Lauren left home an hour ago, which means I'm going to be late if I don't leave soon. But I can't. I can't leave before her. It's become a thing now. I'm determined to stay, until it's just me, David and the cleaners left. David notices I'm there, I know he does. And Helena always says goodbye to me in that cheery, slightly patronizing way, yoga mat slung over her shoulder as she heads off to the gym downstairs for her evening workout. She's not very athletic, though, so I suspect the whole routine is mostly for show, despite her muttering about exercise being the perfect way to clear her head.

Why the hell hasn't she left yet?

She's frowning at something on her computer, sucking on her little finger.

I hear a noise behind me and turn, expecting to see the cleaners. But it's David, marching back from a meeting. He looks across at us, and I turn back to see Helena smiling up at him.

'Working hard, ladies?' he calls, but it's a rhetorical question. He stops by my desk. 'Don't you have a home to go to, Ashley?'

It's one of the first times he's spoken to me directly since the meeting with the bigwigs.

'I'm meeting a friend for dinner,' I say. 'Got a bit of time to kill.' The last bit is a massive lie – I'm going to be so late – but I want him to think I've got some semblance of a social life, as well as being super keen. I overheard them discussing candidates for November's Employee of the Month in the kitchen and was pleased that my name was the first mentioned, but they're an American company and work–life balance is one of their favourite terms to chuck about.

'Enjoy,' he replies, non-committally.

I look back at Helena, and – thank God – she's standing up finally, coat on, and reaching for her handbag. There's no yoga mat tonight. I wonder why she's not going to the gym. A special occasion? Is she having dinner with friends, too? Is it her time of the month? Maybe she has a date with her picture-perfect husband.

She walks towards me, heading for the lift, giving a fleeting glance at David's back as he disappears into his glass cube. His routine is a little less predictable, but he's usually out of the office before seven.

'Night, Ashley,' Helena says as she passes my desk. 'Have a good evening.'

'You too.'

Once I'm sure she'll be safely out of the building, I grab my stuff and rush for the stairs. I text Lauren to say sorry – I'm never late for anything – but it turns out she's been distracted in the massive Primark round the corner and is quite happy to browse while she waits for me to arrive.

It's 7.15 p.m. by the time I finally meet Lauren. She's dressed in a tartan miniskirt and huge high-heeled boots, and her hair is inexplicably pink.

'Ash!' she shouts, a little too loudly. She throws her arms around me and I smell her perfume, the same one she's worn since she was a teenager.

'Oh my God, you've gotta see what I bought. But wait, look at you! Are you wearing . . . a *camel mac*? And your hair! A bob!'

'It's taupe,' I reply, echoing her sarcastic tone, and run my fingers through my hair. *You look like a dark-haired Anna Wintour*, Gary had said when I'd come home with it the week before my interview at KAMU. I was amazed he even noticed, let alone knew who she was. I still wasn't sure the length suited me, but the black fringe set off my blue eyes and white skin quite nicely.

'Is it Burberry?'

'No, don't be thick, it's from Zara. Convincing, though, isn't it? Let's get a table. It's great to see you.'

The restaurant is crowded and the skinny front of house boy tells us it'll be a fifteen-minute wait for a table, but in the meantime we're welcome to perch at the one free bar stool. I let Lauren sit on it, even though my feet are hurting, because she makes a big fuss about her blisters in her new boots. I stand alongside her, being pushed and bumped by the hordes of people who seem to be lost trying to find the toilet.

'Fucking hell, Ash, twelve pounds for a few mushrooms? What's a sweet potato, anyway? One that's been cooked in honey or something?'

'Seriously?' I say, rolling my eyes at her. 'You've never had a sweet potato?'

'Of course I have. But man, these prices ... They'd better be paying you well.'

'I told you, dinner's on me. This is the hottest new restaurant in Soho. My treat.'

Lauren has a job – receptionist at the swankiest hotel on our shitty bit of Hampshire coastline – but she always complains about the cost of her train ticket up here so, whenever we meet up, I pay.

'Right, what are we drinking?' she asks, turning the menu over.

'I won't be drinking,' I say, firmly. 'Early meeting in the morning. But feel free to go ahead.'

Lauren looks at me with concerned eyes, and I feel a rush of love for her. She's my oldest friend, she's been with me through everything. For all her faults, she knows me inside out. She's the only one who really knows what happened with Mum, and she still likes me.

I'm reminded of her face, chubbier back then, when she caught me round the back of the science block, grinding a lit cigarette into my wrist, watching the skin buckle and melt, which was strangely satisfying. I only felt the pain when I looked into her eyes. They filled with tears as she screamed at me and pulled the cigarette away, hugging me and telling me it wasn't my fault. That my mum was a drunken bitch, that she brought it all on herself, and that she'd stand up for me in court, if ever it came to that.

But her belief in me didn't help. Not really. Not when every day I saw the way my brother looked at me, suddenly frightened of the only person he had ever trusted.

I blink hard and focus on the menu again. *Don't let your past steal your present.*

'You haven't been . . . obsessing about your mum again?' she says, as though she can read my guilty mind. 'Surely a vodka and Coke will help you chill out?'

Before I have time to reply, the skinny boy marches over and informs us that there's a table free. As I follow him towards it, I am filled with a strange urge to turn and run. What was I thinking, inviting Lauren here, into my new life, when she knows far too much about the old one? So stupid.

The table is right underneath a speaker that's blasting out music. There's no escaping this dinner now, but at least it's a relief to get off my feet. When I realized Helena wore heels most days to work, and no one else did, I knew that I'd have to up my game, but I'm paying the price for it now. Not for the first time, I wish I'd been born the other gender.

'So anyway, I told him to fuck off, and he said fine, and that's where we're at now . . . I was kinda gutted about it but, to be honest, I've got a bit of a crush on Mike from work . . . remember Mike? He was in Jason's year . . .' There's a pause while she waits for my reaction. I've completely missed the beginning of this story. 'He's working in the kitchens, wants to train up to become a chef.'

'Mike, uh, yeah,' I say, staring down at the menu. 'Ginger, wasn't he?'

'No!' she shrieks, batting at my hand in mock indignation. 'As if I'd go *there*. Anyway, he's got a skinhead now. Reckon he started receding when he was like nineteen, so he's shaved it all off in case people notice. He looks good, though, goes to the gym a lot . . . you'd be impressed . . .' She pauses again. 'Dunno if he hangs out with Jase any more, though.'

'What are you going to order?' I ask. If she thinks I'm going to talk about my brother, then she's mistaken. Sometimes it feels as though, whenever I see Lauren, she only wants to talk about him, as though she's trying to drag me back there, keep my feet on the ground, clip my wings. I suppose it's her way of keeping some control over me – which is what all relationships are about, when you boil them right down to their bare bones.

Well, I'm not going to play that game.

'I think I'll go for the warm duck salad with walnuts.'

A waiter appears and starts pouring water into two thimble-sized glasses.

'Have you heard from him?' she asks, persistent, but I keep my head down.

'Ready to order, ladies?'

'Er, yes, I think so,' I reply, looking up at Lauren. 'Are you ready?'

'You order for me,' she says, snapping her menu shut and looking up at the waiter. 'I'm not really into this fancy stuff. Give me a burger any day. Between you and me,' she continues, twisting one side of her mouth as she looks up at the waiter, 'I might be stopping for a Maccy D's before getting on the train home.'

The waiter smiles in a kind of 'Oh God, I have to be nice to you' way. Irritated by her lack of gratitude – you can take the girl out of Paulsgrove but you can't take Paulsgrove out of the girl – I order us both the duck salad. It's time for her to broaden her horizons. She then orders herself a double vodka and Coke, as if to spite me back.

'So,' she says, and there's a glimmer in her eyes that tells me she's enjoying winding me up, that she thinks I've got above myself, ideas above my station. Despite everything I've achieved, Lauren doesn't do jealousy. She's never thought further than leaving Paulsgrove for Southsea – and she achieved that last year, so she might as well retire tomorrow. 'Tell me about the new job. Is it like *The Apprentice*? Your gran's been going on to everyone at the Regent, saying how your office is so posh they use it as a location for filming telly shows at the weekend.'

'Oh God,' I say, happy that she's dropped the subject of Jason, finally. 'That happened *once*. Yeah, it's good, I'm enjoying it. Here . . .' I reach down and pull out a small paper bag, pushing it towards her. 'This is for you.'

Her eyes light up.

'It's not my birthday!'

'I know, but we get a lot of free stuff – you know, samples and that kind of thing – and you've always loved your make-up more than me.' I look at her now, her candyfloss-pink hair scraped back into a high ponytail, her eyebrows almost black and thick with definition, her face contoured beyond all recognition. A small stud sparkles on one side of her nose. She's pretty, in her own way. But she always goes too far with the slap, and she has no grace, no poise – her posture is terrible – and she teeters about in short skirts and high heels like she's trying to find her sea legs.

She rummages through the bag, her face locked in concentration. Every now and then she gives a little murmur of recognition.

'I haven't heard of half these brands,' she says, pulling each piece out one by one.

'Most of them are new launches,' I say, taking a sip of water.

Unmistakably tap. When the waiter comes back, I'll ask him for a slice of lemon. 'They're all luxury, though. Nothing drugstore.'

'Drugstore?'

'Sorry, it's the American word for chemist. Stupid beauty jargon. It means cheap. So, nothing you'd get in Superdrug.'

'Well, thanks. Ash, you're a mate.' She pushes the bag under the table and there's a silence. I try to will the waiter towards us with my eyeballs, but it's as though he's deliberately ignoring me. Have we run out of conversation already?

'So, how's . . . whatshisname?' she asks, glugging at her vodka and Coke.

'Gary? We broke up,' I say.

'Oh, that's crap. '

'It's OK,' I say. 'It was for the best. He was dragging me down. You know how giving I am in relationships . . . I just kept trying to make things work, trying to help him help himself . . . but you can't make it work if only one of you is putting in the effort.'

She gives a small nod of understanding and pulls out her phone.

'So, Mike, right, he sent me this text yesterday. What do you reckon it means? I can't tell if he's flirting with me, or what . . . I mean, we had a bit of a snog last year at the Christmas do, but afterwards nothing came of it . . . but since then, he's been super friendly, but maybe it's all a bit too narky, kind of teasing me, like I'm his little sister or something . . . even though *he's* younger than me. I don't know what to make of it.'

I stare down at the text. It might as well be written in a foreign language. The ability to deduce what the great men of Portsmouth are thinking about their women is not a skill I have, nor particularly want to acquire.

'Well,' I say, after a pause. 'He'd be mad not to be interested in you, right? He's just scared you'll reject him, so he's playing it cool.'

I've said the right thing.

'Do you think?' she says, beaming. 'Maybe I should text him back . . . maybe in a bit. After our dinner. Maybe on the train home. Don't want to look too keen.'

I give her a short smile and turn my attention to the bowls that have just arrived. I think the restaurant does a cookbook; I must remember to ask about it on the way out.

'So,' Lauren says, pushing the salad around her plate suspiciously. 'Have you been in touch with Jase lately?'

The question is so direct that there's no way out this time.

'No.'

'So you haven't heard, then?' she says, and there's a flash of glee in her eyes. She's going to tell me something she knows will upset me. Even though she cares about me, there's nothing like that thrill. This is the problem, this has always been my problem; the price of being successful. There are too many people in my life who pretend to love me but can't wait to see me cry.

'No. What?' I ask. Whatever it is, I will choose not to care.

'Oh God, Ash. I thought your gran would have said something. It was proper awful. There was a fight . . . Lisa, well, she ended up in hospital. He made a run for it but they caught him trying to get on a boat at Southampton. ABH in the end, I think. But, well, he's back . . . he's back inside.'

NOW

Helena

I blame the boredom.

It takes a split second to arrange – just a quick text and he replies instantly, as though he's been sitting next to his phone ever since he sent the email, waiting for me to get back to him.

Great stuff. This afternoon at 3? At the club?

It's 11 a.m. Even though 3 p.m. is hours away, I am filled with panic. The effort of it all: getting ready, driving to the station, buying a ticket, getting on the train, then the Tube, then walking into the club . . . the thought of talking about *her* with someone who doesn't understand, who can never understand . . . it fills me with a fear I haven't felt since I was a teenager going on a first date. But somehow, I feel I have to prove to myself that I can do it. And the alternative – sitting at home, blanking out in front of daytime television for yet another day – is unbearable.

I text back, before I have the chance to change my mind.

Perfect.

I pace up and down the hallway for a few minutes, trying to decide what to tell Jack. He's 'popped out' somewhere – I think to the gym, but he didn't confirm – but promised to be back for lunch. Again, if I had the energy I'd wonder why he wasn't working today. Perhaps his new furniture business is failing already, and he's too scared to tell me, worried it'll push me off the cliff completely. But if anything, he's been more cheerful recently, so it seems unlikely to be that.

Would Jack mind me going to see David? Probably not; he'd see it as evidence of my recovery, a small price to pay. But to save all the questions, I decide to lie.

I call him. It takes several rings before he picks up.

'Hi,' he says, sounding out of breath. So he's at the gym, after all. 'Everything OK?'

'Yes,' I reply, feeling stupid suddenly. This could have waited until he got home. I don't need to ask his permission. 'It's just . . . Kate – you know, from uni – texted me. She asked if I fancied meeting up with her. This afternoon. You know she moved out of town a while ago . . . she, er, had a meeting there today, randomly asked if I fancied a catch-up. Thought I'd . . . well, thought I'd check you thought it was a good idea.'

There's a noise in the background, a slight screech and a thump as something drops to the floor.

'Hang on,' Jack says, but I can't tell if it's to me or someone else. 'Wait a second.'

The phone line is muffled, as though he's pulled a sleeve over the mouthpiece. Seconds later he's back, but his voice is clearer now, and the background noise has gone.

'Sorry, it was noisy in there, I'm outside now.'

'Noisy in where?'

'So where are you going?' he asks, ignoring me.

'Um, not sure yet . . . I'm meeting her at Oxford Circus. She's

49

got the afternoon off work. I guess she just fancied catching up and . . . I don't know . . . I feel OK today . . . I feel it'd be good to get out, to see people. While I feel up to it.'

'Of course!' His voice lifts. 'Darling, that's brilliant.' I can picture his wide smile and I feel terrible for lying to him, and even more terrible for being able to make him happy with something as simple as going to see a friend. It must be such a relief for him to think of me leaning on someone else for a change. It's been so long since I've seen my friends. So long with just the two of us, stuck in our isolated little bubble of unhappiness. 'What time will you be back?'

'I don't know. I'm not leaving till 1 p.m., though.'

'Great. Enjoy yourself. Spend some money while you're there! Oh and listen . . . I've got a dinner thing after work – do you remember? I told you about it. With Mark and John Hamilton. They might want to invest. I'm afraid it'll probably be a late one.'

'It's fine,' I say, because even though I didn't know he needed investment, it's a relief, really. The loneliness might be grating at times, but it's easier than keeping up the pretence. 'Hope you have a good day, too.'

The train is delayed as it crawls towards London, and I feel that familiar anxiety welling up in me. I'm out of my comfort zone, raw and vulnerable away from the cocoon that I've been hiding in. I wonder what the doctors would say, what my therapist would make of this little expedition. As we pull into King's Cross station I find myself glued to my seat. It's warm inside the train and the carriage is nearly empty. I don't want to get off.

But I have to, because as the train settles alongside the platform

I realize that the concourse is full of people waiting to get on, determined to spoil my peace. I push through them and head for the Underground. I tell myself to hold my head high, that I'm going to be OK, that it's just a normal trip into town to see an old friend, but my eyes are frantic, swivelling around in their sockets, scanning the faces bustling past, always looking, looking, looking. There's no reason for Ash to be at King's Cross at 2.30 p.m. on a Thursday but there's no reason for her not to be, either – the office is still just around the corner, after all.

The Tube is busier than I remembered. At this time of day I expected it to be empty, just a few off-season tourists staring down at paper maps. But instead, it's crammed with people of all ages, luggage, a folded-up bicycle, even a small dog. Has London changed so much since I stopped living here? Or am I just noticing it all with fresh eyes?

At Oxford Circus I emerge. The sun has come out and, despite the cold, I can't help but smile. I feel alive again. Alive with adventure, with possibility and hope. Perhaps it's the house that's been to blame all along. Perhaps we should sell up and move back to London, back into the thick of it, and I should accept the job that David's offering. Maybe this is the answer. Perhaps I don't need the treatment, after all . . . perhaps the answer has been right here all along, just a £20 train journey away! I just need to convince Jack. There must be places he can rent to use as a workshop. Loads of craftsmen still manage to live in cities; they don't have to live in the middle of nowhere, surrounded by woodland.

I step through the great anonymous iron door and into the club, immediately embarrassed to see the concierge is the same woman as before. Judy.

'Mrs Brenton!' she says, smiling. 'You look well. How lovely to see you.'

'Thank you! You too.'

I run my hands through my hair, smiling back at her. She is right. For once, I do look well. And even though I am too thin now, clothes somehow hang better, as though my body is a coat hanger, made for showing them off. And today there are no baggy-bottomed tracksuits or bobbled jumpers. I've made an effort. Slim-fitting black dress, opaque tights, my Saint Laurent boots.

Judy waves me through, without checking whether I am still a member. David first bought me membership about six months after we met, but seeing as we put it through the business, it must have lapsed by now.

'Great to see you back,' Judy says. 'I was ... well ... it's just good to see you.'

He is already there, in his usual armchair by the fire. I see the side of his head first. His hair is greyer than I remembered but he is still so handsome that I have to pause a little before walking towards him. He is staring down at some papers in his lap, frowning, concentrating, turning them over in his hands. For a second, it is as though I've been transported back two years. I stop walking, a few paces away, and just watch him. How I wish I could go back to that time. When I had everything. A husband, an amazing job . . .

When David sees me, he stands up, as he always does. He kisses me on the cheek, and his aftershave is familiar, the memory uncomfortable.

'Just before we start . . . I . . . I don't want to talk about Ashley,' I blurt.

The words take us both by surprise, but he nods.

'Of course. Understood. Here, have a seat. I ordered you an Old Fashioned. You look wonderful, by the way.'

'Thanks,' I reply. 'You don't look so bad yourself.'

'So,' he says, 'I'm not going to pretend I've got any idea what . . . well . . . what hell you've been through, but I did want to say how very sorry I was. It's a terrible thing. Just terrible. Elizabeth . . . she cried for days when she heard.'

I want to snap back how sorry I am for her, but I just give a small nod instead.

'How's Jack and his new enterprise?'

'He's good,' I say. 'Well, as good as can be expected. He's working a lot. It takes time to get these things off the ground, you know . . .' It's a stock answer, and it's only as I give it that I realize it's not true any more. He never seems to be in the workshop, these days, but I have no idea where he is most of the time.

'Oh, but how admirable to be following your passion like that,' he says, sounding as though he might actually mean it. 'Takes a brave man to step away from a steady pay packet and bonus scheme.'

We continue in this vein for several minutes; non-threatening small talk. I ask him about Elizabeth, about his dog, Benji, who was very old and had to be put to sleep. He looks genuinely sombre for a moment; a chink in his Alpha Male veneer. The children, however, are thriving, he tells me. The oldest – ironically, also called Jack – is doing well at boarding school, a big fan of the army cadets. His voice softens when he talks about Penny, his ten-year-old daughter, still the apple of his eye.

I don't ask him about KAMU.

My glass is empty. David gestures for the waiter. 'Another, please,' he says, glancing back at me.

'No! No, thank you. It's too early. I'll have . . . an Americano. Black.'

'And for you, sir?' the waiter asks, picking up my glass and placing it on his tray.

'The same!' David says, clapping his hands together.

The waiter sidles off.

'So,' I say, realizing that we've been here for nearly twenty minutes now and there's still been no mention of his great opportunity. 'What were you so eager to talk to me about?'

'Yes, of course. Are you working at the moment?'

'No,' I reply, the answer making me feel ashamed. 'No, not since . . . well, I've been . . . having a break.'

'Of course. So important to take time out. And you've no plans to – sorry, this is such a personal question, do tell me to get lost – but no plans to have another baby?'

'No,' I say. I'm stunned that David even thinks I'm considering it. Does he imagine that's how you get over something like this? It just shows how little men understand. But I'm more stunned by his boldness. There's something about David's forthright questioning that makes me feel better. And then I realize, it's the tiptoeing around me that's been so painful, all those sympathetic looks, kid gloves and patronizing sentiments. They've done more to erode my sense of self than anything else. In my old life, I wasn't the sort of person that people talked down to, that people felt they needed to protect. I was fearless and respected, known for my achievements in my career.

'No, no plans for another baby.'

'Well then, I've been in discussion with Shopit. A new affiliate programme in the US – you might have heard of them? They're coming over here . . . they're looking for a chief product officer.

I thought, with your knowledge of the market, you might be interested.'

'What's your involvement?' I say, and in an instant the last year has vanished. I am back in the right place, being serious – and, more importantly, being taken seriously.

'Nothing this time, actually. The CTO, Sean, is an old mate . . . we were at Harvard together . . . he asked me if I knew of anyone, and I thought of you. By all accounts it's a hectic place to work, but I know you're used to that. Offices are TBC but they're looking at somewhere east, I think.'

'Remuneration?'

'To be honest, with my recommendation, I reckon you could ask for whatever you wanted. Once you got past their board – it's family owned, and they like to chat to everyone they recruit individually. They'd probably fly you over for a couple of days. They've got investment, though. Money isn't the problem, they're just looking for the right people now.'

'Share options?'

'Of course.'

I sit back in my button-back chair. The waiter sets down our coffees.

'So we wouldn't be working together?' I'm cross with myself for even asking.

'Not this time,' David replies. 'Still chained to KAMU . . . But like I say, Sean's an old mate. I've been helping him out, so I'm sure our paths would cross. Listen, why don't I get him to drop you a line? You're on LinkedIn, right?'

I nod, and take a sip of my coffee, wishing I'd ordered something alcoholic, after all.

THEN

Ash

Networking is an essential part of building wealth.

Just a shame I'm so shit at it.

I survey the Christmas party. There's money in the company, that's for sure. A three-course meal (with champagne) at a swanky hotel, followed by an open bar and a vaguely famous DJ. Of course, I have no idea who he is, but Helena assured me he wasn't cheap. I think he's a friend of hers, in fact, or an ex-boyfriend. She seems to know so many people. And not just any people, but the right people.

'Phew!'

I turn to see David's PA, Lizzy, holding out an upturned sparkly bowler hat full of tiny pieces of paper.

'Pick one!' she says, shaking it in front of me as though panning for gold. 'It's the Secret Santa, with a twist. Remember? We all pick a number and then get to choose a present in that order . . .'

I zone out as I reach in for a number, thinking not of these tedious instructions but, instead, how much her face has changed in only a couple of weeks. Is this what pregnancy does to you?

Doubles the number of chins you have? She looks tired, too – none of that glow they bang on about. I wonder how old she is. Definitely late thirties. Must have worried she was running out of time, wanted to squeeze one out before her ovaries gave up on her.

'Admiring my pregnancy ball gown?' she says, hoicking her black tube dress down over her hips. 'It's as comfortable as it looks. Can't wait to get the effing thing off. No one told me that when you're pregnant the underside of your boobs starts to sweat, especially when wrapped in tight black Lycra. In fact, I'm mostly just one big sweaty mess, these days. It's *great*.'

'Oh,' I say, embarrassed that she's caught me looking. 'No, I was just . . . thinking how lovely you look.'

'Liar,' she says, but her eyes are twinkling. She's the most good-natured PA I've ever worked with. 'I'm a fat whale. It's OK. Apparently, it's all going to be worth it.'

And with that she wobbles off towards the accounts team, bowler hat aloft.

I turn back to the room, watching Helena as I stand by the bar, making my one glass of champagne last. It's a concession, for Christmas. I gave up alcohol a week after starting my job at Kiss and Make Up. After Gary moved out, I found myself settling into a routine of red wine and work, instead of an actual supper, and it began to affect my complexion. I've never had the best skin tone – what the copywriters at KAMU would call 'deathly'. I'm too pale, and dehydration gives me the sort of dark circles under my eyes that a forty-year-old would be horrified by.

It's all right for Helena, of course. Good genes. I might be younger, but when the two of us walk into a room together, she's the one that gets the first glances. She's so much *smaller* than me; the definition of petite. Tonight, her body is encased in a satin black jumpsuit, her hair loose in waves across her shoulders, a trademark slick of dark lipstick bringing definition to her face.

It would be so easy to hate her.

I don't hate her, though, because I've realized over these past few weeks that she likes me. She likes my ambition, the fact that I don't let my age and relative inexperience hold me back.

The trouble is, you think you have time.

People think it's a Buddha quote, but there's no proof. More likely, it's something thought up by a greetings card company. Still, I like it, and it feels relevant for today.

Steve from the sales department has sidled over to Helena like an unattractive snake. He's drunk already and it's only 9.30 p.m. The music is loud and I feel for her as I watch her lean towards him to catch what he's saying. A flick of spit lands on her shoulder as he speaks. She's like some Disney princess, standing there surrounded by frogs, all trying to kiss her, to see if they're 'the one'. But, of course, she's married. I've seen a photograph of her husband, on the screensaver on her phone. He's ridiculously good-looking, in a rather conventional way. He probably has some very eligible friends.

No use to me, unfortunately. Because, at the end of the day, she's my boss. I'm her direct report. We've been getting on well – she's made some cringe-worthy jokes about girl power and taking on the Americans – but it's always going to be tricky to cross that professional line into friendship. She's just signed off my probation, said everything I've done is excellent and that I've gone 'above and beyond'. But there will always be that barrier between us.

Not for the first time, I wonder what she's earning. She has an expensive-looking watch on her slim wrist, but her husband is obviously well off, so that doesn't necessarily say anything.

My head thumps with fury when I think of my own salary. Just enough to pay for the studio flat in Mitcham – thank God I've been able to give up working in the shop, finally – but it's hardly impressive. After I passed my probation, Helena announced my two grand pay rise as though it was some kind of massive deal, and I had to bite my tongue and accept it gratefully. Two grand? I asked her when I could expect another review, and she looked surprised, but not cross, and said she'd look into it.

I've only been working here for three months and I'm already restless. They promised ample opportunities for promotion, but I can't see any obvious next step. I'll have to wait for Helena to leave, but that might be too big a leap. The short-sighted powers that be won't promote me from Digital Executive to Creative Director. I'll have to work my way up the digital team first. It isn't what I want to do. I'm better than that.

I want to lead a team, to effect real change, to have an impact. As Helena has done.

I look back over at her. She glances up and meets my eyes, giving me a broad and beautiful smile. I smile back and watch as she leans forward and excuses herself to Steve, making her way over to me.

'Champagne!' she says, nodding at my glass. 'I'm impressed. Don't tell me you're letting your hair down for once.'

'Only at Christmas,' I say, drinking the last mouthful in one gulp. 'There.' I put the glass down on the table next to me. 'That's me done.'

'You are funny,' she says, smiling. 'Why don't you have another? I'm quite tipsy myself, Jack will be most unimpressed.'

'Is he controlling?' I ask, the words out before I have given them proper thought.

'What?' She frowns slightly, and when she frowns she looks like a cross child. 'Not at all! I just mean . . .' She leans forward conspiratorially. 'He finds me rather hard work when I've had a few drinks. I have a tendency to come home, put music on – you know, a bit of old-school trance – and dance around the living room. He's more of a blues fan.'

'Oh,' I say. 'I don't know . . . I'm not really into music.'

'Oh, Ashley, you do make me laugh!' she says, but she isn't really listening now; she's watching Lizzy trying to balance the glittery hat on her distended stomach, a performance for an appreciative bunch of drunkards from sales. 'What have you been doing all your life?'

'Working,' I say, under my breath.

She smiles again and gives a half-nod, and I know she's not listening to me at all.

'Doesn't Lizzy look amazing?' she says. 'Eight months pregnant, and all that energy.'

'I think she's hating every second of it, actually,' I say.

Helena's head whips back towards me.

'Really?'

'She just told me how uncomfortable she is.'

There's something in the way Helena's staring into space. Perhaps she's pregnant herself, or trying?

'I think she looks brilliant . . .' Helena continues, but her voice is even dopier now and her attention has been diverted towards David, who's busy chatting to Rebecca, a round-faced brunette from the content team.

That's when I realize. I'm just a cover; an excuse for her to be on this side of the room. She stares at David, as he drapes his arm around Rebecca's shoulders.

'She's after a promotion,' I say, unthinkingly. Rebecca's shiny bob is swinging back and forth as she simpers in David's arms.

'What?' Helena replies, looking back at me. 'How do you know?'

'I heard her talking to Lizzy. She thinks there's room for a more senior editorial role. Reckons she can work alongside you.'

This isn't strictly true. What she actually said was that she wished she had more editorial work, her background was in journalism and she was bored of classic copywriting. But this is what happens to me when I'm left to do small talk; words just fall out, usually the ones I think will get the most dramatic reaction. Blame the champagne, blame my dysfunctional childhood. It's been a lifelong curse: I'll say anything to make sure people don't forget me.

'Work alongside me as what?'

'Well, she wants to be a kind of editor, I guess,' I say, shrugging and reaching for another glass of champagne. If I've started on this road, which it looks like I have, I'll need some more Dutch courage.

'Hmm.' Helena bites her lip. She doesn't look worried, exactly, more confused. 'I don't think David would be interested in creating a role like that. It'd make the structure too top heavy. And we need her, she's a good copywriter.'

'Yes,' I say, taking another sip. 'She is, isn't she? Really good at her job. I really enjoy working with her, in fact.'

'Do you?' Helena says, her eyes suddenly sharp. 'That's great. I'm glad to hear you're happy here. We're lucky to have you. I hope you know that.'

And with that, she has snapped back into work mode like the professional she is. There's seemingly no way of penetrating her glossy shield.

She makes her excuses then, and leaves. I remain in my corner as she quickly and carefully works the room, meandering her way over to David and Rebecca as if it were the most natural thing in the world. The three of them chat for a bit, and then Rebecca slips off to the toilet. David and Helena talk for a while, and then their chatting grows more animated, until Helena is throwing back her head and laughing, her cheeks bright and shiny.

It's clear that David is thinking exactly what I'd expect him to be thinking.

When it seems an acceptable time to leave – *top tip: not too early, not too late* – I join the queue for my coat at the cloakroom, with my Secret Santa present (a blow-up boyfriend – *hilarious*) tucked under my arm. As I stand waiting, my bare legs caught in icy blasts each time the revolving door turns, I hear a familiar laugh behind me. I glance over my shoulder briefly to see them walk past, oblivious to everything but each other. David, with his arm around Helena's satin waist. Helena with her back to me and her face tilted up towards him. She's laughing, leaning in close. Too close.

How disappointing.

I take my coat and hide behind a column, watching them as they linger in the reception area. David takes out his phone, puts it to his ear for a few minutes, then slips it into his pocket. Helena's cheeks are red now, inflamed by alcohol, and the eyeliner on one of her eyes is smudged, sending a skinny black tear down the side of her face.

They wait together in the corner of the reception area, but who knows what for? His arm is still around her waist. She looks down, then back up, her eyes big and puppy doggish. A little laugh, all feigned embarrassment, and then her eyes widen again, before she and David turn to leave the hotel.

NOW

Helena

The sound of Jack's car crunching through the gravel driveway wakes me. I peer at the bedside clock. It's 8.07 a.m. Two things about this don't make sense: 1) that I have slept past six, and 2) that Jack should be coming back from somewhere at such an early hour. Where has he been?

It takes several minutes for my brain to emerge from its slumber, then I remember that yesterday he was meant to be having dinner with his parents' friends, the Hamiltons, about the possibility of them investing. He'd never said anything about staying overnight. The dinner must have gone on later than expected, and he missed the last train, decided to stay with a friend. But something about this disagrees with me. He would have let me know if this had been the case.

The strangest thing of all about this morning, however, is the fact that I don't feel like crying the second I wake up. Instead, there's a knot at the pit of my stomach; a knot that I recognize with nostalgia as excitement. And then I remember why: David, the job offer, a potential future beyond this repetitive misery. No doubt Jack and the doctors won't share my enthusiasm. They'll worry that I'm not up to it; that it's too much to take on.

I decide to stay in bed, to pretend to be asleep, to see what he will do next. I wait, my eyes closed but my ears desperately straining to pick up on any clues. Our bedroom is above the kitchen. I hear him switch on the coffee machine, the aggressive vibrations piercing the silence, followed by a heavy sigh and the clatter of china on the worktop. There is silence next, and then the dull, uncharacteristic thump of his footsteps on the stairs, moving more slowly than usual.

The door to our bedroom pushes open, fighting with the thick carpet we had laid when we moved in, the sound like a groan. And then there is the smell; something I haven't smelled for years, something that takes me back to the days before Ash, before the baby, before I had any notion that you could lose control of your own life, if you just weren't careful enough.

Jack has been smoking.

'Darling?' he says, his voice soft, reminding me of the days after I gave birth, when he started stroking my hair as though I were a child. 'Are you still asleep?'

I carry on with my pretence, and don't reply. He pads past me softly and through to our en suite bathroom. The door shuts and the shower pump kicks into life. Minutes later, he's back in the bedroom and I go through the motions of waking up: a little twitch, rolling over, opening my eyes.

'Morning,' Jack says, sitting on the edge of the bed. He's wrapped a towel around his middle, and his bare chest – which I haven't seen in what feels like years – is hairless. I think of the forest that's taken root on my legs, and wonder where he finds the vanity to bother with such things.

'Hi,' I say. I wait for him to explain where he's been, but he doesn't say a word. Instead, he just looks at me, as though I'm a total stranger, and he has no idea what I'm doing in his bed.

'Hope I didn't wake you,' he says, eventually. 'That's the longest sleep you've had in a while.'

I want to sit up and tell him everything: that I lied about seeing Kate, that David is putting me forward for a job, that I'm going to be OK, that he doesn't need to worry about me any more. But I don't know how he'll react. I need to plan this properly, so instead I nod and murmur and pretend to pull the covers back over my head.

'We have your follow-up appointment today,' he says, gently pulling the duvet back down. 'They're going to talk to you about the next step. I don't want you to feel pressured but . . .'

'It's OK,' I say, sitting up. My nightdress is damp under the arms and I realize I've been sweating. All night, or just since hearing him come home? 'I just want to get it over with.'

'Are you sure?'

'Well, nothing else is helping, is it?' I say. Even though David's offer has lifted my spirits more than anything else I can think of, I'm too scared to back out now. They might take me away again. 'So I might as well try.'

'You're very . . . brave,' he says, his eyes serious. He kisses me on the forehead.

'What are you doing today?' I ask.

'I—' He stops short, fiddling with the towel at his waist, wrapping it around himself more tightly. 'I have some things to do later . . . I've got a bunch of photographers to get in touch with about shooting the stuff for the website. Your appointment is at 11 a.m., right? I can have lunch with you, then go off.'

Go off where?

'How was your meeting with the investors last night?' Emboldened, I lay my hand on the fabric over his legs, remembering a time when I would move my hand higher and higher, and we'd fall into bed together and both be late for work. The idea of doing that to him now is somehow inconceivable. I can picture the shock on his face if I did such a thing, and am half tempted. 'I didn't hear you come in.'

'I . . . it was late. It didn't exactly go to plan. Waste of time, to be honest. Nothing for you to worry about. I didn't want to wake you, so I slept across the hall.'

Liar, liar, liar a voice inside my head thunders, but I stay perfectly still, the corners of my lips frozen in an uptight smile, my hand on his leg, despite the thundering in my chest. After all, this morning he's not the only one who's lying. After so many months of having my every waking thought, action and feeling laid bare, to be picked over by others, it is strangely satisfying to have my own secret.

'I prefer it when you're there when I wake up,' I say, using guilt as my weapon instead. 'I don't like waking alone. I always worry you've been in an accident.'

He looks genuinely remorseful then, but instead of breaking down and confessing all, he pushes my hand away and stands up.

'I know. But sometimes it just can't be helped.'

He walks towards the dressing room, pausing briefly before disappearing into it.

'You'd better get dressed darling,' he says, as though he's talking to a five-year-old. 'We don't want to be late.'

We are never late. We are, in fact, half an hour early, and sit side by side on white leather sofas in a vast waiting area. The floor is white marble, the coffee table glass and vast. The walls are white, with choice pieces of ceramics sitting proud on downlit plinths. Above our heads a huge glass skylight floods the room with light, despite the clouds above. There's a coffee machine in one corner, with a choice of different-coloured capsules lined up like jewels on a dark wooden tray. There's bottled water: still and sparkling. A row of neatly stacked glasses. A bucket full of ice. No plastic cups in wobbly towers by a water cooler here. The magazines on the coffee table are cased in plastic folders, and there's a selection to suit all tastes.

This is what you pay for when you go private. Not the expertise, but the trimmings, the stuff that shouldn't matter at all. But Jack had insisted on finding *the best out there, no matter what the cost.* He had sold his sports car to pay for my treatment. Disloyally, I wondered if it was just a badge of honour to stick on his cap.

The waiting area reminds me of the one at KAMU; that first time I saw David. The way he said my name, the whiteness of his smile, the smell of his aftershave.

I glance sideways at Jack, who is frowning at something on his iPhone screen. An email, something about the shop he's interested in renting, the agent requesting a callback with details on the lease. Since he started his business he always has somewhere more important to be, somewhere that's not with me. It was the same with his old job, of course, but I never used to resent it, because I always had somewhere else to be, too. But now I am irritated, and I find myself making a clicking sound at the back of my throat. He puts his phone away and reaches for my hand, squeezing it.

'Not too much longer, darling,' he says. 'Don't worry.'

'I'm not worried,' I say. 'I just want to get it over with. It's just a referral, anyway. Could do it on the phone.'

'Hmm.'

'Do you have a cigarette?'

He looks at me, surprised.

'What?'

'I could smell it on you earlier. Don't pretend. Can I have one?'

There's a split second before he chooses his response. Blink and you'd miss it, but I didn't and I don't.

'Busted,' he says, beaming at me. 'Your bloodhound nose again.' The insensitivity of his comment is lost on him. He doesn't remember that it was only after I became pregnant that I started to smell things more intensely, not before. He reaches into his pocket and pulls out a small packet of Marlboro Lights, handing them to me. 'Not menthol, I'm afraid.'

It used to be a running joke between us. When we first met, we both smoked, but Jack's habit was considerably worse than mine. I'd started at boarding school, because, let's face it, what else was there to do as a seventeen-year-old girl locked up with a load of other girls? It was the only act of rebellion that we could both afford and do every day. But I'd never taken to it properly, not really. It was always an affectation for me – and when Jack found out I smoked menthol cigarettes, he had laughed and told me I was ridiculously adorable.

'I'll cope,' I say, flicking open the lid and pulling one out. 'Lighter?'

He presses a flash of silver into my open palm, and I gasp.

'Wow,' I say, stroking the engraving running across it. 'I forgot all about this.'

'The best present you ever bought me,' he replies, winking.

'I won't be long.'

Outside, I watch people coming and going as I inhale the cigarette slowly. There are characters from all walks of life: young, old, male, female, fat, slim ... Depression is an indiscriminate hunter, picking off its victims like a sniper shooting into a crowd. There's only one thing that unites the sufferers in this particular clinic, and that is that they all have money, or health insurance. Whoever said money can't buy you happiness must have hung out here a lot.

I stub the cigarette out on the ground, half finished, and walk back into the waiting area, towards the sofa we were sitting on. But Jack's not there. In his place is only the imprint of his body, leaving a shallow impression on the white leather. I turn round and scan the room. The receptionists are both on the phone. Other than that, there's no one here but an older couple sitting in one corner.

Jack has vanished.

Instinctively, I pull my phone out of my coat pocket and switch it on. It's frustratingly slow to come to life, and then I am bombarded by the usual notifications of missed calls, which I dismiss in an irritated panic. There are several from my mother, and then a text message from her that keeps popping up, over and over, even as I try to close it. Just three words, pinging in my face repeatedly.

Don't do it.

Eventually, I manage to delete the message and scroll down to find Jack's number. But there's a tug at my shoulder and I turn, and he is there.

'That was quick,' he says. 'Sorry. I just went to stretch my legs.'

He's holding his phone again. When your own behaviour can no longer be considered normal, it's difficult to work out whether or not other people are behaving strangely.

'My mum . . .' I hiss. 'She texted me . . . How did she know . . .?'

'I'm sorry,' Jack says, pushing his phone back into the pocket of his jeans. 'I spoke to her yesterday. She's just worried about you, that's all. Don't worry. It's all going to be OK. It's for the best. We've talked about this. It's going to be OK.'

'Helena Brenton?' a voice echoes across the white cave.

'It's going to be OK,' Jack says, again, squeezing my hand as we walk towards the voice. 'I'm here. You can do this.'

THEN

Ash

Today is my last day in the office before a mandatory Christmas break, and I might be the only person in London who's excited about going to work. After the party, I made my way back to the flat, but found I couldn't switch off. So instead, I got up, pulled on my leggings and started to run. My brain was racing with my legs, the possibilities whirling in my mind. It was 3 a.m. by the time I got back and finally fell into bed, into a fitful sleep.

This morning I woke earlier than normal, and instead of hanging about, I've decided to head straight into the office. It'll be good to be prepared, to take my seat and wait for the show to unfold. As always, I phone Gran on the way to the station and try to advise her as best I can on today's critical issue: where to buy a top for the Zumba class she's starting next week. She agrees to try H&M again – 'Upstairs, Gran, the sportswear is upstairs' – but I make a note on my to-do list to order her something cheerful from Pineapple and have it delivered as a surprise.

Sportswear crisis averted – 'I don't want to look like an old twit, Ashy, Grandad's already told me I won't keep up with all that loud music' – I climb on to a far emptier train than usual and try to work out how I can use the information about Helena to my advantage. Surely, surely, it'll all blow up and eventually one of them will have to leave? And I know which one will be most likely, paving the way for me to move up the ranks . . .

There's no one in the office as I exit the lift, and I'm not surprised. The detritus from yesterday's pre-party drinks – plastic cups, empty bottles, bowls of crisps and some shrivelled olives – is still scattered around.

In the kitchen, I fill the kettle and switch it on, reaching for the mug I always use, the one with a thin rim and the logo of one of the more expensive brands. I'm still caffeine-free, but I've grown used to it now – the mid-morning headaches have subsided and I actually look forward to my cup of peppermint tea.

Back at my desk, I open my laptop and flick through my emails. I don't have any, of course; no one at KAMU is doing any work today. It's 8.30 a.m. – usually, Helena is in by now, but there's no sign of her. Her desk sits across from me, empty and immaculate. After twenty minutes spent reading the latest headlines on *The Drum*, the lift pings to life and I look up, expecting to see her, or David, marching through. But it's neither of them. Instead, it's one of the developers, the one with the clean-smelling T-shirts. Joel, I think he's called.

He smiles at me, but he doesn't have much of a choice – I'm staring right at him.

'Morning!' he says.

'Hi.'

He walks towards my desk. We've never really spoken before, and I don't remember seeing him at the party last night.

'No hangover, then?' he says.

'I only had a couple of glasses,' I reply. 'Usually I'm a teetotal bore.'

'Same,' he says. 'I feel like I should high five you or something.'

I laugh.

'Best not.'

'Was it good, then?' he asks.

'The party? It was . . . a bit dull but it livened up near the end. I didn't see you there?'

He looks embarrassed, all of a sudden.

'No, I couldn't go . . . I had to take care of my mum. She's not very well.'

'Sorry to hear that,' I reply.

He pauses, lingering a little too long, his thumb hanging off the corner of my desk.

'Er, so . . . want a coffee? Ashley, isn't it?'

'Thanks, but I'm good,' I reply, signalling to my mug.

'Ah yes, the peppermint tea girl,' he says. 'You know, my granny drinks that. Enjoy!'

He ambles off to his corner of the office and I am struck by how silent the room is. It's usually a buzz of activity: phones ringing, constant chatter, machines whirring. But eventually, they begin arriving – in dribs and drabs, as Gran would say – like defeated soldiers marching back from war. I sit at my desk and listen to them all, in competition for the worst hangover, for the latest night, for the most dramatic story.

'I fell asleep with both shoes on.'

'I ordered an Uber and then got distracted and carried on dancing – that's the end of my five-star rating!'

'I vomited on the night bus home.'

And the worst one of all, to these princesses of the beauty

world, accompanied by much squealing from the audience: 'I slept in my make-up!'

By 9.35 a.m., there's still no sign of her. No one seems to know what I know, so I keep my mouth shut and, instead, just listen to their one-upmanship. No one seems to be missing Helena, or care why she's not in yet, and I scribble circles on a Post-it note in frustration.

When Lizzy arrives, I feign an excuse about believing I had a meeting with David, and she tells me that he's not in today. That's it for him now, he's gone off to spend Christmas with his wife's parents in their chalet in Switzerland.

'Won't be back till 3rd January, lazy bugger,' she says, but I know she's fond of him – he's a charmer, everyone loves him – and she says it with affection. She tells me she's off herself, in a bit. Another antenatal appointment, apparently. 'Might as well sleep at the hospital, these days!'

Freckles seems to have abandoned the Dukan for today, and is tucking into a bacon roll, thoughtfully provided by the head of sales. His team seem to be faring the worst of all, and one of them has already gone home, claiming food poisoning after throwing up again this morning in the office loos.

No one is doing any work. I am finishing off my end-of-year review, detailing my ideas for engaging more with boutique brands. There are so many opportunities we're missing when it comes to trendy beauty start-ups and niche cruelty-free brands. It's not something I was asked to do, but I'm pleased with it – it's taken me weeks, and I had intended to send it to David and Helena this afternoon, but it's beginning to look like there'll be no point.

It's 10.07 a.m. by the time she finally arrives. She's wearing jeans, as she often does on a Friday, biker boots and a black silk blouse, a bright red geometric necklace adding a flash of colour. I try not to stare as I watch her making her way to her desk, coffee in hand, her coat slung over one arm, her handbag over the other. To the right of her, two of the developers are actually playing ping-pong on that ridiculous table that takes up half the office, and she laughs as the ball flies past her. There's no outward sign that something out of the ordinary has taken place.

'Morning, Helena!' Freckles squeaks as she passes our bank of desks.

'Morning!' she replies, equally sunny. 'Oh God, bacon rolls. Don't tell me I missed them. Dammit.'

'We were wondering where you'd got to.' I can't help myself.

Freckles stares at me with admiration.

'I know! Typical of me to book a dentist appointment the day after our Christmas party, right?' Helena replies, rolling her eyes. 'I was not impressed with myself at 7 a.m. when I remembered.'

Freckles grins. 'Oh, you poor thing!'

'I didn't see you leave last night,' I say, unable to stop myself. 'Did you get home all right?'

Helena shoots me a look then; one I can't interpret. Does she know that I saw her, or does she just think I should mind my own business?

'I just mean . . .' I continue, 'I was a bit worried. Daft. Sorry. My, er, mum always used to fuss over me getting home safely, guess I just . . .'

Helena gives a short, sharp laugh. 'Bless you, Ashley,' she says. 'But I think you'll find I'm old enough and ugly enough to take care of myself.'

Freckles gives a snort. She thinks I don't hear it but I do, and I have to stop myself from kicking her under the desk.

'That put you in your place,' she says, as soon as Helena is settled at her desk and out of earshot.

My foot shoots forward on instinct.

'Ow!' Freckles says, her eyes wide with outrage.

'Oh – so, so sorry,' I reply. 'My foot slipped.'

At 12 p.m. Helena sends an email round to the entire company.

From: HelenaB@kamu.com
Subject: It's beginning to look a lot like . . .

Hi team
Thanks for all your hard work this year! I can't believe how much we've achieved – and we're only five months in. Next year is going to be magnificent. But for now . . . it's time to go home and spend some time with your loved ones. So bugger off, the lot of you, and I'll see you (some of you, at least) after Christmas, and the rest in the New Year.
*   Loads of love*
*   H xxx*

A Mexican wave of excitement ripples around the office as everyone reads it. I do not join in.

The kisses, for one thing, still annoy me. But I've grown used to this new, familiar way of behaving – Helena ends most of her emails with kisses, even the ones to the developers. I know we're new media and most people working here (myself included) are godawful Millennials, but seriously, how can she expect people to respect her when she talks to them like a bunch of needy children? Even though it's not something I've ever experienced, I feel nostalgic for the old days of business, when women wore suits and men wore ties, and people shook hands instead of air-kissing, and everyone took their work seriously.

The other thing that gets on my wick is that I don't want to go home yet. I am contracted to work until 5.30 p.m. I haven't finished proofing my proposal, and now – even if I do manage to finish it within the next five minutes – Helena won't have any time to read it before the break. I've offered to work in between Christmas and New Year, which won me huge brownie points from the rest of my team. But I know there will only be what Helena referred to as a 'skeleton staff' in at that time, and she herself has somehow managed to wangle most of the time off to spend it clay-pigeon shooting with her husband and his family in the Cotswolds. I don't know what they're doing exactly, but it's bound to be something like that.

I look over at her. She's standing by her desk, chatting to one of the developers. There's nothing there, no hint, to suggest what she did last night. Maybe they just had a kiss, left in separate taxis, and she's justified it to herself as a bit of harmless fun at the Christmas party, nothing to be proud of, of course, but something that makes her a bit more human. Maybe she went home last night and tearfully confessed all to Mr Conventional, and he laughed and hugged her and pretended to want to go and punch seven bells out of David, and then they both laughed again and he thanked her for her honesty and told her not to drink so much next time. Maybe they had vigorous sex up against a wall in their hallway afterwards – his way of stamping his scent back on her – and this morning he feels like even more of a man than he did yesterday.

Maybe she really did have the dentist this morning, after all.

By the time I turn back to my computer, half the office has disappeared, and the other half are shrugging on their coats and heading for the lifts. Cheery calls of 'Have a good one, mate!' and 'See you next year!' punctuate the air. Freckles has vanished.

I continue with my work.

By 12.30 p.m., it's just Helena, Joel and me left. Joel seems to be working, like me, and I find myself warming to him even more. Helena, meanwhile, is flicking idly across our competitors' websites – I can see her screen reflected in the window behind her. She'll justify it as research, but I know she's just killing time. She doesn't want to leave before us, thinks it'll expose her magnanimous gesture for the self-interested move it really is.

A few minutes later, her phone rings and she grabs it as though it's a child about to run into the road.

'Hi,' she says, but her voice is so soft I have to strain to hear her. 'Hang on . . . hang on a second, David.'

She stands and strides towards the meeting room, pulling the huge door shut behind her. Inside the glass cage, she rests her bottom on the table, absent-mindedly rubbing the armrest of one of the chairs with her free hand. Her body language is defensive, worried – but, of course, I can't hear anything she's saying. After several minutes, she pulls the phone away from her head and just stares into space, before pinching her nose and returning to her desk. As she passes me, I can see that her eyes are watery, and she gives a not-so-subtle sniff. What has David said to her?

'Drink?'

I look up. Joel has appeared at my desk.

'Sorry?'

'Well, it's Christmas, right. And I'm done with my work, and you . . . well, you look like you've lost interest in yours. So. Do you fancy a drink?'

Nothing is more expensive than a missed opportunity.

I smile, and close down my PowerPoint presentation. I can always finish it tonight.

'Why not?' I reply, offering him my biggest and best smile.

As we leave, Helena looks up.

'Bye, guys,' she says, but her voice is that of a child's: small, faraway, confused. 'Have a good one . . . enjoy.'

'You too!' I reply, and as the lift doors close, I can just about make out Helena resting her head on her hands, as though she's about to weep.

NOW

Helena

Five days to go until my treatment. I have been marking them off on my calendar. Last night, I felt overcome with hysteria at the ridiculousness of life, my situation, everything, and nearly grabbed my marker and scrawled 'Calendar of Doom' across the top of it, but then I saw all those little As, all the red ones, and I realized it's not funny, it's not funny at all.

Jack has been doing his research. Each evening as we sit in front of the fire he pulls out his iPad and I can see over his shoulder he's looking into the side effects, into the possible out-comes. Memory loss – I think that's the one that scares him the most. It doesn't scare me. It would be a relief not to be able to remember the experience. And as for loss of appetite, headaches, nausea, fear, anxiety and confusion . . . I have them all, already.

It's 10 a.m., and Jack disappeared into his workshop at 7. I've been in bed since he left, not sleeping, but not completely awake, either – trapped in a strange kind of insomnia, as though groggy from an operation. I have nothing particularly to get up for, and it's so cold outside. But then the doorbell rings and I know it's the postman – I heard him walking up the lane, whistling. The windows in our bedroom are the original ones, thin panes of glass that barely separate us from the sounds of tyres skidding across tarmac, followed by those incessant shrieks that follow me into my dreams.

I consider ignoring him but he presses our doorbell again, more insistently this time. It's the anniversary of the first day we met. Perhaps Jack has ordered me something; he'll be upset to miss its delivery.

I pull on my dressing gown and tread downstairs, pressing the intercom to open our gates and catching sight of my reflection in the large hallway mirror. A few years ago, I'd have been humiliated to let anyone see me like this, but I don't care any more. And it's good preparation: after what I'm about to go through, I won't have any dignity left.

'Morning!' the postman says, as I open the huge arched door. He thrusts a small bundle into my hands. 'Just a signature here, please.' He's so cheery, so *awake*, so content with his lot in life, I can't help but smile at him.

I scribble something on his little device and take a parcel from him, along with the mail. It's addressed to Jack, as suspected.

'Thank you,' I say.

As he turns to leave, he pauses and looks back.

'You all right, love?' he says. His eyes, watery with age, are the brightest blue I've ever seen. 'None of my business, but I've got a daughter about your age . . .' He gives an anxious smile, and I want to run towards him and throw my arms round him and ask him to be my dad, too.

Instead, I smile again and shrug my shoulders, cradling the post in my arms.

'I've not been well,' I reply. 'But I'm on the mend, thank you. I'm . . . I'm getting some new treatment next week, in fact.'

He's embarrassed now. He didn't want all these details.

'Ah right. So long as someone's looking after you,' he says, softly, as he walks away.

'Yes, my husband, he's just in his workshop, actually . . . but . . . thank you,' I call after him. 'Thank you for asking.'

He nods and I stay at the doorway until he's disappeared down the drive and through our gates. I wish I could invite him in, ask him to tell me all about his daughter, what she does, where she lives – is she married, does she have a career she loves?

In the kitchen, I make tea and toast and perch on a bar stool, looking through the post. Three letters: two of which are addressed to us both, so will be about the mortgage or the house insurance or something equally mundane, but one addressed just to me. I know it's from the Council even before I've torn the seal.

Dear Mrs Brenton

We write regarding your letter to this office of 2 October 2016. We are sorry to hear you still have concerns about road safety in your area.

As you are aware, the Council undertook a risk assessment of Forest Lane last year and took measures, including new signage and removal of the original stone wall on your neighbouring property's land, which was replaced with wire fencing to improve visibility. We also recently filled in several large potholes on Bushwicks Lane. We note your comments about surface water pooling in the road. However, we do not feel this is a sufficient issue to warrant further investigation at the current time.

*We appreciate your concern and assure you we are committed to
road safety within the Pease Valley area.*
Best regards
J. L. Thompson

The contents of the letter are just an echo of what they keep
telling me on the phone; a bureaucratic way of telling me to get
lost. It's the name at the bottom that makes my heart quicken.
Her surname – a common enough one, of course – but the coincidence slaps me around the face, all the same. I cannot escape
her, even when I am trying to. But more than that, I am sure,
so sure, that she mentioned a brother once, that his name was
Jason. I squint at the signature above the printed name, but it's
just a squiggle, like the one I left on the postman's device. It gives
nothing away. It could have been made by a toddler.

I rip the letter into small pieces and sprinkle them into the
recycling bin. What is the likelihood of Ashley's brother suddenly
having a job working at Pease Valley Council? Slim to nonexistent.
I know nothing about him, only that he's younger than her, that
the two of them aren't close.

I turn my attention back to the small square parcel, sitting squat
in front of me on the kitchen worktop, postmarked London. I pick it
up and give it a little shake. Something inside rattles; another box.
Jewellery. It's light, so it's probably a pair of earrings, or maybe a
pendant. I push it into the corner of the counter, by the fruit bowl.

We are going out for dinner tonight. Table for two at the poshest
restaurant in our nearest town. Jack has been excited about it for
days, downloading the menu and reading TripAdvisor reviews as
though he's planning a long holiday. He thinks it's the start of

something new, the celebration of a change. Post-treatment, he hopes I'll be back to my old self. But is it that easy to erase the damage to your brain, to rub it out like a misspelled word on a page?

When he gets home, I am in our bedroom curling my hair with tongs in the way I used to when we first met.

'I've booked us a cab!' he shouts up the stairs. I hear him then, bounding up them like a puppy. 'Oh!' He stops short in the doorway of our bedroom.

'What?'

'Nothing,' he says, smiling. 'It's just . . . well, you look nice. Really nice.'

I am wearing the same dress I wore to meet David. It's pretty much the only thing that fits me, these days; everything else is too big.

'Thanks,' I say, doing a hesitant twirl. I catch sight of my reflection in the dressing-table mirror and all I can see is a bony rake of a woman, all the vitality sucked from her. But my hair, at least, looks good. The clumps that fell out after I gave birth have nearly all grown back. And the corners of my mouth are almost completely back to normal. My tongue darts to them reflexively, running over the once-cracked skin. The iron supplement has worked; I might even risk lipstick.

'I feel . . .' Jack says, coming towards me. He puts his arms around my waist, rests his head on my shoulder. 'I feel like things are changing. Changing for the better. Don't you agree?'

'Yes,' I say, but he catches the hesitation in my voice.

'What?'

'Nothing,' I say, switching off the hair tongs and setting them down on my dressing table. 'It's just . . .' I try to find the words to tell him about David, about the job, about the LinkedIn profile I spent two hours meticulously brushing up this afternoon, but I know it'll be the start of a bigger conversation, and I don't want to ruin the moment. I want us to go out for dinner, and eat a meal and chatter meaninglessly, like we used to.

'Tell me,' Jack says, letting go of my waist. 'What's the matter?'

'Nothing,' I reply. 'I was just . . . just thinking about maybe getting back to work. Some kind of work.'

'Darling, you know you don't need to do that. Are you worried about money? Because we're fine, we're absolutely fine. It won't be long now before I start bringing some in again, I promise. And surely, surely, you have some left, even if you don't want to rely on me?'

'It's not the money,' I say, stunned by his ignorance. Doesn't he understand that we don't just work for money? That it's so much more than that: that it's fundamental to life, having a purpose, self-esteem, an identity. What's the point otherwise? I'm a mother without a child. I'm a career woman without a job. I'm literally pointless. 'I haven't thought about the money at all. I want . . . I *need* to be doing something with my brain.'

'But the house . . .' He tails off. This has been his designated project for me, for the past few months. His way of helping me; giving me something else to think about, to put all my attention into. Minimal risk. I think it was my therapist's idea, in fact. I swear the two of them email each other about me, even though I know that's against her code of ethics. But giving me something to focus on is supposed to save me from myself. The only problem is, I have no interest in interior design – and Jack's the one with all the talent in that department, anyway.

'Jack,' I say, and from nowhere I feel the stirrings of my temper. It's so unfamiliar now, so utterly *missed*, that I want to seize it, drag it out of myself and let it erupt. 'I don't want to do the bloody house up!' It's not quite a shout, but it's the closest I've come in a long time. 'It doesn't need doing up, anyway. It was all done when we got here.'

'It's not our taste,' Jack says. 'I wanted it to feel more "us".'

'It'll never feel more us!' I am shouting now, and the sound is so surprising I want to laugh with nerves. 'We don't belong here. That's why it all went wrong . . . We never belonged here. We're Londoners.'

'I'm from Cirencester,' Jack replies, his voice deliberately calm as he walks towards the wardrobe. 'Actually.'

I give a whine of frustration. 'That's not what I mean . . .'

'I thought you liked living here,' he says, sulkily. 'I thought you understood how important it was for me to be able to give the business a shot. It's not failing, if that's what you're worried about. It just takes time. And anyway, you agreed that we wanted more space . . . better air quality . . . fewer people around . . .'

'That was because—' But I stop talking, because he knows why I wanted to move here, and I don't want us both to start crying. Not tonight. Not when it's meant to be our evening, the start of a promising new future.

Jack gets dressed in the en suite, which feels like he's trying to make a point, but by the time the cab arrives and I am ready, full face of make-up, high heels and no tights, we have both calmed down. In the back of the taxi, he squeezes my hand and I watch the rain drizzle its way down the windows. Tonight is important. Lately, I've felt Jack shifting away from me again. It's as though we've broken down in the middle of a deserted road somewhere and he's walking away to get help, but I'm stuck in the car, and all I can see is him fading into the distance, becoming smaller and smaller, until there's nothing left but a tiny speck. A tiny speck that's about to disappear.

It's twelve years to the day since we first met. We don't really celebrate our wedding anniversary, because we got married after being together for so long and our anniversary was already set in our minds, an annual tradition, something we couldn't change: 30th October.

I reminisce as the taxi winds its way down our lane. For once I am not thinking of the accidents, or the number of times I've found myself standing out in the cold waiting for an ambulance, my heart breaking all over again. Instead, I'm thinking of the party at Barney's.

Barney was Jack's friend from Cambridge, and the son of one of my mother's oldest friends. Of course, the first time I saw Jack, I wasn't that impressed. He was shy, a bit geeky, good-looking but with terrible dress sense. But he was kind. Not one of those Eton or Harrow alumni, but instead the product of a decent grammar school. Pushed by his parents, who wanted more for him than they had had, into a life in the City, but philanthropic with it, keen to change the status quo, to bring some compassion to the financial world. Barney knew – he knew me and he knew Jack, and he knew we'd get on. Within twenty minutes of meeting him, I was hooked. At the end of the evening, we were both a little tipsy. He told me I was beautiful and asked for my phone number. We exchanged a peck on the cheek, and arranged to meet the next week.

I smile when I think of our first date. A slightly less sedate affair;

I got blind drunk and shagged him in a doorway in Notting Hill. He seemed a bit taken aback at the time, but more than happy to participate. So many times we tried to revisit that doorway, but we could never quite remember exactly where it was.

Those days are far away now. Twelve years. It might as well be a lifetime.

We pull into the car park. The restaurant is exactly as I'd hoped: quiet, intimate, with generous spacing between the tables. A converted coaching inn, all low-beamed ceilings and flickering fires. Our fellow diners are grey-haired, stolid and hushed.

'Shall we go for the tasting menu?' Jack says, looking across the top of his menu. 'It's the reason for the plaudits, after all.'

'Five courses?' I reply, scanning the dishes. 'I'm not sure I can manage . . .'

'It's a tasting menu, darling,' he says. 'You only have to taste each. And the portions are tiny.'

And like that, the matter is decided. The old me would have railed against such behaviour, told him that I was well aware what a tasting menu was *thank you very much*, but I've grown used to letting Jack make decisions for me. The inevitable side effect of not being able to trust your own choices any more. It's so much easier when someone else can take the blame.

'So,' I say, when we are halfway through the second course, which seems to consist of half a raw scallop swimming in orange juice. 'How's work? You haven't talked about it for a while. How's the prototype?'

Jack is the first British furniture-maker to incorporate coppiced wood in his designs – the stubby young tree stems cut down during woodland management and usually considered a waste product. It was his passion, something he'd told me he wanted to do ever since I'd met him. When he was stuck in his desk job, he used to talk about it endlessly: the designs he would create, the difference he would make. Now he's actually doing it, he no longer seems to want to talk about it at all. At least, not with me.

'It's frustrating,' he says. 'That's why. Slow progress . . .' He tears a piece of bread from his roll and pops it into his mouth. 'But do you remember Pete Higgins? Short chap – he was on the desk next to me? He came to our engagement drinks, I think . . . I found out today he topped himself. Gassed himself in his garage a few weeks ago. His wife found him. God, am I glad I got out of that place.'

'Oh goodness,' I say. 'Poor woman.'

'Yes, although I'm sure his life insurance has set her up nicely. By all accounts they weren't very happy together, anyway.' He calls the waiter back over to order more water, as though this man's suicide means nothing, and I wonder where the Jack I first met has gone. The one who set up a series of mindfulness work-shops at the bank, to help bring stress levels down. The one who told me to always be kind, because everyone is fighting a battle you know nothing about. Or am I overreacting? Is it all right, him speaking like this, or is it nasty? Does it mean, deep down, he's a total shit, or is he behaving like anyone would, indulging in a little idle gossip about a man that neither of us really knows?

I used to imagine what they'd say about me over dinner in their restaurants, in the kitchen at work and during Friday night drinks in the pub.

'Can you believe what happened to Helena?'

'Never thought she was mother material, anyway. Too career driven.'

'Bet she didn't know what she was letting herself in for.'

Would people be that vicious, or was it just my imagination tormenting me?

Most of all, though, I'd wonder what *she* was thinking. As I lay there sedated in the unit, my arms sore from all the needles, my eyes raw from the tears, bruises all over my body from where they had to hold me down, I'd lie there and wonder if she even cared. I'd wonder if she was lighting a candle for me, looking at the sky and asking whoever was up there to look out for me, as I would have done for her.

'Darling!' Jack says, bringing my attention back to the present.

The only thing that exists is the present.

That's what she would have been thinking. I'm in the past – chucked on the rubbish heap, yesterday's news. She wouldn't have given me, or my predicament, a second thought.

'Yes?'

'Where were you?' he says, rolling his eyes. He's relaxed now – maybe it's the wine, or the fact that I've curled my hair and put a dress on. Whatever it is, he's been reminded of us as we were, and it's making him happy.

'Sorry.'

'I was just saying. Tell me more . . . about what you've been thinking. About going back to work.'

I grab my glass of wine and take a huge swig.

And then I fill my lungs with air and begin to tell him every-thing.

Well, nearly everything.

THEN

Ash

The email arrives only an hour after I sit down.

From: HelenaB@kamu.com
Subject: Chat

Hi Ashley
I'd like to take you for a coffee at Ted's (OK, not a coffee, a cup of warm coconut water or whatever is your current preference!) to have a quick catch up at 11 a.m. today, if you're free.
  Thanks
  H xx

I write back without hesitation.

From: AshleyT@kamu.com
Subject: Re: Chat

Of course.
A

We are all back in the office after the 'holiday season', as the revolting bigwigs referred to it in their corporate 'Thank you, worker drones, you have served us well' message. David has been hosting various people in his glass enclosure all morning. Helena, wearing a silk shirt dress, Alice band and suede over-the-knee boots (Christmas present from Mr Conventional?), has been typing furiously. Freckles is dieting again: 'I'm trying the 5:2 now, better not talk to me on a 2 day!' And Joel has been emailing me, asking me about my New Year's resolutions, and whether any of them involved giving him a second date. Even though, technically, our first one wasn't a date at all – as I have painstakingly pointed out to him. Although I've been enjoying the attention, I am getting a little frustrated with the constant distraction.

There's a card going round for Lizzy. KEEP CALM AND ENJOY YOUR MATERNITY LEAVE, it shouts, complete with a drawing of a stork that looks more like a duck, dangling a takeaway box from its mouth. Inside, David's scrawl implores her: *Good luck and all that, but remember: KAMU was your first love! Enjoy yourself but not so much you don't come back! Hope I can survive without you . . . xx* I suppose he thinks he's being funny, or cute, or affectionate. Thinks he's showing her how much she means to him, rather than guilt-tripping her for choosing biology over office management. Still, it's a shame she wasn't able to resist the call of the Motherland. I'm actually going to miss her. There's a warmth about her, the touch of Essex in her accent, the way she always offers you paracetamol if you say you're feeling under the weather . . . She makes you feel safe, like she actually cares.

She'll be a brilliant mother, I think, and so I write this in the card and push it towards Freckles.

93

There has been no reply to my twenty-six-page boutique brand proposal from either David or Helena. I had 'read' receipts for both of them, so they've definitely opened the emails: Helena, on 27th December; David, not till 31st December – what a way to spend New Year's Eve! I'd like to think that Helena wants to talk to me about it this morning, but it makes no sense that she would do so at Ted's, rather than in the meeting room, or the canteen.

The only other possibility, of course, is that she wants to talk to me about David, and what I saw at the Christmas party. My toes tingle with excitement and I find myself rashly accepting Joel's offer of a date on Friday.

At ten to eleven, I go to the ladies' toilets and examine my reflection. My skin is pale, my eyes bright, my lips almost invisible. My hair is jet black, along with my eyebrows, and if it wasn't for my blue eyes, my face would look like a black-and-white photograph. I've never worn a lot of make-up – never really got the hang of it – and I've always wanted to be taken seriously for my work, rather than my appearance. But I am beginning to appreciate the value in that awful expression: power dressing. I think of Helena's suede boots, and what an impact they make.

On the way to the coffee shop, we chatter about our holidays. Well, Helena chatters and I listen. When she asks me how my Christmas was, I skim over the surface, telling her that Gran had a fall, and that we spent most of it in the hospital by her bedside. Despite Helena's sympathetic murmurs, her attention is focused elsewhere and I am glad I haven't given her any more details.

Ted's is one of those artisan-type places on the canal towpath. I take a sip of my hot chocolate as I smile at her, anxious to hear the purpose of this meeting. She insisted on paying for my drink, and for a second I am illogically terrified she is going to fire me.

'Right, then, I'll get to the point,' she says. 'I have some news. And I wanted to discuss it with you.'

'Oh,' I say. This is not what I was expecting. 'Sounds intriguing.'

She looks at me, suddenly hesitant, as if she isn't sure she can trust me.

'Well . . .' There's a pause. So much for getting to the point. 'God, I don't know why I'm so nervous about telling you.' She's talking more to herself than me. 'It's just a coincidence, really. Or a sign we're both geniuses. Ha, ha. So, the news is . . . in February I'm going to be moving across to a different role.'

'Really?' I say, careful to keep my voice measured. 'That's exciting. Doing what exactly?'

'It *is* exciting,' she replies, and then she starts beaming again, that same angelic smile that made the barista blush when she paid for our drinks. He clocked her wedding ring straight after, though, and I saw his face fall.

'David's asked me to head up a new division,' she says. 'He agrees with me that Kiss and Make Up are doing amazing things, but also that they're missing a trick for the London market, in particular. So I'll be launching a standalone site, still under the KAMU umbrella, of course, but . . . well, this is the funny thing. It's been in the pipeline for months, I promise you. Just shows you have your finger on the pulse!' She gives a strangled laugh. 'It's a site for niche brands, brands with provenance, brands with a story behind them. As you rightly pointed out in your proposal, there are so many smaller brands out there just waiting for an audience. So we're going to give it to them.'

She's. Stolen. My. Idea.

I take a deep breath, trying to get my feelings in some kind of order. My eyes narrow as they meet hers, scanning them for sincerity, trying to work out if she's truly done what I think she's done, or if it's just a coincidence, as she's so merrily protesting.

'Well,' I say. She's still my boss. I can't lose control. I need this job. And I did send the proposal, after all. What did I expect? That she'd give me a budget and the free rein to set up a new site on my own?

But still, the injustice of it . . . her taking all the glory, probably getting a massive pay rise.

'That's . . . certainly interesting.'

She smiles awkwardly. At least she's aware of what she's doing.

'That's why I wanted to talk to you about it personally,' she says, 'away from the office. I didn't want you to think anything untoward had gone on. I promise that this has been on the cards for a while now – I first approached David with the idea in the summer. We were just waiting for the OK from the American team . . . They took some persuading, but they green-lit it just before Christmas, and I'll be announcing my new role to the rest of the office later on today. Best of all, if it's a success, there's the possibility of rolling it out over there, too.'

'Right,' I say.

Back in your box, Ashley, where you belong.

What's the point of telling me this? Some kind of weird boast? To try to make herself feel better?

'Well, good for you. I hope they have the budgets to work with you. Always a challenge with smaller brands.'

'Ah, listen, Ashley,' she says, smiling. 'That's another reason I wanted to talk to you. I know you're wasted in that job. I appreciated your proposal, it was so near the mark. Considering you've no experience in this area, your insights were . . . ambitious but impressive. Not to mention the fact that your business instincts are almost spot on. If a little naive, at times. I think getting the bigger brands to sponsor an event championing their smaller competitors is just a *little* bit unlikely!'

She rolls her eyes at me, laughing. I want to hit her.

'But you're far too bright to be writing Instagram captions all day,' she continues. 'I'm going to suggest to David that we promote you to a new role as Head of Influencer Marketing. I'd like to harness those business instincts, put some proper targets against your work. And Jodie needs support with the digital stuff, she's admitted as much. We might even find the budget for an assistant – or an intern, at least – to help you with the donkey work. What do you think?'

I've never been very good at hiding how I feel. It's my strength and my weakness. I don't have time to mess around. I don't have time to spare people's feelings.

What do I think? I think she's being incredibly patronizing.

'Yeah,' I say, gathering myself together. 'I'm not sure, actually. I'm not sure it's what I want to do.'

She looks genuinely puzzled. It doesn't occur to her that I might want more than some crappy new job title accompanied, no doubt, by a crappy two grand pay rise again.

'Oh,' she says. 'Right. Sorry. I thought . . . I thought you were looking to get promoted. I must have got the wrong end of the stick. I thought you were fiercely ambitious.'

'I am fiercely ambitious,' I reply, and I realize I am glaring at her just in time to soften my features. 'I'm just not fiercely ambitious to work my arse off doing what other people tell me to. Just like you, really.'

She smiles at me, and there is a silence. We are like two cats, sizing each other up before a fight.

'I've underestimated you,' she says, after a while. 'I'm sorry. But . . . I mean, realistically, working your way up at a company like KAMU can only be a good thing . . .'

'Do you have any idea what it's like?' I can tell I'm about to rant, and there is no way to stop it. The coffee shop and all its noise somehow fall away, until I can see nothing but her huge eyes, blinking at me. 'To have come from the kind of place where no one amounts to anything, where getting a job in management in Tesco is seen as a success? To be constantly told that people like me, people with backgrounds like mine, don't go anywhere? My gran . . . my gran would have been pleased if I'd married a postman and had two kids. That would be seen as a great achievement. Anyone who hasn't done a spell in young offenders is considered a catch.'

She shifts about in her seat, her eyes wandering towards the exit. 'I'm sorry.'

I let out a great sigh, running my hands through my hair in frustration, messing up my fringe. The twinkly barista chooses this moment to come over with a tray and collect our cups.

'Anything else I can get you?' he says.

'No,' Helena says. She's eyeing me, nervously. But with something else, too . . . a kind of curiosity that I haven't noticed before. 'We're good, thanks.'

'In that case,' he says, leaning down towards me, 'I hope you don't think I'm being rude but you have the most beautiful eyes.

Can I take your number? I would love to take you out sometime.'

'No,' I say, looking away. Brilliant. Just to rub salt in the wound, now I'm getting Helena's sloppy seconds. 'I'm not interested.'

'Ashley!' Helena cries, flicking me on the arm as though we are old friends. 'That's so mean!'

She gives him an apologetic smile and he shrugs, before walking away, looking remarkably unaffected by the situation. Perhaps he does it all the time.

'Listen,' she says, considering me. 'I'm starting this division from scratch, and I'll need a team around me who are as passionate about it as I am. And it'd be great to have someone feisty, ballsy alongside me. Someone who isn't afraid to be ambitious, who doesn't apologize for it. So, forget what I just said. How do you feel about joining me?'

'Joining you?'

'Yes. Forget the promotion. Why don't you come to work for me at the new website? I'll need a second-in-command.'

'Thanks,' I say, sighing. She still doesn't get it. I don't want to be an iron in someone else's fire. 'Thanks, but I think I'd find it too frustrating, Given that I had my own ideas for it . . . I want to be able to manage something of my own.'

'OK,' she says, looking thoughtful. 'I understand . . . but what if we created a role for you?' she says, and I can tell that even as the words come out she's not entirely sure of them, she's just trying them on for size. 'Something for you to take ownership of. David and I are both agreed that events will form a huge part of this new site's strategy. We need to take it offline, to really get the message out there. Pop-up shops, that kind of thing. How would you feel . . . how would you feel about running that section alongside me?'

NOW

Helena

I don't tell Jack, but sometimes I dream that I am with her. We're in the park and she's bigger now – no longer a baby, but a small person, fists clenched and determined to make her own way in the world. Her face is round, her arms under her jumper soft and doughy, coated in skin as white and fragile as chalk. I watch her: fighting for independence, a gummy mouth set in a line as she hauls herself upright, pushing unreliable feet through the wet grass, trying to reach me herself. Those tiny brown eyes fixed on mine, shining like glass, telling me fiercely not to help, but to let her do it on her own.

I cling to these dreams, but they don't come often enough. And when they do, they're always marred. Because my mother is always there, too – hovering in the background, at first, then coming between us, trying to take her from me.

Sometimes dreams are more painful than reality.

It has been three days now, and I haven't heard anything about the job. I am back to obsessively checking my LinkedIn page, to see if this Sean Taylor chap has looked at my profile. But nothing.

Not a peep since he accepted my invitation to connect, from my shiny new grown-up email address.

Now, I feel like a fool. After all the fuss, all the excitement, what if he never gets in touch? What if David had some other reason for luring me back? What if the whole thing was a set-up, what if he was just trying to find out what I was up to, to feed the information back to her?

I realize I am pacing the living room, in the way I did the days after I lost her. Walking round and round in circles, clutching my mobile phone, now switched on at all times, desperate for news. My mind is filled with phrases, snippets of potential things I could say, ways I could get in touch, opening lines for emails . . . the words swirl around and around, shouting in my ears, until my head hurts so intensely that I have to sit down, pushing my palms into my eye sockets, trying to make everything go away.

But there is only one way to make that happen.

I call David.

It's two rings before he answers, and I feel my breathing slacken again, like a released spring.

'Well, hello!' he says, and the clarity of his voice tells me he's in his office, surrounded by glass, no interruptions.

'Hi,' I say, trying to speak slowly. 'How are you?'

'Knee-deep in Q1 budgeting,' he replies, as though my phone call is the most natural thing in the world, as though it was in his diary, he's been expecting it. 'You remember how it is. Gavin's trying to get us to align with Australia, who apparently are producing twice the amount of content as we are – with half the headcount. Anyway . . . how are you?'

'I'm fine, I'm well, I'm . . .' I tail off. 'Well. I was just wondering,

I mean, I haven't heard.' I stop speaking for a few seconds. My hands are shaking and I feel nausea creeping up the edges of my insides. 'I haven't heard anything from Sean. Just wondering . . . I'm about to go away. Er, Jack and I. We're off on holiday next week. Just wanted to check before I leave . . . in case there's no Internet . . . Jack's big on digital breaks these days . . . leaving the iPads behind . . . '

'Where are you going?' David asks, and of course he's more interested in my holiday plans than anything else.

'What?'

'On holiday? Surprised he's able to have a break from his new project so early on . . . although it is the perfect time to visit Asia of course. Thailand?'

'Yes,' I reply, unthinking. 'Thailand.'

'Going for the beaches? Even so, make sure you make a trip to Chiang Mai. Unmissable. Don't let Jack get involved with the water sports, or you'll never see him again . . . so cheap out there.' He gives a little laugh, as though he knows Jack and his type, as though they're old friends, as though they've done water sports together.

'Yes,' I say. 'Will do. But listen, any idea what's happening with . . . the position you, er, mentioned?'

'Sean not been in touch?'

'No.'

'Hmm,' he says. 'I can give him a ring for you, if you like? Or why don't you just ping him an email now? Here . . . hang on . . . there you go, I've sent over his address.'

'Great,' I say. 'Thank you. I will.'

I stride to my office, pulling open my laptop. I type hurriedly, check the email once for errors and then send it, before I have the chance to talk myself out of it.

Of course, Sean replies the morning that I am due to go in for my treatment: 6 a.m., so it's there when I wake. An email dashed off before a busy day in the office, or perhaps he's going to the gym first, setting himself up for another day of *doing something* with his life, of making his mark.

It's just a few lines. That's all it is to him – a few lines to get rid of that niggle at the back of his mind, to tick it off the to-do list. But a few lines are all it takes, these days, to shatter my delicately reconstructed self-esteem.

> *From: SeanT@shopit.com*
> *Subject: David Marlow*
>
> *Helena*
> *Thanks for your email. David spoke very highly of you and I appreciate you taking the time to get in touch. We've filled this role now, but great to know you are looking for a new challenge and I'll certainly touch base again if we have any other suitable openings.*
> *Regards*
> *Sean*

There is nothing to be read into this, not really, not if you are a normal human being. It might just be that I took too long to get back to David. That actually my skillset wasn't quite what they were looking for. That someone else Sean went to Harvard with recommended someone else, and they got in there first. That they wanted a man for the job instead of a woman, despite how sickeningly unfair it is. But still. All I read is that I am tainted, that no one wants to work with me, that my business card is marked, that I am a mother without a child, that I am a career woman without a career, and that the sum of all these facts is that I am a failure.

Jack finds me staring into space in my nightdress in the en suite, my legs curled under me on the cold tiled floor. The underfloor heating is switched off, and my toes are frozen. The dial to turn the heating back on is barely an arm's stretch away, but it's still too far, too far for me to reach, like everything else in my life. Or maybe I just don't care enough any more. Let my toes freeze – what does it matter when my brain is atrophying, anyway?

I'm so tired of myself.

'This is why I didn't want you involved,' Jack shouts, standing in the doorway. He doesn't rush to comfort me, as he might once have done. He knows better now. He knows that he can't stop my feelings with a simple hug, a promise of a brighter tomorrow, a cup of extra-strong tea. He is frustrated instead, kicking the door frame in irritation.

'That fucking man. I should never have told you he'd called. Getting your hopes up. He has *no* idea, *no idea*, what we've been dealing with. What you've been through. Raising your hopes. And today. Today of all days!'

He disappears then, through to the bedroom, and I hear him kicking something else – probably the bed frame – and thumping his fists on the windowsill. I let him get it all out, and then I straighten up, blow my nose, wipe my eyes, and walk towards him.

'Jack. We have to go,' I whisper, touching his back. 'Please. Let's go. I'm going to have the treatment. It's a good day. We need to try to be positive. Let's go. Let's go and get this done.'

He turns to face me, and I see that he is crying.

'I just want you to get better,' he says, and then he falls towards me, burying his face awkwardly on my shoulder. His sobs grow louder as the dampness from his tears seeps through my nightdress. 'That's all I want, Helena. I just want you to get better.'

PART TWO

THEN

Ash

There's an unfamiliar mug on my desk in our new office; I notice it as soon as I come in. Stamped in bright pink letters around the outside of it is a slogan: *Teamwork makes the dream work*. I left Helena in the office alone last night to go on a long run: 12km. I wanted to make it to 15km but it started to rain and my knackered trainers began to fill with water. It was the first time I'd left the office before Helena since we started working on KAMU Boutique, six weeks ago – usually, I stay till at least 8 p.m., and she always leaves before me, muttering that Jack will be calling the missing persons helpline. I know the truth is that she's just tired, or bored of work, and then I remember: not everyone enjoys working as hard as I do.

But yesterday morning I stood in the shower and felt the skin over my hips was softer than before. Not much, but enough for me to notice. Too many late nights, too many unhealthy dinners. I even resorted to eating chips one evening last week, when my stomach felt like it was about to eat itself, and they were the only thing I could bear to buy from the fried chicken shop on the corner. I'm trying, but it's so hard to mix business with exercise.

Helena and I ran together at lunch yesterday, but with her slowing me down I felt like I hadn't exercised properly. There's been so much work to do: wire-framing the website, branding, compiling spreadsheets of potential clients, sending feelers out. My new job title is Events Manager, but that hasn't stopped Helena asking me for advice on pretty much everything. Thankfully, David and the Americans have been happy to let us do our own thing, and so far Helena and I are mostly on the same page. She's actually quite compliant, I'm beginning to realize.

'What's this?' I say, taking my seat, picking up the mug and waving it at Helena. The rim is far too thick, the handle uncomfortably narrow.

'Do you like it?' she says, smiling at me. 'It's a present! Thought it could be a kind of motto for us, seeing as we're going to be a brand-new team. I got five of them, so we can all have one.'

'How will we know whose is whose?' I say, but then I see her face fall. I don't want to upset her. So I give her a beaming smile, instead – not quite as good as hers, but I'm working on it. Copying her mannerisms is a recent project; I've written them all down in my notebook, and am pleased to have mastered the annoying art of 'coyly tucking hair behind ear while gazing up confidently'.

But where was I? The mug.

'But no, I love it,' I say. 'Thank you. It's great. And very organized of you to get all the staff one before you've even recruited them . . .'

I jerk my head and scan our empty corner of the office, sweeping my eyes over the empty chairs at empty workstations. I was pleased when David said we'd be co-located with the rest of KAMU, but on the floor below – far enough away that we feel pretty much independent, even if he has insisted on weekly management updates.

'Ha!' Helena replies. 'Yes. They'll appreciate them SO much. First on my list for today: meeting the recruitment agents. It's why I got in early, actually.'

'Knock, knock.'

I look up to see David peering round the door to our office.

'Am I allowed in?' he says. 'Or is it women only down here?'

'Hilarious,' Helena says, but she stands up, flushing slightly at the sight of him. 'Come and meet all our staff. Jeff did a great job with the set-up – do thank him for me. I'm so excited to start filling these desks.'

'I think you have a better view,' David says, walking towards the window. 'Definitely not fair. Might have to see what we can do about that.'

'You mean you can see how busy the pub is from here,' Helena says, moving closer to him.

'Yes,' he replies. 'Like I say, a much better view.'

Are they flirting, or am I just clueless? Whatever's going on, I feel distinctly uncomfortable. I give an involuntary cough and they both look back at me.

'How are you getting on, Ashley?' David asks, apparently only just aware of my presence. 'Is she working you too hard?'

'More like the other way round,' I say, my big mouth running away with me again. Shit. 'I mean, I've been getting a bit carried away. Just very enthusiastic about the project, as I'm sure you know.'

'Oh yes,' he says. 'Helena mentioned that you'd had a similar idea yourself. Great to have you on board.'

A similar idea myself? Did he not even bother to read my proposal, then? A wave of misery washes over me, that tide of self-doubt again, telling me I'll never matter, I'll never achieve anything, it's all too stacked against me.

I give him a tight smile, my passive aggressive way of showing him I don't care what he thinks, and look down at my computer. I wish that Joel hadn't been poached by a financial software firm but was upstairs so that I could have a little moan in the stairwell. I pick up my phone, consider texting him my frustration, but put it back down again. It's still early days, don't want to frighten him off by whinging too much.

'So,' I hear David say, although I keep my head down. 'Budgets. Do you have time to chat now?'

I look back up, but he's staring directly at Helena. She nods, grabs her notepad and flicks her hair behind her shoulders, before sauntering out of the office without even giving me a backward glance.

THEN

Helena

The best part about Ash working for me is that she actually *likes* doing sales. When David told me there was only enough in the budget for one account exec until we've proved our business case, I realized I'd be expected to do a huge chunk of the legwork myself. But when I mentioned this to Ash, she happily volunteered to take ownership of our lead list, saying she'd need to be in touch with them all for the first pop-up event, anyway.

I knew I did the right thing getting her on board.

My most pressing task is recruitment, and I am deeply engrossed in forms sent to me by the agent when I hear the office door push open. I look up, expecting to see David, or Jodie – my best friend from KAMU upstairs – but, instead, I see my husband.

'Jack!' I say, and I can't help but smile. It feels like an age since I've seen him in the daylight. I think back to our teary conversation at New Year, how we promised to make more of an effort to make time for each other. We're only a few weeks in and we're failing already. 'What are you doing here?'

'Just had a meeting round the corner, couldn't face going back into the office . . .' He pauses for a moment, and I notice the bruise-like shadows under his eyes. His insomnia is back, then. I feel a rush of tenderness for him. 'It's nearly four, anyway. And I told you I'd come and see your new empire! All this space for your new project. But where's your minion?' He nods towards Ash's empty desk.

'She's scouting locations for our pop-up. I was going to go too but I got caught up in this and thought it best to finish . . .'

'Oh, shame,' Jack says, pulling out her chair and sitting in it.

'She won't be back today but you'll meet her soon, I'm sure. In fact, I was thinking of inviting her over to Dad's at some point. Bizarrely, she mentioned he was one of her business heroes. I think she's read his autobiography – how embarrassing is that?'

He nods, his face twisting slightly as his trouser pocket vibrates.

'Sorry,' he says, pulling out his phone.

I turn back to the forms on my desk.

'Oh!' he says, and I look back up again.

'What?'

'Alicia has had her baby!' His voice is strange, unfamiliar, high-pitched and excitable. He holds his phone up to me, shows me a picture of a tiny, wrinkly-faced infant. 'Six pounds seven, whatever that means. Isn't she cute?'

'Gorgeous,' I say, obediently. 'What's its name?'

'Her. It's a girl. Olivia Rose Huntingdon-Clark.'

'Lovely,' I reply, eyeing him. He's gazing off into the middle distance, his eyes unfocused, despite the phone in front of them. 'Barney must be thrilled. Say congrats from me.'

Jack nods again, types a reply and then puts his phone back in his pocket.

'It'll be us next,' he says, and I notice the vein on his neck is pulsating slightly. I watch it as it moves back and forth, like a tide coming in and drawing back, the same tension.

I laugh, loudly and heartily, to let him know that I appreciate his joke.

'You barely sleep as it is,' I say. 'Listen, what are you up to? It's a bit early for me to leave but Ashley won't be back today and I've nearly done these forms, anyway. Why don't we go and get some sushi and go home? I feel like it's been ages since we did anything together . . . anything that's not, well, rushed.' I wink at him, and immediately regret it. It feels seedy, condescending, entirely wrong. Yes, our sex life isn't what it used to be, but at least we still have one, unlike so many people who've been together as long as we have.

He stands up and walks towards me. In his shirt and suit jacket, the light from the window casting a glow around him, I suddenly see him as all the women he works with must see him. Sexy. My husband is sexy.

He takes my hands and hauls me to my feet, pulling me against him and finding my mouth with his. Gently at first, and then with more insistence. It takes me back to years ago, to how we once were, before we got old and familiar and saw each other more often in our slippers and pyjamas. Before sex was just a mechanical procedure done under a thick duvet, something to be crossed off the to-do list, an exercise in good health: three times a week, like the gym.

'Jack!' I say, squirming a little, but then an image flickers through my mind. Me, in a taxi, an unfamiliar aftershave hanging in the air. I squeeze my eyes shut, blink it away. Thank God he's in the US this week and there's no chance of him popping down to my office. I kiss my husband back, pushing him on to the desk, clearing the day's clutter with one swipe of my arm, as though I'm in a film.

We take the Tube home after five minutes failing to hail a taxi. I suggested getting an Uber, but Jack had read something about the way they were treating their drivers and gave me a very well-intentioned lecture as to why we should no longer use them. His social conscience, one of the reasons I fell in love with him, is both endearing and alien to his type.

The carriage is relatively empty and we sit next to each other, hand in hand, as the train rattles through the stations. I rest my head on his shoulder, fighting the urge to get my phone out and check my emails. In the restaurant, I sneaked off to the toilets and managed to reply to three from Ash, making sure to delete the automatic *Sent from my iPhone* message at the bottom of them. I don't want her to think I'm slacking off already, not when I'm her manager. Even though I'm itching to find out if she's replied to my suggestion that we try to lure Joel back as our developer, it can wait till tomorrow. Enough work today, my relationship deserves some time, too.

'It's a bit fiddly from Kings Cross isn't it?' Jack says, as we get off at Finchley Road to change trains. It's cold on the platform. The early spring sunshine has disappeared, leaving a chill in its wake.

'I told you we should have got an Uber!' I say, stamping my feet up and down. 'Goodness me, it's cold. I should have put a scarf on this morning.'

Jack takes his off and puts it around my neck. It smells of him and I lean up and kiss him as a thank you.

'Barney and Alicia are moving out of town you know,' he says, staring over my head at the departure board.

I turn round. Seven minutes till the next train.

'Hmmm,' I say, already aware of where this conversation is leading. 'Are they going to get chickens?'

'Maybe,' he replies, smiling. 'Their place was valued at one point two million. Crazy. Never could understand the appeal of Putney myself, all that aeroplane noise. But they're looking at Buckinghamshire, apparently. Can practically buy an estate for that in some of the smaller villages.'

'Right,' I say, scrabbling around for a new subject. A train trundles past on the opposite platform and unveils a huge billboard for a new film, much lauded, nominated for seven Oscars. 'Fancy seeing that sometime?' I nod at the billboard.

'Uh, yeah, maybe,' he says, refusing to take the bait. 'I think it'd be nice to have a bit more space. Not to have to do . . . this . . .'

'Getting the Tube home was your idea! And anyway, how do you think people who live in the suburbs get to work? Helicopter?'

'I'm just saying. All the people. Don't you wish for a change of scenery sometimes? A bit of space?'

'That's what holidays are for,' I reply, bluntly.

'We couldn't stay here if we had a kid,' Jack says. 'For a start the flat's too small, and for another, I wouldn't want them growing up with all this pollution.'

'Best not have a kid, then,' I say, relieved to see our train slowly pulling up to the platform. Subject changed. Confrontation avoided.

Or so I think.

He presses on, in the carriage, his eyes suddenly a little bloodshot, as though he's exhausted or had too much to drink.

'But darling, you said we'd try this year . . .'

'Yes, but that was before.' Bubbles of irritation start to pop in my mind. *I thought* we were having a nice evening. Not doing this. Again.

'Before what?'

'Before I got promoted,' I say, my voice strained. 'I'm working on a new launch. It's not exactly a great time to be disappearing off to have a baby, is it?'

Jack slumps back in his seat, dropping my hand, like a sulky teenager.

'What?' I say, twisting in my seat to frown at him.

'I just . . . I told you before, I don't want to be an old dad.'

'You're thirty-seven! That's not old. That's young, these days.'

'Yes, but we should get a move on . . . you're thirty-five this year . . .'

'Oh great, thanks very much. Now I'm too old! Brilliant.'

'I'm just saying. I don't want to be like my father. Dead before my kids turn twenty. I want to be around for them while I still have the energy to do things with them. I want to see them grow up. I want to see them have kids of their own.'

'You're getting a little ahead of yourself,' I say.

The woman sitting opposite us is blatantly eavesdropping on our conversation, her eyebrows moving up and down with interest.

'Anyway, can we talk about this another time? Another place? Like home . . .'

'It just feels like you've gone off the idea entirely,' Jack says.

'Don't be ridiculous! It's just not the right time at the moment. It'll happen when it's meant to.' My fingers shoot to my upper arm, digging about under the skin for the little tube, making sure it's still there.

The woman opposite me notices my fiddling, and I really want to tell her to mind her own business, but she's having far too much fun listening in. I wonder if she has kids. She's about my age, but her clothes are crumpled, her hair scraped back into a ponytail, highlights long outgrown, her eye make-up smudged with tiredness. Perhaps she's silently willing me not to back down, trying to tell me that I'm right. I meet her eyes for a second and she smiles at me. Yes, that's it, female solidarity. *It's your life that will change, not his*, her eyes seem to be saying. *Don't do it unless you really want to.*

Jack slumps down even further, pulling his phone out from his pocket. I watch as he opens his emails, flicking through them quickly, as though they are ants that need to be disposed of. He pauses on one. I let my eyes travel further and read the subject line, a split second before he closes the app. *Termination of Contract.* He sucks air through his teeth, then puts his phone away, staring through the opposite window at the blurry tunnel walls as the Tube hurtles along.

So that's what he's been dealing with today. I sink back into my seat, put my hand on his knee and squeeze it. I remember how hard he finds having to sack people; he's far too compassionate for his own good. Sometimes I forget how stressful his job is – the more money you earn, the more responsibility you have – and I know that, deep down, he wants to be like his dad, putting up shelves for a living, working with his hands and with the grateful rather than the greedy. But it was all mapped out for him, by his teachers, his parents, whether he wanted it or not, and Jack is nothing if not eager to please.

There's nothing new I can say to him. I've told him before that he can give up work if he likes, that I can support us both, but his pride won't have it. And so I let him brood as I pull out my phone and go through Ash's emails. All eighteen of them.

THEN

Ash

Google Maps reliably informs me that Helena's dad's house is a twenty-five-minute walk from the station. I should have remembered from Gran's cleaning jobs; people who live in houses like this don't need to live near a station. Or a bus stop. They drive everywhere. Or are driven.

I wish I could drive. Last week I read an interview with someone who said that adults who couldn't drive or cook were immature, that they needed to grow up. It pissed me off – but then again, I kind of see their point. Now I can afford to, it's time I learned – something else for the to-do list.

Thankfully, I allowed myself plenty of time and I have half an hour to spare before I am due at the Cawstons' house. I leave the station and turn right, heading for the high street. There's an Asian man sitting in a car outside the station; he winds the window down when I approach and it's only then that I realize he is a taxi and expects me to want a ride. I shake my head at him, although part of me is slightly tempted to turn up in a taxi. I suppose that's what they would expect.

Using my phone as a guide, I head towards the centre of the

town. It's cold, but my feet are bearing up despite the four-inch heels, and I am listening to Arianna Huffington's book *Thrive* through my headphones. I am especially enjoying her thoughts on the need to disconnect from technology in order to reconnect with ourselves. I just wonder when I'll have time to do so. In my bag, I have a bottle of red wine – a Châteauneuf-du-Pape, classy but not too expensive. I've learned enough to know what good manners are.

Helena said her husband will be there for lunch, and I'm looking forward to meeting him, finally. He's always been too busy before and I've, perhaps unfairly, taken against him for it. I don't need to meet his eligible friends any longer, not now I have Joel, but I'm still interested to see what Jack is like. I smile as I think of Joel, watching me get ready earlier. I've decided that I'll let him move in with me in a month or two, if things are still going well. It'll be great to have some help with the rent, and he seemed to take the hint when I cleared a space for his stuff in my wardrobe and told him to consider my place his home.

The high street is a pretty affair, all carefully planted hanging baskets and hand-painted shop signs. So this is what the women of Hertfordshire do on their Saturdays: push their brood of perfectly dressed children down the high street to the baker's, trailing their Labradors behind them. Most of them seem to have a husband in tow, too. I wonder if any of these cashmere women have jobs, or if they're just employed full-time by their offspring.

My left foot starts to chafe slightly and I stop for a second to stick a plaster over the back of my heel, fiddling with it to make sure it's not visible. When I finally arrive at St Andrew's Hill, I am stunned to find a little man sitting in a small hut, in front of a long, white, firmly closed gate.

'Hello,' he says, not unfriendly.

'Hi,' I say, kicking myself for not taking the cab, after all. 'I'm here to visit Sandbanks. The Cawstons' house?'

He nods at me.

'Right you are,' he says. 'Come on through. Although it's a walk, I'm afraid. You need to continue up South Road, then when the road forks, take a left. It's on Golf Club Road, about halfway down. Or up.' He chuckles. 'Bit of a hill, unfortunately. Lovely road, though. One of the nicest.'

I nod at him, steeling myself for the walk. My foot is hurting now. Properly hurting. I'm also freaking out that my underarm area is beginning to feel a little damp. I decide to walk far enough that I am out of the sentry man's sight, and then refresh myself with the deodorant I have in my bag.

I arrive at the house exactly five minutes early. It reminds me of a doll's house from the outside: perfectly symmetrical, with an overbearing black front door, flanked by two enormous stone pillars. The brick is a kind of sand colour, and the windows are Georgian in style, with timber framing. Gran would be so impressed.

But this isn't Helena's house. It's her dad's. I am yet to be invited to Helena's flat. All I know is that it's a stone's throw from West Hampstead Tube. I wonder if she has any idea just how lucky she is.

I make my way up the long driveway, taking in the perfectly symmetrical olive trees forming a V shape each side of the front door. It's all a bit paint-by-numbers. But I still feel a thrill of anticipation as I approach the front door. Mr Cawston grew up in the roughest part of Essex – his parents were publicans, he didn't go to university, and he made every penny himself through hard graft. Proving there's hope even for me. He's one of the reasons I applied for that job with Helena in the first place and now, finally, finally, I'm going to get to meet him. She invited me when we were out jogging together last week – it was pretty thoughtful of her, really. I can't quite believe I'm here.

The brass doorbell is mock Victorian and looks entirely out of place. I can see through the panes of glass either side of the front door that the hallway is tiled in something shiny and deathly looking, and I know even before the door opens that I'll be faced with a sweeping central staircase, curving out at the sides to greet me.

The door is opened by a stocky woman in a smart suit.

'Hello,' she says, with a faint trace of an accent. 'Please come in.'

'It's Ashley,' I say, wondering whether I'm meant to shake her hand. Does one shake hands with the staff? Probably not.

'May I take your coat?' the woman replies, smiling. 'Everyone is in the drawing room. It's just through that door on your left.'

I don't know what I was expecting exactly, but it's like going into a really posh hotel. A really posh, modern, soulless hotel. He could move out tomorrow: contents, artwork and furniture all included in the sale. He would take only his clothes and his watches and not miss a thing.

I hear Helena before I see her. Pushing open the large double oak door that the housekeeper indicated, I step through into one of the biggest living rooms I have ever seen. You could fit my studio into it twice, and there'd still be room left over.

Helena smiles at me, rushes over.

'So glad you could come!' she says. 'Dad, Jack, meet Ashley.'

It's only then that I notice the other people in the room, clustered around the fireplace, champagne glasses in hand. Jess, our new copywriter. Toby, our account exec. My excitement and happiness dissipate. How could I have been so stupid? This isn't a special lunch for me and Helena. This is a special lunch for the whole team. What an idiot.

Get your game face on Ashley.

I pull myself together. This will be my world. It's only a matter of time. I will have it all; I will make it, just like Alan Cawston has done. I will have the great big house, the housekeeper to keep it tidy, the choice of cars in the driveway, the chef preparing meals in the kitchen I never set foot in. I will have a granny annex for Gran, and she'll never have to see Jason again.

I will have your life one day, I think, as I shake his hand. *Just watch me. Just wait and see. I'll have it all.*

Only I'll have more taste.

THEN

Helena

'Ashley's quite ... upfront, isn't she?' Jack corners me in the kitchen.

'Yes, that's what I like about her,' I reply, glancing over at a plate of chicken Caesar salad which Marta has just set down on the kitchen island. 'Is there anything else?' I ask her, wincing slightly. 'Any, er, salads without dressing?'

'Why would you want it without dressing?' she says, looking cross. I've never got on with the idea of having staff – the whole thing makes me feel awkward. But Dad always told me it's a privilege to be able to provide employment for people, and that you should do it whenever possible. I look down at the salad, sighing.

'My colleague is lactose intolerant.'

Marta gives me a puzzled look.

'She can't have milk ... nothing dairy ...' Jack is grinning behind Marta's back. 'Could we just get a salad like this, without the dressing? Or the cheese!'

'Fine,' she says, turning her back to me. In my mind's eye I picture a scowl forming in response to me and my spoilt friends. I want to say that, actually, Ash didn't grow up with money, but the truth is I don't know much about her upbringing at all. I've tried to ask her several times, but she always deflects the question.

'Are you intimidated by her?' Jack grins, taking a fresh bottle of champagne out of the fridge.

'Don't be daft,' I reply. 'I just don't want her to feel uncomfortable.'

'She doesn't seem very uncomfortable to me. I've just left her embroiled in a debate with your dad over the long-term consequences of a potential EU referendum. Did you know she was a capitalist?'

'Of course she's a capitalist. What, you didn't think she could be, because she didn't go to a public school?' I roll my eyes and follow Jack back into the drawing room. Dad is leaning over the fire, prodding it with a long poker. Ashley is standing next to him, clutching a glass of champagne, which I notice is exactly as full as when I first filled it nearly an hour ago. The other two are staring at something on Toby's iPhone, looking uncomfortable. Damn, I really hoped today would help us all bond.

'Lunch is ready,' I say, and they both turn to look at me.

'About time,' Dad replies, grinning. 'Come along, then.'

Dad seems old, suddenly, and shorter. Ash is tall – very tall for a girl at five foot ten – and she stands shoulder to shoulder with him. Perhaps it's her youth that makes him look older, but something stirs in me: a strange sensation that I need to protect him, that he is somehow growing vulnerable as he ages. Which is ridiculous, given that he is one of Britain's most successful entrepreneurs and, as far as I know, fears nothing.

We settle around the long dining table, Jack and Jess next to me, and Ash and Toby opposite, next to Dad. Marta brings in the salad, plus a bowl of new potatoes, some coleslaw and then a mini salad, which she places with badly concealed attitude in front of Ashley.

After a few minutes of mindless chat about the food, there's what Jack would call 'one of those silences'. I realize my dad's attention has wandered elsewhere. This is the problem with my father. He lives too much inside his own head. All he thinks about is work. It isn't that he doesn't love me, because I know he does, it's just that he has nothing in common with me and nothing to say to me. He loves me, but he isn't very interested in me.

'Has Dad told you guys about his plane?' I hear myself ask. It's a desperate attempt to draw him back in. I've used it hundreds of times before and it usually works.

'No,' Jess pipes up. 'I'm terrified of flying myself. Ever since my cousin Laura got caught in a – what do you call it? – crosswind and had to do an emergency landing. She said the entire aircraft was screaming.'

'Oh dear,' Dad says. But I know that we've got him back – temporarily, at least.

'Helena told me that you have a pilot's licence,' Ash says, shooting a warning look at Jess. 'Tell me more?'

Dad starts then; off on one of his usual lectures about the original Tiger Moth he bought last year. Ash smiles, nods, laughs at the right times, takes sips from her glass of sparkling mineral water, and generally charms him until lunch is over. It's easy enough to do: Dad likes young, attractive women, after all.

Marta comes to collect the plates, and brings in a huge bowl of strawberries for pudding.

'Oh, excellent,' Jack says, rubbing his hands together. 'Strawberries in March. Not very seasonal but . . .'

'Don't be so rude,' I reply, elbowing him. Ash is watching us, and I remember that she's never met him before. Given how closely we will be working together, I hope the two of them get on. But there's never anything to worry about with Jack. He's kind, universally liked, and well behaved. He really is one of those 'too good to be true' men. He might be a banker, but he's not posh and he's not a twat. He can relate to anyone, no matter what their background.

'Not complaining,' Jack says, 'just wondering where these strawberries have come from. Did you know that in the winter the vast majority of strawberries are imported from Egypt? Something very un-British about that, don't you think? An Egyptian Eton mess!'

'What does it matter where they came from?' Ash says, and there's an edge to her voice. 'They're just as good as other strawberries.'

Jack looks surprised. He isn't stupid – or not listening, like my dad, who is now staring over the top of my head to the window beyond.

'I don't think . . .' I say, keeping my voice light, wondering how to make a joke out of it.

'Wherever they're from, they look delicious,' Ash says, beaming, helping herself before passing them to me.

I smile at her, relaxing a little as I take the bowl. Everything is going to be fine.

After lunch, we congregate in the living room again. Ash and I are perched next to each other on one of the long sofas underneath the window. My dad and Jack are chatting about furniture, as they always do, and Jess and Toby are giggling in the corner. They're both slightly older than Ash, but they seem so much younger, somehow. No, not younger, that's the wrong word. Immature. They're much more immature.

'So how are things going with Joel?' I ask Ash.

She smiles, looking down at her lap. I think it's the first time I've seen her look shy. Maybe she's just private and that's why she hates small talk. Nothing wrong with that.

'He's great,' she says. 'Really great. Thoughtful, too.'

'I really like him,' I say. 'He seems like a decent guy.'

'He is,' she says, and her eyes are shining as she gazes into the middle distance. 'We're off to a concert tonight, actually, at the Albert Hall. I've never been before. He arranged it as a surprise.'

'Oh, wow, very romantic. It's funny, really – he's not the person I would have pictured you with.'

'Why not?'

'He's just so . . . laid-back, I suppose,' I reply. 'Sorry, none of my business, I know. I guess I just saw you with a real ball-breaker. God, that's awful, I'm really sorry!'

'He might be quiet, but he's still ambitious,' she says, lifting her chin slightly. 'He's an amazing developer, too. They've already made him head of a team at his new place, and he's about five years younger than most of the other techies. He's really bright.'

'Well, you're a dangerous couple, then!' I want to reach out and pat her on the shoulder, but thankfully I realize in time just how patronizing that would be.

'Thanks,' she replies, smiling. 'That's nice of you to say. I'm really happy – I'm enjoying the job, and I'm lucky to have Joel. It's been an amazing year so far. And it was really great to meet your dad – like I said, he's been a real inspiration to me.'

She's such a funny one, such a tough outer core. But who knows what's underneath it?

Before we leave, I pin Dad down in the kitchen for his thoughts.

He smiles at me and there's a look in his eyes – a split second of magic when, finally, I have his attention, he is fully engaged and locked on to our conversation.

'They're great. Very smart, very ambitious, very motivated. Toby's very likeable – which obviously helps, if you're a sales guy. Jess is a bit of a talker,' he says, giving my arm a little squeeze. 'But Ashley is certainly determined. She'll keep you on your toes.'

I smile – it's what I wanted to hear, what I always want to hear: Dad's validation. I turn towards the door, to collect my coat from Sam.

'But Helena,' he says, pulling me back. He drops his voice slightly. 'Just one thing. Ashley. She's very insecure. Very desperate to prove herself. Nothing wrong with that, of course, but . . . well, just watch her. Insecurity can make people do terrible things.'

THEN

Ash

It's her birthday today. She would have been forty-one. Not that much older than Helena, really. It's crazy to think about it. Which I have been, all morning. And as if to drag my thoughts right back there, Lauren just texted me to tell me that Jason has been let out. On good behaviour. I nearly laughed out loud.

I've been up since 8 a.m., working on the plans for the first pop-up. Last week I found the venue and even got sponsorship from one of the bigger brands looking to promote their latest collaboration – a new eyebrow pencil 'developed' by a YouTuber who looks about sixteen. The stands are filling up slowly but surely. The marketing team at KAMU have been surprisingly supportive – Helena's friend Jodie has been helping us out after hours. But now I need to work on the PR list and the invitations for the launch party. Helena provided me with a stream of 300 names. 'We don't have to invite them all, Ash, maybe just the ones you've heard of?' But of course I've only heard of a handful of them. The world she moves in is still way out of my reach.

Instead of working on the guest list, however, I'm sitting at my tiny desk in the corner of the studio, watching Joel as he sleeps, which is making me feel uncharacteristically soppy. He's good at sleeping – better than me. He's beginning to worry me a bit, getting too much under my skin. I'm not normally one to let my emotions run away with me. After all, relationships are just business transactions of sorts.

My laptop screen keeps fading to black as I sit here thinking of my mum, and my brother. The only two people who can ruin my day without even being in it. I wonder if he's thinking of her too, if he remembers it's her birthday. I need to focus on this list, but instead I'm itching. To do something, but I don't know what. *Ants in your pants.* Gran's voice in my head. She's still in hospital. Peeking out from under my bed is a bag of things I've picked out to take her this weekend, to try to cheer her up. If only a copy of *Woman*, some slipper socks and a bag of chocolate eclairs were enough. I look over at my trainers, and then at the pelting rain outside. Sometimes running in the rain is refreshing, but most of the time it's just annoying, sloppy, dangerous, uncomfortable.

Joel turns over in the bed, gives a dull mumble. The sex is still good, the best I've ever had, although there hasn't been that much competition. But still, I'm getting fed up of waiting. It's pointless us both wasting money on rent, but he's not mentioned the possibility of us moving in together at all. He's lucky to have me . . . doesn't he realize how lucky?

I open Twitter, examine my profile.

Ashley Thompson, London.

Events Manager, KAMU Boutique.

No-nonsense feminist. The harder I work, the luckier I get.

I click to edit it.

Events Director, KAMU Boutique. No-nonsense feminist. Passionate about small businesses with big ideas.

Satisfied, I sit back in my desk chair, admiring my work. I feel calmer now, more determined, and Helena will never notice the slight tweak to my job title. I'm headed that way, anyway. It's time to move things along. Keep the pace up.

I glance over at my vision board, propped up on the radiator, smiling as I take in all the things on it that are coming to fruition. I usually keep it in the wardrobe, away from prying eyes, but Joel doesn't seem to have noticed it – or care, if he has.

'Good morning.'

I turn to the voice. Joel is sitting up in bed, rubbing his hair with his hands.

'Hello.'

'Last night was awesome,' he says. I watch as he reaches over the bed and lights a cigarette. I don't particularly like him smoking in the flat, but I let it go. Years of growing up surrounded by fag butts and worse mean I find them easier to put up with than most non-smokers.

The art of being wise is knowing what to overlook.

'Thanks,' I say, despite the fact that being given feedback on my performance in bed is both sexist and patronizing. Mustn't get distracted. Perhaps a cigarette will help, give me courage. I shake the thought from my mind. It's ridiculous. I haven't smoked since . . .

'Listen, Joel, I've been thinking.'

'Do you ever do anything else?' he says, exhaling slowly.

'Quite a lot, actually!'

I walk to the window and open it, before sitting beside him

on the bed. The rain bounces on the windowsill, sprinkles of it landing on the carpet, but the blast of fresh air gives me the energy I need.

'I know, I was teasing you,' he says, kissing me. 'Come back to bed, grumpy.' I can tell that I'm one step closer to getting what I want. I just need to be brave and come out with it. What's holding me back? The fact that I actually, really, really like this one.

Everything you want is on the other side of fear.

I take his free hand, squeezing his fingers in mine.

'We've been seeing each other for four months now, right?' I say, and he nods. 'And I don't know if you remember me saying, but my contract is coming up for this place and . . .' I have a momentary loss of confidence. What if I've misjudged the situation completely? What if he sees me as nothing more than a fuck buddy? I think of Helena, of her boring but, yes, I'll admit it, handsome husband. The perfect man: well connected, good job, intelligent. Kind too, if kindness is your thing. Clearly in love with her. Impressive taste in engagement rings. Ugh. How did she manage it? She's no cleverer than me. Better looking, perhaps, but not much.

I feel my fists balling and my fingernails digging into my palm as I think of Jack at that awful lunch, of the way he looked me up and down, like a lab rat, not good enough for his precious princess. There has to be something about him, some flaw, some chink in his armour. He's probably screwing his PA. They're both as bad as each other.

Concentrate, Ashley.

'I was thinking . . .' I say, my heart starting to thump in my chest. 'Seeing as your mother is better now—'

'You were thinking you'd like me to move in with you,' he says, finishing off my sentence.

'Yes,' I say, surprised. 'Exactly. What do you think?'

'Are you going to make me pay half the rent?'

'What?!'

'Well, it's a fair question – are you going to expect me to help out with the bills?' he says, lying back against the pillow and putting his arms behind his head. 'Seeing as, at the moment, I don't have to pay my mum anything.'

Recognizing when someone is teasing me has never been my strong point. I can't tell whether he's being serious or not.

'You have to be kidding me!' I say, and I stand up, slinging my dressing gown on over the stupidly skimpy silk nightdress I pulled out especially for this occasion. I fold my arms in front of my chest and glare at him.

Joel leans over and stubs out his cigarette on the small glass ashtray I bought him, after I got sick of finding cigarette ends in my mugs.

'Fuck's sake,' he mutters. 'Ashley . . .'

I feel a huge wave of regret. Why have I pinned my hopes on this man? He might be bright, he might have a good job but he's essentially too laid-back, just like Gary, just like all the others . . . Why am I stuck, dating pointless, pathetic man-child after man-child? Where are the fucking providers?

It takes me a few seconds to realize that I've said the last two sentences out loud.

'Jesus,' Joel says. 'I didn't think you were the sort of woman who wanted to be provided for. I was also pretty confident that you didn't need to be. I've clearly misjudged you. Sorry.'

136

He stands up and starts ramming his legs into his trousers. Everything has gone wrong, suddenly.

'Stop, stop!' I shout. Tears start to fill my eyes. 'I didn't mean . . .'

'Oh, you meant it all right,' he snaps. 'I heard you. I know you, remember? I know how you work. And in case you hadn't realized, I'm in love with you!'

The last sentence is a roar.

'Joel, listen to me . . .' I say, reaching across the bed to grab him, to make him stop getting dressed, to make him stand still and look at me. 'You're being ridiculous.'

'Forget it, I'm off,' he says, and he storms past me.

'Wait!' I shout, following him. 'I feel the same – I feel the same!'

He stops by the front door and stares at me.

'Do me a favour, Ashley,' he says, and the words come out accompanied by spit. 'You think I don't know you? I know you. You don't love me. You don't love anyone. You don't love anyone but yourself.'

And then he's gone.

THEN

Helena

'So, what we're saying is,' Martin looks around at his colleague Louise, 'we'd like to go ahead. With your third package. The, er, full shebang, as it were. Including taking over the designs for the entrance foyer at the pop-up.'

Ash wasn't meant to be at this meeting – she volunteered to come, rather forcefully, and I couldn't quite think how to tell her she wasn't needed, but now I'm so glad I have someone to share my excitement with. I want to kick her under the table, but that would be difficult as we are perched on achingly trendy but incredibly uncomfortable bar stools underneath a Perspex tabletop, and my legs are clearly visible. Instead, I give a short cough and flick my eyes across at her. She is already beaming.

'Well, wow, wow, that's just great!' she says, and her enthusiasm makes them all smile, too.

'We're very excited to be working with you,' I say, thinking we don't want to appear too keen, or it'll look like we've never closed a single deal between us. 'And so glad you're interested in taking part in the event, too – it really will help you maximize your ROI as quickly as possible.' I try to ignore the little voice in my head that's telling me Ash's event is going a little *too* well.

'That's what we want!' Martin says, clapping his hands together. 'I was very impressed with you both, and the industry has been crying out for this kind of event. It was such a refreshing change from the usual people we have pitching to us. Half of them don't seem to know what they're talking about. Now, let's celebrate with a drink. Why not?'

Louise, whose voice reminds me of all the girls at Bentley Ladies College whose only ambition in life was to be thin and beautiful, gives a little tinkle of a laugh. I wonder if she's sleeping with him, and then kick myself for it. Of course she isn't – she's maybe twenty-five at most, he's in his late forties, she'll see him as practically geriatric.

'Thirsty Thursday!' Louise says, smiling around at us all. 'That's what they call it, these days, you know . . . practically mandatory to have a drink.'

She slips off her bar stool and disappears into the kitchen area, returning with a bottle of champagne and four glasses.

'Thank you, Louise,' Martin says, opening the bottle, his teeth gritted slightly as he does so. 'I hope you girls both like Bollinger. I prefer it to Moët.'

I nod, although I don't particularly want to drink this early in the day. It seems a little excessive, even if we have just verbally agreed a £75,000 deal. I look over at Ash. It's an interesting test – will she drink the champagne or not?

'Great,' I say.

'Cheers!' Louise says, clinking our glasses. Ash picks hers up and joins in. I watch as she puts the rim to her lips and tilts but, as suspected, she doesn't actually swallow any liquid. I feel a little let down – where's the ballsy Ash, telling them she doesn't drink alcohol?

'One thing, Martin,' she says, as though she's read my mind. She puts her glass back down on the table. Perhaps she's going to go for it, after all. 'If we're going to work together. Please. We're not girls. We haven't been girls since we left school.'

Martin flushes then – so suddenly and immediately that I am worried he might start shouting, or have a heart attack. It occurs to me that no one has ever said anything like that to him before – and certainly not any of his suppliers. I am proud of her for speaking out but, at the same time, mortified and terrified he'll change his mind.

He doesn't, of course. How can he, sitting here surrounded by women? He's both in the minority and in the wrong.

'Oh, of course, of course, I do apologize,' he says, but his neck is still bright red. 'Slip of the tongue. Not an indication of how I see you both, I assure you. None at all, none at all.'

'Thank you, I appreciate the apology,' Ash replies. 'I'm sure you can understand, as women in business, it's something we have to deal with a lot. And it can get tiring.'

'Of course,' Martin says, swallowing, pulling at his shirt collar.

Louise is staring at Ash with an open mouth.

'Right,' I say, trying to bring things back into focus. This is my meeting, after all. 'I'll have the contract drawn up later this afternoon for you to sign, along with some forms for the event, which we'll need you to fill in. Has Ashley shown you pictures of the venue? It's stunning – really atmospheric and incredibly Instagrammable! I'll ask my assistant to send some across to you later.'

'Perfect,' Martin says. His champagne glass is already empty.

We finish up the meeting with small talk on where we all live – Martin says he knows my road in West Hampstead, explaining that one of his ex-girlfriends lived there when he was in his twenties. Ash sits in silence as we chat about how the area has changed in recent years. I know she lives in Mitcham, but she's never spoken to me about it, except to say that her commute to the office takes ages. I wonder why she doesn't simply move closer.

We leave their office and manage to hold ourselves together pretty well until we get outside. And then, Ash gives a giant squeal, so shrill it nearly pierces my eardrums.

'Oh. *My. God!*' she says, flinging her arms around me. 'Boutique D'Arblay! Oh my God, Helena, can you believe this? This. Is. Epic!'

I give her an encouraging smile, trying to imagine what my industry friends will think the next time I see them and drop into casual conversation that we are now working with Boutique D'Arblay. It's easily one of the most popular niche brands among the team at KAMU – the skincare brand I used in my proposal to the Americans, and the one I most wanted to get on board.

But there's a little niggle of doubt that tells me Martin wasn't as convinced by my pitch as he was by Ash's. Perhaps I was naive, giving Ash all the responsibility for the events. They were meant to be part of the whole package, not a separate proposition, and certainly not an alternative one.

'Jesus,' Ash is saying, while texting on her phone. 'You realize what this means? It means that Celia and Co and Lila Rose will be desperate to do the event! And I was worried I wouldn't be able to get meetings with them . . . the second I tell them I've signed these guys . . . seriously. The only way is up.'

She continues smiling at me, spinning in circles, and when I glance at her phone I realize she is tweeting something.

'Wait, what . . .' I say, trying to see what she's writing, 'what are you saying? Don't tweet anything yet! Ink's not even on the page yet, let alone dry. You'll jinx it.'

She twists her forehead into a frown, her finger hovering mid-air above the screen.

'OK,' she says, quitting Twitter. 'You're right. Just got carried away.'

I put my arms around her shoulders and give them a squeeze.

'OK, no tweeting, but what shall we do to celebrate? Come on, it's lunchtime, let's go somewhere lovely. Put it on the company.'

'Can we?' she says, and her eyes are sparkling and I remember how very young she is. It's easy to forget most of the time – in many ways she's more self-assured and confident than me.

'Not really,' I say. 'But I won't tell David, if you don't. We'll claim we were taking Martin out for lunch.'

'Excellent,' she says.

She loops her arm through mine, and we walk together along Glasshouse Street towards the Underground. I can still smell her perfume from when we hugged – something strangely masculine yet sickly – and for the first time since we met I feel truly fond of her.

'How are things with Joel?' I ask.

She makes a non-committal noise.

'Think I might have overestimated him.'

'Oh, really?' I ask, giving a pause, waiting for her to add to her story. But she doesn't, so I carry on. 'I think he broke up with a long-term girlfriend just before starting at KAMU.'

Her eyes flash.

'Really?'

'Yes, that's why he had to move in with his mum. She left him high and dry – they bought a flat together and she basically kicked him out. He seems lovely, though. Perhaps he's just a bit bruised from his experience, wants to take things slowly.'

'Hmmm.'

My phone rings and I pull it out. It's Jack.

'Sorry, I'd better get this.'

'No worries.' We have stopped outside Boots. Ash's eyes are already scanning the aisles just inside the door. 'I need to get some bits in here, anyway. I won't be a minute.'

She disappears into the shop.

'Hi,' I say, into my phone. Jack rarely rings me in the daytime. 'Everything OK?'

'Yes. Just wondered if you'd seen my message?'

'Sorry . . . I've been in the meeting with Boutique D'Arblay. They are going to sign! I'm actually so shocked. They were very excited about the pop-up, which is great for Ashley. Really boosted her confidence. What was it?'

'That's great! Congratulations. It was just to let you know that I've got an agent coming round tonight to value the flat. Seven p.m. Doesn't matter if you're not home by then. I'll make sure I'm back.'

'Jack . . .'

'He's doing next door's, anyway, and I thought he might as well do ours at the same time. It's good to know how much it's worth, don't you think? Did I tell you how much Alex sold his for?'

'Jack . . .' I don't have the energy for this conversation. Not now.

'Look, we don't have to do anything. I'm not saying we put it on the market tomorrow. It's just to give us an idea. You know. So we can start planning a bit more . . . for the future. When we'll . . . well, we'll need more space when there are three of us. I'd better go . . . meeting someone for lunch. And on that note, I hope you girls are celebrating! I'll see you later on. Love you.'

He rings off and as I wait for Ash on the busy street, I'm not thinking about the estate agent, or moving house, or the baby that Jack suddenly seems so obsessed with having.

Instead, I am thinking of Ash's voice saying we haven't been girls since we left school, and I'm wondering why I never noticed my husband calling us that before.

THEN

Ash

Day two of radio silence.

Where is he?

Who needs a man, anyway?

It's my own stupid fault. Falling in love is for fools.

The price you pay for love is grief.

Look at Gran. Professing to love a man who's put her second to everything else his entire life. Where's that got her? There is nothing more important for a woman than to be independent, both financially and emotionally.

These are my thoughts as I run around Mitcham Common, waiting for the sun to finish rising. Everywhere I look, I remember moments we shared together. I hope, if I keep on running, eventually the sentimental nonsense in my head will disappear. But it doesn't, so I carry on. I carry on until I've run 15km, and my left calf starts cramping.

I'm cold as I limp back to the station. That kind of horrible sweaty cold, my leggings sticking to my crotch and my socks damp inside my trainers. It's only 6 a.m., I have time to get home, have a shower, and still be in the office by 8.30 a.m.

Back at the block, I let myself in and climb the concrete stairs to my flat. The stairwell smells of urine again – someone drunk last night, probably, or that ancient dog that lives downstairs with the skinhead who never seems to leave the flat, except to let the sickly creature go to the toilet in the 'communal garden'. The dog's clearly on its last legs and winces in pain as it limps out of the block, but there's no evidence that the owner has taken him to a vet. Clearly, putting it down is the most humane thing to do. Sometimes you have to be cruel to be kind, and the poor thing needs to be put out of its misery. Thankfully, the stuff I ordered online has arrived. I just need to get home in time to leave it an irresistible snack – that will be one less thing to worry about, at least.

I shower quickly, one eye constantly roving towards my iPhone, which is balanced on the edge of the basin, to see if Joel has been in touch. But it doesn't light up once.

I dry my hair, and take out my new Isabel Marant dress. Helena will recognize it as designer – she has the sort of mind that can tell whether an item of clothing is high street or not. And she cares about labels. She told me that first impressions are everything, that labels show you are successful, that you've made it, that you are someone to be respected. In many ways, confidence and appearances are more important than brains or hard work. I hate that this is the way the world works, but I have to admit there is something to be said for non-verbal body language, and clothing is part and parcel of that.

Plus, the dress is awesome. I found it in a charity shop last week and haven't worn it yet. It's in mint condition, too.

Before I get dressed, I weigh myself. Down to eight stone

exactly. That's something, at the very least. I make myself a kale and banana smoothie with the machine that Joel bought me, allowing myself a second or two of nostalgia as I plug it in, and then head out of the door with my flask.

On the train, I read *CITY A.M.* from cover to cover, then put it on the seat next to me in the hope that it stops anyone from sitting there. I can't afford to get ill at the moment, and London trains are the worst. All that breathing in enclosed spaces, sitting on top of each other. People are disgusting.

I flick through my calendar on my iPhone, trying to ignore the fact that he still hasn't got in touch. It's the first day since I moved across to KAMU B that I'm not looking forward to going to work. We have one new client meeting this afternoon – another one that I set up – but other than that, I'll be talking to our new staff all day. Helena has asked me to give them a rundown of the ethos of the company, which pissed me off, as surely that's her job? But I had to show willing. The more indispensable I make myself, the more opportunities . . . We hit our target last week, a whole month before the projection. Apparently, David was very impressed, although he didn't bother to tell me that, of course – I had to hear it second-hand, through Helena. Even so, I know it was mostly down to me. It's the pop-up that's got them all excited. One mention of Instagram booths and model ambassadors and they're sold.

I take a look at the photograph of my vision board on my phone. I've been working on the proposal for my promotion in the evenings, detailing all the reasons why I should definitely be promoted to Events Director, and I just need to decide whether to show it to Helena, or go straight to David.

I'm first in the office, as usual, and I sit at my desk and enjoy the peace. My phone is lying next to my computer keyboard, black and silent, as if it's sticking two fingers up at me.

As I finish off my kale smoothie and start to rewrite my to-do list in capitals on my notepad, listing jobs in order of priority and urgency, the door swings open. I look up, expecting to see Helena, but instead it's Amy, the newest member of staff. Large of hip, meek of nature. Underneath one arm she's carrying a huge bunch of white roses.

'Morning,' she says, her voice small and shy.

'Hello!' I say, my heart lifting, even though the gesture doesn't seem Joel's style, somehow. 'Those are rather lovely.'

She nods, sets them down at the desk next to me.

Helena's desk.

'Yes, Karen on reception asked me to bring them up. They're for Helena.'

'Oh,' I say. 'Lucky her.'

I swallow my disappointment and try to concentrate on my pipeline spreadsheet, but Joel is in my head and he won't leave. I can't believe his silent treatment has lasted this long. I also can't believe he said he loved me, even though it hadn't felt entirely genuine, more like a shock tactic to get my attention. And what meaner way to tell someone you love them for the first time than when you're having a massive row?

After five minutes, Amy announces she's off to get a coffee, and I take the opportunity to rummage about in the green and white foliage and fish out the tiny handwritten card. It's not sealed (thank you, florists) and the message is not what I was expecting.

Congratulations, you. I knew you could do it, D x

Nice of her to give us *any* of the credit, then. By the time Helena gets in, it's game over: my negative mood has set in for the day. She's late, again. Most of the other staff members are here, although Guy – Helena's assistant, who prefers to entertain the others with his camp bitchiness rather than actually do any work – is nowhere to be seen.

'Hi,' Helena says, crashing down opposite me, all bags and coats and scarves and bouncy hair. She looks flushed, her skin somehow shinier than normal.

'Afternoon,' I say, but I give her a bright smile, just to show that I'm joking, even though I'm not.

'Oh, get lost, it's six minutes past!' she says, switching on her computer.

I have about five minutes before she asks me to turn the radio on. She claims she hates working in silence, that it's too intense. As though intense is a bad thing.

'There was a massive queue at the coffee bar,' she continues. 'Otherwise I would have been early. How's it going?'

'Good, thanks,' I say, typing gobbledygook into a blank email so she realizes I don't have time for this conversation. 'Those flowers are for you, by the way.'

She looks over, barely even acknowledging them.

'Oh,' she says, as though they are a nuisance. She reaches over and yanks them closer, finding the card, as I did. I watch her intensely as she scans it. There's a flicker of something like embarrassment, and then she smiles. 'Nice.'

'Who are they from?' I ask.

There's a slight pause – just a millisecond – before she tells me what I already know.

'David. Just congratulating us on hitting our target,' she says, and her voice is impressively deadpan.

'How thoughtful of him,' I say.

She gives a murmur and turns away from the flowers, pulling her iPad out of her bag.

'Listen, I made some notes on this afternoon's presentation – nothing major. Shall we go over them at some point this morning?'

'Sure,' I reply. 'How about ten?'

'Perfect. Love your dress, by the way,' she says, before leaning over her desk and pulling my phone charger from the back of my computer. She plugs her phone into it and connects it to her machine. I grind my teeth together.

I look back to see an email notification flashing up in the corner of my screen, clicking to read it without looking.

It loads, and a familiar feeling of dread washes over me.

A small square image.

That face. That smirk.

Jason K. Thompson is now following you on Twitter!

He's back. What does he want this time?

'Oh,' Helena says, again, and I look up at her, unblinking. 'How about some cheesy Magic FM to get us all going? It's way too intense in here.'

THEN

Helena

'Look at this place . . .' Jack says, shoving his iPad on to my lap. Outside, the rain is persistent, drumming a beat that I'd usually find relaxing but today is making my temples sore. It's been a long day, nearly the end of a long but successful week. 'It's a hundred grand less than this flat, and it has outbuildings.'

I stare at the house. The type of place you'd expect your parents to own. Thirties styling. Half hung with tiles, a bright red roof. A detached workshop. A log store. Sweeping lawn at the front. Five bedrooms. Two bathrooms. Three miles to the station.

'We don't need five bedrooms,' I say, handing it back to him. 'And it's too far from the station. What station is that, anyway?'

'It's direct to Kings Cross. An hour and fifteen minutes.'

'And the rest,' I say, pulling my laptop out from under the coffee table. Perhaps if I start to work he'll leave me alone. 'You know those commuter trains never run on time.'

'You could work from home sometimes,' he says, flicking back through the property site. 'It's a tech brand, after all. Supposed to be at the forefront of flexible working.'

'I need to be in town. I can hardly manage a team from a shed in the woods.'

Jack snorts. 'I'm sure the wonder child, Ashley, would be happy to stand in for you.'

I breathe in sharply.

'Well, I wouldn't be happy,' I say, opening my emails.

There's one from her. It's 10 p.m., I haven't seen her for a few hours. Of course there is.

From: AshleyT@kamu.com
Subject: Threading!!

So, Helena, I had an idea. I know we've got a nail bar already, but I was thinking if we shave a tiny bit off the coffee area we can squeeze in a threading station, too! I've spoken to this really cool new brand who . . .

The message fills my screen and spills over beneath it. I don't scroll down to read the rest. The headache settles in, so I shut my computer and stand up.

'I'm going to bed.'

Jack looks up at me, hopeful.

'Shall I join you?'

'No,' I say, and my voice is harsher than intended. 'I've got a headache.' I want to laugh at the cliché as I say it.

I take longer than usual in the bathroom, cleansing my face twice and leaving on a hydrating mask as I sit on the toilet. My stomach feels tight, pre-menstrual, but I haven't had a period since I had the implant fitted. There's a message from David, of course, asking if I received the flowers, and I reply quickly with my thanks, even though I'm desperate not to encourage him any more.

I end up scrolling through Twitter, killing time before returning to Jack. Ashley has been tweeting all evening, teasing with promises of big news from *KAMU B! All to be revealed soon!* She deleted her personal Twitter account today, asking if she could manage the business one instead, from now on, rather than letting Guy do it. She gave me a list of ten reasons why his perfectly engaging tweets weren't up to scratch, and so I gave in – for an easy life – and handed it over. To be fair, Guy didn't look too disappointed to have lost the responsibility.

Ashley seems given to momentary changes of direction; unexpected behaviour like this bubbles up out of nowhere. She's hot-headed, and a starter not a finisher. I've also noticed there's some tension between her and Toby. I'm not entirely sure what happened, but I need to keep more of a handle on her. After all, my job is to channel her talents, and help her be the best she can be. I wonder if this is how David felt about me, before . . . I throw the thought from my mind.

I click on our Twitter profile, reading through it, and stop at one of her more boastful outbursts, telling the world we now have sixty-eight exhibitors for the pop-up. She's gone crazy with her hashtags: #onfire #nothingworksunlessyoudo #womenwhowork.

Not sure how Toby and Guy will feel about that last hashtag.

Scrolling back, it's clear that all the tweets she's posted relate to her event, rather than the site itself. She's made the venue look incredible, and the engagement is fantastic, with an impressive number of shares from big-name beauty folk. Although it's fine for her to focus on it for now, I must remind her to switch to promoting the actual site itself, once the event's over.

It's half an hour before I leave the bathroom, and the lights are off in the hallway. I push open the door to our bedroom. Jack is sitting on the bed in his boxer shorts and T-shirt, holding his toothbrush, texting someone.

'You didn't have to come to bed,' I say, and he locks his phone screen. 'I told you.'

'I'm tired, anyway,' he says, tossing his phone on to the bed before walking towards me. 'And you were ages in the bathroom.'

'Sorry,' I reply. I don't want to get undressed in front of him tonight – not that I think he'd try anything, but my stomach is really hurting now, and I feel possessive of my body, as though he hasn't earned the right to see or touch it today. I linger by the wardrobe, waiting for him to go.

'If you don't want to leave London completely,' he says, pausing with his hand on the door, 'then perhaps we can consider moving a bit further out? Wouldn't you like some more space?'

I stare around at our bedroom. My bedroom. I have lived here for eight years. It's more than a home: it's the backdrop to my adult life. There are memories in every inch of every room. It's the only place I remember being happy. Why would I want to leave?

'I love you,' I say, because I can't tell him what he wants to hear, but I don't want to hurt him. I want to make him happy, but right now I'm not sure I can.

THEN

Ash

Two days since he followed me on Twitter. I deleted my account as soon as I got the notification, but I know it's too bloody late.

I get off the train at the stop before mine. I was going to run home – I even got changed in the toilets at work, hoping to shut up all these voices in my head – but I can't find the energy, so instead I walk, saying a silent prayer that Joel will be waiting for me when I get there. I need him. I need his admiration, his attention, his love. And right now, I need his support, too.

He's back. Of course he is. I wonder if it's Lauren, if she blabbed, gave the game away. Probably. Possibly. Who knows?

I think back to the last time I saw him at Gran's house. Drunk, or worse. Outside in the rain, hurling her flowerpots at the windows. Begging at first, then crying. Finally, screaming. Rage – her rage, Grandad's rage, so familiar to me – funnelled through him and then her and then him, handed down through the generations. What an inheritance. Grandad's mates from the Legion coming in and holding him back as he tried to break down the door. Gran watching from the window, clutching her cheap beaded necklace as her fingers shook with fear.

The day has been a struggle. Some days are harder than others, and I still find it difficult from time to time. Self-pity is a dangerous swamp that will suck you under if you so much as dip a toe in. I know this, but there are still times when I just want to bury my head beneath the sand and slowly suffocate, surrounded by nothing but darkness.

What goes up must come down.

The universe is having a right old laugh at my expense, this time round. *Throw everything at her!* it seems to be saying. *Go on! More shit and more shit! Let's see how much she can take!*

As my thoughts get more crazy, I pick up pace until I'm basically marching. Nearly home. I focus on my breathing as I walk towards my block. I have to get myself together, just in case Joel's there. Helena took my work charger home with her yesterday – 'So sorry, hun, thought it was mine!' – and my phone has run out of battery. I knew I shouldn't have let her use it, should have said something at the time when she yanked it out of my computer. It's killing me that I can't check whether Joel has been in touch.

Perhaps I should have gone over to his place, instead of blindly hoping he'll show up here, but backing down would be catastrophic for our relationship. He has to make the first move, so I can keep the upper hand.

I'm a few steps away when I hear it. The dog. Round the back of the bins, I can see its owner chatting to someone on his phone. He's clutching a joint, the smoke unfurling from his nostrils, the stubble on his face the only thing that defines him. I realize the reason I can't stand him: he reminds me of Jason. He is shuffling his feet, kicking a stone about, trying to stay warm. The dog, meanwhile, is liberally pissing all over the walls. There's a gash on its upper leg that I haven't noticed before, and it's oozing something green and unpleasant. After a few minutes, the pathetic creature just gives up, slumping to the ground, lying in a puddle of its own wee.

I stopped at the Co-op on the way home. I put my hand into my bag, squeezing the thick slab of meat, feeling it ooze underneath the pressure of my fingertips. It's an offcut, going out of date tomorrow. Nice and cheap, but not a bad last meal for a dog, really.

The owner sees me as I climb the steps to the entrance. He gives me a brief nod, some kind of acknowledgement of my existence. He probably likes me; he can tell that, despite the posh second-hand clothes, I fit right in here. Probably wants to sleep with me, but can't be bothered to do anything about it.

I smile back, broadly, resisting the temptation to wave. I even give the dog a smile.

I let myself into the building using the key fob, stepping carefully over the patch of warm piss staining the concrete. Even though it's spring now, it's always so cold inside the hall – there's no heating, no carpet, no paint on the walls. No decoration except for a glass-fronted noticeboard, with reminders about bin days and our obligation to only allow entry to authorized persons. Like all council buildings, the stairwells are concrete, topped off with a rusting metal banister that makes your hands smell of blood if you use it. My legs are tired as I climb the first flight of steps to the studio.

As I turn on the first landing, I immediately spot a shadowy figure standing outside my door. My heart leaps. It's him, after all. He has come back. Thank God. Something of today can be salvaged.

I punch the white light switch with my knuckles, flooding the stairway with harsh strip lighting. The shadowy figure is a shadow no more. He turns to look at me, and then I see that it isn't him.

It isn't him, after all.

'Hello,' Jason says. 'Long time no see.'

THEN

Helena

I am dreaming of my mother when a sharp, stabbing pain deep inside my abdomen wakes me. It feels like a needle is being inserted into my womb, and the sensation is so intense I almost gasp in shock. But just as quickly as it arrives, it's gone.

I've fallen asleep on the sofa. I pull my phone out from where it's wedged underneath me and check the time: 9.30 p.m. Jack is slumped in the armchair opposite me, fixated on some television programme. The pain returns, making me catch my breath. As quickly as I have felt it, it has gone again.

'You all right, sleepyhead?' he says, smiling at me. 'You haven't done that for years.'

I pull a face at the television.

'It's *Top Gear*, what do you expect?'

'Yeah, right. I think it's more likely you've been working too hard. Go to bed, darling, I won't be much longer.'

I haul myself off the sofa.

'Yes, I will in a bit. Just going to the loo.'

In the bedroom, I grab a clean pair of knickers from my drawer and tiptoe down the hall to the bathroom.

It's been so long since I've had a period, I'm not sure I even have anything to use. I wrench open the bathroom cabinet door, forgetting that the hinge broke a few months ago, and it complains with a metallic crunch as the door breaks away at the bottom.

'Shit,' I say, to no one, as the contents of the cabinet start to spill out into the basin. There's plenty here, but not what I'm looking for, although I do find a packet of paracetamol, and quickly swallow two with water.

There's no way around it, I'll have to improvise. I sit on the toilet and pull down my knickers, ready for the carnage that awaits, but there's nothing there. Not a speck of blood – nor anything else, for that matter. What a relief. I've forgotten that the cramps sometimes start before the bleeding.

When I wipe myself, there's a tiny spot of pink, but it's so faint I wonder if it's just a mark on the tissue paper, a scrap of something that got churned up with the paper in the machinery. Just to be safe, I fold up some toilet roll and stuff it into my pants, putting the second pair over the top to keep my makeshift nappy in place. I vaguely remember the doctor saying that when my periods returned, it would mean it was time to have my implant replaced with a new one. I think of Jack's obsession with us having a baby this year, and wonder if the fates are on his side. How can I buy more time? There must be something I can do, some way I can put him off. It's not that I don't want kids at all, just *not now*.

Admittedly, it's been 'not now' for the last five years, but surely that's normal? This is the twenty-first century, after all. And there's so much to get done before you have children. To interrupt my career now, when it's in full flow and I'm at my peak . . . Women pretend we can have it all, if only we're organized enough, but it's not true. I remember Nicky, one of the account managers at KAMU, the way she always left at 4.30 p.m. on the dot to collect her son from nursery, leaving the rest of us to deal with any problems that came in after she'd left. I had to do so many US conference calls for her. I once mentioned it to Ash, who said she hoped Nicky's shorter hours were reflected in her wages. Nicky herself told me most of her salary went on nursery fees, and I wondered why she bothered working at all.

Back in the living room, I feel more awake than I do first thing in the morning. My stomach is no longer aching, but my mind is animated, desperately trying to recall the details of the dream that the strange pain interrupted. But all I can remember is that my mother was unhappy, and young and alone.

Perhaps it's my guilt that is taunting me. It's been at least four months since I last saw her, about a month since we spoke. I owe her another visit, but I know she's keen to become a grandmother, and she'll just pile the pressure on, and I won't be able to handle it. Ironic, really, that my mother is so desperate for grandchildren, when she once told me her first and only pregnancy ruined her life, professionally and personally. She seems to have forgotten that; forgotten that she told me getting pregnant was the worst thing to have happened to her. 'Not having you, of course, my darling. Not becoming a parent. You were a blessing. But getting pregnant, that was the worst thing. The two things are quite separate. After all, a man becomes a parent but doesn't have to get pregnant to do so. And I was just too young. My modelling career was over before it had properly begun.'

It's a convenient excuse, but it doesn't explain the fact she never went on to have any more children, that she stopped at me, and that she was a half-hearted mother at the best of times. It's only now that she's an altogether calmer and more content woman that she seems to find any appeal in children at all.

'Don't put it off for too long. You don't want to be one of those women who turns around at forty-five, with only a cat for company, and wonders which friend they can impose on at Christmas this year. And I don't want to be an old granny!'

The unjust irony of our last conversation. One rule for you, one rule for me, eh, Mum? But still, her words have affected me more deeply than she, or anyone else, realizes.

I grab my phone, unwilling to follow this train of thought. As I press the main button, the screen lights up, telling me I have a new message, and I know who it's from even before I read it. Sent only ten minutes ago. David's just lonely, I suppose. And still hopeful.

Jack is still glued to the television. I have a strange urge to cry. I have to sort this situation out, once and for all, but I don't know how to.

THEN

Ash

The first thing I notice is that he's holding a huge black holdall and that under his zip-up hoodie, his T-shirt is too tight for him, showing off the muscles across his chest.

Oh, and there's a new scar running down one of his cheeks.

'They let you out, then,' I say.

'Yeah,' he replies. 'Why don't you invite me in for a cup of tea and I'll tell you all about it?'

I can't help thinking about the steak in my handbag and my plan for the dog. I need to get rid of Jason. He probably wants money; it's usually about money.

'Fine,' I say through my teeth as I open the door with my key. 'But I only have decaf – and I'm knackered, so you can't stay long.'

'Always a pleasure seeing you, too,' he says.

Once inside, I take my coat off, plug my phone in to charge it, and he helps himself to a spot on the sofa, dumping his bag on the floor as he checks out the studio. Of course, everything's immaculate, as it always is. Immaculate and . . . sterile. Thank God I put the vision board away last night. Aside from my pur-ple-painted wall and the cheap Escher print hanging on it, there's nothing personal here. That's how I like it. It gives him nothing to use against me.

'How did you find out where I live?' I ask.

'Followed you back from the office last night,' he says.

I sigh. 'Of course you did.'

I fill the kettle and switch it on with a fierce click. Then I unpack my bag, taking out some beetroot and salad I bought for my tea, along with the steak. He notices that, of course.

'What's that?' he says.

'Nothing,' I reply.

'I haven't had a decent meal in days now.'

'Poor you.'

'So. Can I have it?'

I think about it, I genuinely do. Just for a few seconds. I think about the bottle under the sink, imagine how easy it would be to slip a few drops on to the steak as he watches me cook it. But of course, the idea is ridiculous. Not the sort of thing you can get away with – not like with a dog. And I don't want him dead, after all. Do I?

'Trust me, I don't think you'd like it,' I say, turning and handing him his cup of tea. 'Here.'

'Ta,' he says, taking it from me and cupping his hands round it. His fingernails are dirty and uneven, as though he's scraped them along the side of a building. He pulls off his beanie, revealing a very recently shaved head. He looks like the thug I remember; the sort of person people cross the road to avoid. He smells, too; not of alcohol, thank God, but of sweat and laziness.

'Fuck, it's cold out there,' he says, blowing on the tea. The steam settles on his nose.

I pour myself a cup of water from the jug in the fridge and sit opposite him on my tiny footstool. How can I get rid of him?

'I've been waiting for hours. I thought you were never coming home. Still a workaholic, then? I guess that's how you've done so well for yourself.'

'What's in the bag?' I say. It's huge. I hope he doesn't think he's coming to stay.

'Got a new job, didn't I?' he says, kicking the bag with his foot. He rests his tea on the arm of the sofa bed. 'While I'm at it, can I interest you in . . .?'

He unzips the bag and pulls out a bright orange duster on a plastic handle.

'It's flexible,' he says, bending it. 'For cleaning behind radiators.'

'I think that's known as a solution that's looking for a problem. How much?'

'Twelve pounds.'

'Twelve pounds? You're having a laugh. That'd be a pound in the local shop.'

'Tea towels?' he says, yanking some out from underneath the dusters and handing them to me. 'Or how about a hazard warning triangle for your car?'

'I don't have a car,' I reply, handing them back over. 'And I have enough tea towels. Thank you.'

He chucks them down in a heap by his foot and picks up his tea again.

'You're just like the rest of them,' he replies. 'All those posh bitches in Balham. Looking at me like I'm dirt, desperate to get rid of me, calling their pathetic husbands to try to scare me off.'

'No, I'm not. I just don't want to buy a load of crap,' I reply, sighing. 'Is this really the best you can do?'

'It's decent enough money,' he says, sounding subdued. 'They bus us all up here – twenty lads at a time – give us the gear and leave us to it. You can make a fair bit, so long as you're polite. I give them some sob story about trying to get my life back on track, how I'm about to join the Marines. Usually does the trick. Especially if you turn up before the wanker banker husbands get home, and they're alone bathing their kids. They'll chuck fifty quid at you just to make you piss off. '

'It's not a job, though, is it?' I say. 'It's just glorified begging. Or theft by intimidation.'

'Better than robbing,' he says. 'Guess we can't all be as clever as you, Ashley. What's with the "L, E, Y", anyway? *Ashleigh* just too chavvy for your new workmates? You might be trying to pretend you belong on *Made in Chelsea* now, but I don't think much of your neighbourhood.' He gives a sideways sneer at the damp patch above the kitchen units.

'What do you want, Jason?'

There's a pause. I wonder if I have any cash in the flat, or whether I'll have to trudge outside to get some. If so, I might get an opportunity to leave the steak. I know the dog gets its final toilet session at about 11.30 p.m., so I have a couple of hours to go.

He shrugs. 'Nothing. Just thought you might want to chat. Seeing as it was her birthday this week.'

I breathe out, rubbing my eyes with my fingers. I'm knackered. The last two days haven't gone to plan at all. I want to go to bed. No, it's worse than that; I want to cry.

'What do you *want*?'

He sighs, and for a second he looks like the brother I once loved; the one whose bottom I wiped when Mum had disappeared on an eight-hour bender and we hadn't eaten properly for days. The one I went to the corner shop and stole baked beans for. The one who sobbed and held me at night, asking me to promise I'd never leave him.

The one who, aged fifteen, punched me so hard in the face I broke a tooth.

'I haven't got anywhere to stay right now,' he says. 'They haven't exactly been welcoming, the grandparents.'

'Not my problem,' I snap. 'Don't you have a parole officer, or something, looking out for you? You're a grown-up. About time you sorted your own life out.'

'Where's your bedroom?' he says, changing tack.

This is why I'm in no hurry to leave this place. Because I knew that this would happen at some point. Staying in the studio means that I'm safe from him; there's no room at the inn.

'I don't have one. You're sitting on my bed.'

He looks down at the sofa.

'Look, what do you want?' I say, again, losing patience. 'I can get you some money, I suppose. Enough to get you a hostel, or whatever, for a few nights. But you can't stay here. As you can see, there's no room. And I'm tired and I need to go to bed. I've got a long day ahead . . .'

My phone starts to ring. I grab it. It's Joel. Finally. *Finally*. But fucking hell, he doesn't half pick his moments. I stare at the phone, feeling it vibrate in my hand, like a grenade about to go off.

'Fuck,' I say.

'Don't mind me,' Jason replies, leaning back on the sofa and giving me another smirk.

I want to punch him. I cancel the call, muttering under my breath.

'No one important, then?' he asks, and I can see, despite the needling, that he's actually interested. It's those flickers of humanity that are usually my downfall. I have to remember who he is and what he's done. He isn't the little boy who used to wet the bed, terrified of Mum and her drunken outbursts. Not any more.

'How much?' I ask.

'What?'

'How much to make you go away?' I'm exasperated now – I'll give him the entire balance of my bank account, if it means he'll leave.

'Jeez, Ash, that hurts,' he says, feigning a tear. 'We haven't seen each other in, what, eighteen months, and you just want to get rid of me? Thanks. Thanks a lot.'

'Please,' I say. I wonder if I should call Gran, whether that would be any help at all. But it's late; she'll be asleep, and she's only just out of hospital. I can't stress her out any more, it wouldn't be fair. 'I'm just getting things sorted for myself, I'm busy at work . . . it's late.'

'I just need somewhere to stay for a few days,' he says. 'That's all. While I'm up here selling. I won't get in the way of your oh-so-successful life.'

'I told you, I'll give you money for a hostel,' I reply, flatly. 'That's the best I can do.'

'I don't want to stay in a hostel. That's exactly the kind of place

I need to get away from. Fuck, you're my sister. Can't you put me up for one night?'

I fumble in my bag for my purse. 'Here, take my bank card. The pin number is 2902. Take out what you like. I'll call the bank tomorrow and say I've lost it.'

He stands, and I remember how tall he is, how much bigger than me. And then, with a frustration I've seen before so many, many times, he throws the mug he's holding at the wall behind me. It smashes behind the kitchen sink, breaking into pieces and leaving a brown stain on the wall.

'Fuck's sake, Jason!' I shout, but he storms out, yanking his bag from the floor and slamming my front door behind him. It bounces back open, then creaks on its hinges to a close, without shutting properly.

Nothing changes.

I allow a few unwanted tears to trickle down my face before blowing my nose on a tissue. And then I hear it, the front door creaking again.

'Ashley?' a voice says.

I look up to see Joel, standing there, his fingers wrapped around a bunch of roses. His eyes take in the scene: the luminous duster, my blotchy face and the huge tea stain on the wall.

'I tried to ring you to tell you I was here . . . Some guy let me in downstairs. Why was your door open? Are you OK? What's happened?'

'I'm fine,' I say, 'don't worry. It was nothing.'

'Who was he?' Joel asks, reaching out and smoothing my hair. He lays the roses down on the coffee table, and I smile at them sadly.

I walk to the sofa and sit down, looking at the tea stain behind the sink. The pieces of mug are still scattered across the worktop, the largest chunk on the drainer. I feel Joel's arms around me, pulling me towards him, and it's only then that I realize I'm shaking.

'He was . . .' I begin, my brain racing to concoct a story. I haven't got the energy to tell Joel about Jason, the fact I have a brother who's been in and out of prison since he was seventeen. Not yet, anyway. 'He was just some lad selling stuff.' So much, so true. 'I was stupid, I felt sorry for him. I invited him in, but then he tried to sell me all these crappy cleaning products for twenty quid. And when I told him that they were too expensive, he just went ballistic.'

'You need to report him,' Joel says.

'No,' I say. 'Not . . . not now . . . I'm really tired.'

'But he smashed the place up!'

'He only broke a mug,' I say, pushing Joel off and walking towards the kitchen area. I collect the pieces carefully and pile them up on the drainer, then take some kitchen towel and try to blot up the tea stains on the carpet. 'My stupid fault for inviting him in and giving him a cup of tea. I just felt sorry for him and I wanted to give him a break.'

The words are an act, but as I say them the tears start to return. I think of Helena, her perfect life with her glamorous parents, no black sheep siblings turning up to wreck things all the time.

It's not fair.

He looks at me.

'I can't believe you'd be that . . . trusting,' he says, a hint of suspicion in his voice. 'Is there something . . . anything else you want to tell me?'

I shake my head. Does he think I fancied him? Is that it? He thinks some bloke turned up at my door selling dusters and I thought he was fit, so I invited him in?

'I just want to go to bed . . . please. He'll be long gone now, anyway.'

He stands up, wraps his arms around me and pulls me towards him. I'm going to cry again. It's inevitable, as it was earlier. I can't escape Jason. We're all that's left of each other's pasts, bound together forever, no matter how far I try to run.

'You came back,' I whisper, as Joel strokes my hair.

'Of course I did,' he says. 'I was worried when you didn't answer your phone. It's OK. You're going to be OK. I'm sorry for storming off.'

'It doesn't matter,' I say. 'Let's go to bed.'

He makes me a cup of peppermint tea and I sit on the footstool again, watching as he makes the bed up. It's uplifting to see this new side of him, more serious and sensitive than I thought he could be. Today's not all bad, then.

And perhaps that'll be it for the next eighteen months or so. Perhaps now I've stood up to him, Jason will leave me alone.

THEN

Helena

I can't escape the atmosphere in the office this morning. When I first arrived, Ash and Toby were sitting in the breakout area, having far too intense a discussion for 9.20 a.m. Ashley's face was flushed, her cheeks and neck bright pink, her nostrils flaring. Toby was gesticulating wildly, all arms and hands in her face. But as soon as I came in, the two of them stopped speaking, and Ashley stalked off to the toilets.

'You missed all the drama,' Jess says, dropping a page of proofs into my in-tray as I sit down at my desk.

'Looks like it,' I say, keeping my eyes on the screen as my computer drags itself into life. If I give Jess even the teeniest of windows she'll be here for the next fifteen minutes, chewing my ear off about some row she had with her colleague at her previous job. She's sweet enough, but definitely an oversharer.

'I think Toby might quit, you know,' Jess says, lowering her voice.

She wins; I look up at her.

'He's that annoyed. He was telling me in the pub last night. She doesn't care who she treads on to get what she wants.'

'Right,' I say, straightening up in my chair. 'Thanks for the heads-up. I'll have a word.'

She gets the message and wanders off to Amy, to try her luck at a chat there.

My computer gives a gentle bleep and I see a new email from Toby.

From: TobyJ@kamu.com
Subject: Ash – sales tactics

Hi Helena

It's not in my nature to 'report' my colleagues, but I just wanted to make you aware that Ashley has been offering my leads discounted prices (and in some cases reduced contracts) on their listings if they take out space at the pop-up. As far as I understood from your and David's brief, the listing fees are non-negotiable. As a consequence of several of her discounted 'deals', word has been getting round and it's not only undermining my position, but making it increasingly difficult for me to do my job.

I'd appreciate it if you could speak with her, or clarify the position to me, if indeed I have misunderstood our discounting policy/the priority of the pop-up.

Cheers

Toby

I flick my eyes up, and glance towards Toby's screen. He's frowning, clearly still upset – and understandably so – his fingers fighting with the keyboard, no doubt venting all to a friend. I take a deep breath, try to put myself in his position – one of David's top management tips – and reply to his message as empathetically as possible.

My period hasn't arrived. After spending what feels like the whole morning locked in a meeting room reassuring Toby that I will have words with Ash about her tactics – that we do, indeed, value him and that she has, indeed, been behaving out of turn – I head out to the small chemist on the corner of our building. It takes me a while to find what I am looking for, and I buy two – just in case. The woman behind the counter gives me a curious smile as I pay. She must sell these things all the time, to all kinds of different women experiencing all kinds of different emotions.

Afterwards I go next door to Pret and stare at the racks of sandwiches and salads and soups for what feels like hours. Busy worker bees jostle to get the things they want, pushing in front of me, tutting when I don't get out of the way. A child is wailing in a high chair in the corner, throwing all his mother's offerings on to the floor, as though the small pieces of baguette and cheese are the most disgusting foods he has ever seen. I walk up and down, trying to find something to suit my gnawing stomach, but none of it is what I want. I settle on some chocolate-covered rice cakes and a peppermint tea. They aren't going to fill me up, but they might stop this dreadful churning feeling.

Back in our building, I press the button and wait for the lift. I usually take the stairs but my legs are unwilling today. At our floor, I have to turn left for the toilets and right for our office. There's no one in the corridor, and I stand there for a few seconds trying to decide what to do. Get it over with now, or wait until tonight?

I've never been good at waiting. I walk a few paces and push the toilet door open. Ash is standing in front of the mirror, leaning on the basin, breathing heavily. There's a small make-up bag in front of her – something else that's new. I want to tell her that she doesn't need it, that there's barely a blemish on her clear white face, that too much make-up makes her look unnatural, clown-like. But I don't dare. She jerks her head towards me when she hears me come in. From the way she's standing, I expect her to be crying, but it's the opposite: she's angry.

'What's the matter?' I ask, staring.

She relaxes her arms, and her face follows.

'Nothing,' she says, looking back at the basin and turning on the taps. She starts washing her hands, a little too thoroughly, turning them over and over in the water. 'I'm just pissed off with Jess. That's all.'

'What's she done?' I ask.

'Just a stupid fuck-up, making us look like idiots,' she says, wiping away some smudged eyeliner with her finger. She zips open the make-up bag, pulls out some face powder and starts patting it on her face with a ferocity that makes me wince.

'Listen,' I say, remembering my promise to Toby. Ambition is all well and good, but not at the expense of others. 'Let's have a catch-up later. I have something . . . something I need to talk to you about.'

'Sure,' she says, keeping her head down, the heavy fringe in front of her eyes preventing mine from meeting hers. She pulls four paper towels from the dispenser, screwing them up into tiny balls in her hands, then throws them into the bin.

'Just grab me when you want to,' she says, her voice flat, and then she's gone.

I try to get Ash out of my mind as I go into the cubicle, lock it and hang my handbag and coat on the back of the door. I pull the white paper bag out, open the box and carefully take out the test.

I've never had to do this before, but I know the drill. But the whole experience is nothing like I expected. Not least because, deep down, I know I don't need to take the test at all. I know my own body. I know I'm pregnant. It took me half an hour of rummaging through my bedroom to find the leaflet they gave me when I had the implant fitted, reminding me in the strongest terms to get it changed after three years.

The irony of it all is not lost on me. I only have myself and my own stupidity to blame.

I pause for a second, checking there's definitely no one else in the bathroom. It's a small toilet, only three cubicles, and the only sound I can hear is the gentle whir of the air-conditioning vent above my head. I rip open the foil wrapper, and then I crouch as best I can over the small white stick. I've held myself all morning for this moment and my urine comes out in a gush of relief, splashing my forefinger in the process.

So much for having to wait three minutes. There's no doubt about this result.

My first thought is relief – I do understand my own body, after all. All the things that didn't make sense, suddenly do.

But then the magnitude of the situation hits me. The timing couldn't be worse. I've only been in this job for a few months: a job I created, that I had to fight for them to give me.

What the hell am I going to do?

THEN

*

Ash

Helena closes the door behind me, as though she's trying to provide me with some privacy, but everyone knows why we're in here. The meeting room is literally a goldfish bowl, for God's sake, glass on all sides. It's taken her four days to finally pluck up the courage to talk to me, and I'm keen to get it over with.

'Have a seat,' she says, gesturing at the chairs.

'I've got a call with the catering team in ten,' I say, but I know my voice sounds too aggressive. 'Sorry, I mean . . .'

'This won't take long.' Helena sighs, running her hands through her hair. As she does so, I notice the roots are slightly greasy. 'I had an email from Toby.'

'God, what a coward,' I say, sitting back in my chair and crossing my arms.

Helena frowns at me.

'That's not the word I'd use to describe him.'

'No,' I say. *Shit, me and my big mouth.* 'Sorry, I just . . . I just don't understand why people don't talk to people face-to-face any more. I read a really interesting article online about it yesterday, actually, how email is killing productivity—'

'Yes,' Helena interrupts. 'Listen, you seem to know what this is about. I wanted to give you the opportunity to put your side across. Toby's very upset.'

'The discounts,' I say, shrugging. 'It was a misunderstanding.'

'Really?' Her voice is laced with sarcasm. 'A misunderstanding?'

'Yes. I misunderstood the priorities, that's all. I thought, as it's a launch, it was important that we filled the stands at the pop-up. As it's the first event. You know, build long-term loyalty, get them excited so that next time they'll be more than happy to pay full price . . .'

What does it matter about Toby's paltry commission now, if it means we'll be raking it in, in the future? I want to add. But I manage to contain myself.

'That wasn't your decision to make,' Helena says. 'The prices are fixed, and we made it very clear what they were at the beginning of this. It's also unprofessional to undermine your colleagues in front of clients. Do you have a personal issue with Toby?'

'No!' I say, taken aback. 'Not at all.'

There's a pause. I expect her to back down, but there's a hardness in the way she looks at me that I haven't seen before. Perhaps I've pushed her too far this time.

'I'm sorry,' I say, even though it's an effort. I smile at her, give her a 'What am I like!' eye roll. 'I promise not to offer any more discounts. I'll apologize to Toby. And if you like . . . the ones that aren't fully committed yet, I can always go back and say there's been a misunderstanding, that I got the price wrong?'

I watch her face as she considers this; see the way her mind rolls the idea around. She knows how humiliating it would be to have to go back to them all – I've promised cheaper rates to at least five major brands.

'It's fine,' she says, and there it is again: that weakness, that need to be liked. She tries so hard to show authority, but she just can't master it. A tougher boss might have sacked me for this. 'It'll make us look even more unprofessional. But listen, just make sure this doesn't happen again.'

My phone buzzes on my desk and I click to read the message. It's from Joel: a photograph of some burgers, accompanied by the words 'Barbecue tonight?'

I text back 'Yes' immediately. God, I love the start of summer. And I love sharing the studio with Joel. I might even pick up some white wine on the way home from work tonight.

Appreciate what you have, before it turns into what you had.

Everything is going so well at the moment.

For me, at least. Helena, on the other hand, seems positively miserable. She's barely spoken to me since my telling off two days ago, and it's clear that something's up. I look over the top of our computer screens. She's staring at something on her desk, but I can't see what. Emboldened by my good mood, I skype her.

Are you OK?

Her computer pings. She looks up, sniffs slightly, starts to type.

Yes, all good, thanks. Just lots to do at the moment. And it's my mum's birthday next week, too; she wants us to go over for lunch.

Oh? Is that not a good thing?

Yes, it's fine! Don't worry! It's just that my mother and I don't really get on.

Not sure how to respond to that one. I could tell her I know how she feels – that when the problem of my mother was solved, it just led to a whole load more problems – but that probably wouldn't be a good move.

Mums, eh?

Are you close to yours?

I pause.

Not any more. She died. When I was fifteen.

She shifts in her seat, meets my eyes over the top of our screens. This time they're full of sympathy, reminding me of the funeral, the stares they all gave us. The way Jason cried when we got back to Gran's house. Confused and asking for answers, telling me it didn't look like an accident, that he had seen me at the top of the stairs. His voice was strained as he asked if I was trying to help her, if that's what he saw. Me reassuring him. Yes, of course I was.

Oh my goodness, I'm so sorry to hear that. I had no idea . . . I feel terrible for complaining about mine now.

How do I get off this subject?

Don't worry. She wasn't well. It was a blessing in some ways.

There's a pause before she types the inevitable. So much for feeling terrible.

Do you mind me asking what happened?

I tell her what she wants to hear. She wants the drama, she wants the details. She can have them.

No, it's OK. She fell down the stairs at my gran's house. Broke her neck on Christmas Eve. She was an alcoholic. Accident-prone, as they tend to be.

She meets my eye again and gives me her sickly-sweet smile.

Oh, Ashley. I'm so sorry.

Thanks. Long time ago now.

Unsurprisingly, she has never told me the whole story of her and her mother. I know she had some kind of breakdown and disappeared, and the family was reunited when Helena was about ten. But it sounds like Helena has never forgiven her. Which is fair enough. Ironic, really, that my mum abandoning me would have done me a massive favour, whereas she actually wanted hers around.

I stare at her again, wondering about her mental state, how tough she really is. She's all bravado in public, all flouncy hair and air kisses and super smiles, but there's more to her than that. She's no Princess Barbie. She's smart, for one thing, nearly as smart as me. But I know nothing about her private life, her relationships. I think back to the Christmas party; the way she was flirting with David like some stupid teenager . . . the day afterwards, when it looked like she was crying at her desk. The flowers, his inappropriate card.

He's what Gran would call a 'lothario'. I spotted him with Jodie earlier, when I was waiting for the lift. They were lingering on the stairwell, deep in conversation. I couldn't hear what they were saying but there is definitely something going on – it was clear from the way Jodie was gasping and giggling at him. Unsurprising that he's moved on already. Jodie's almost as attractive as Helena, and Helena has certainly let herself go lately. I feel a little sorry for her. But whatever went on between them, it hasn't done her career any harm.

My computer screen fades to black; my reminder to take a break. Important for your eyes, as well as the muscles in your neck and shoulders. I stand up, stretching my arms above my head, and walk towards the kitchen area. As I pass Jess's computer, I notice her quickly flick between her personal Facebook and our content management system. She clicks on one of the tabs at the top but it's too late, she's redirected to the login screen, meaning she's been inactive for more than fifteen minutes. I pause deliberately by her desk to let her know I've seen.

It might be a thankless job, copywriting product details for hours upon hours, day after day, but it's a job and she's paid well. I wonder if Helena would mind if I requested Jess give me some help. I'm sure she'd be fine about it; she's always telling me to ask if I need some support. I think asking her to fill all the goody bags for the pop-up isn't too unreasonable. I was going to do it tonight. But why should I have to stay late if Jess has time to piss around on social media? Helena's all about the teamwork, after all.

THEN

Helena

Distraction and denial are keeping me sane, at least for now. I just need the launch party for the pop-up over and done with, and then I can tell Jack and together we can formulate a plan. It's going to be all right. It has to be.

I stand near the entrance to the venue – the achingly trendy Islington Metalworks, a former nineteenth-century stable building tucked behind Angel station, scanning the crowds. Everyone looks happy – they are talking, boozing, networking. Buzzing. So far, so good. No one has noticed I'm not drinking. We had a couple of journalists turn up, keen to chat to me and Ashley, which delighted her. There are several high-profile make-up artists here, along with a few fashion designers. In one corner, near the coffee-area-turned-bar, Ashley is chatting away to one of our clients. She's pinned her hair up in a kind of 1960s chignon and it looks great, although it does make her look about ten years older than she actually is. I wonder why she's so keen to look older, but then I remember I was the same at that age.

I should join them, but I'm exhausted, and I can't keep up with her sales patter. I'm finding her quite annoying tonight. It's not her fault, of course, rather the situation I've got myself into, but she's one of the tangible reminders of what a mess I've made, and every time I look at her I struggle to imagine what on earth I'm going to do. Added to this, I've heard her talking about the event and her vision for it, and it's always in the singular, as though the rest of the team don't exist. I know it's just how her mind works – she'd say she doesn't want to speak for all of us – but even so, I don't like it. She's getting a little too big for her boots. She's supposed to work for me, after all.

It's the first time she's really irritated me. No, that isn't strictly true. She irritated me the day we moved into the downstairs office, by announcing that the desk next to the window would be hers, without even asking if it was OK by me. To keep the peace, I didn't object – even though I would have quite liked the window desk myself and thought it was pretty outrageous of her. I couldn't imagine behaving like that in front of my manager.

She also turns the radio off the second I leave the office, even if I'm only popping downstairs for a coffee, despite the long chats we've had about it and the unanimous agreement among the rest of the team that we like to work to a bit of Magic FM.

Don't sweat the small stuff.

Not one of her phrases, incidentally. She seems to sweat the small stuff all the time. So God knows what she will do about the big stuff.

I am lost in these thoughts, watching the people trickle through the entrance, their eyes darting around, lighting up as they take in the exposed brickwork and neon lighting, when I feel a little tug at my elbow. I turn round, and there Ashley is, her face flushed with excitement.

She holds out a glass of champagne.

'Are you OK?' she says. 'You look a little peaky.'

I take the glass from her, wondering if she'll notice me using the same trick she always does.

'Absolutely fine, thank you,' I say, my voice coming across like an imperious schoolteacher's. 'What about you?' I fling the question back at her, nodding towards her glass of suspiciously clear liquid.

'Need to keep a clear head,' she says. 'I haven't drunk in so long that if I had a glass of that stuff, I'd be all over the place. Anyway, want to hear the good news?'

I nod, pressing the glass to my lips and feeling the bubbles against my tongue, wishing I could down the whole thing.

'Tilly Mae are interested in taking a double stand at the next event, apparently. One of their PAs is here – I went to uni with her, so thought I'd invite her along – and she literally just did the minutes for the meeting in which they discussed my proposal. She's sure they're going to get in touch on Monday. At this rate, I'm going to have to find a bigger venue for the next one.'

'Wow,' I say, and despite the tinge of excitement, there's something else there. Not just the exhaustion, but the fear that this is all going a little too well for Ash. There's no denying that the website's progress has been less immediate, whereas the pop-up shop has been an instant success. 'Let's hope that this week's event goes well, then. It's all very well getting the exhibitors in, but without any punters, it'll be a disaster.'

'I know,' Ash says. 'Of course, you're right. But I think it's going to be fine. Please don't worry, Helena, I have it under control.'

She is smiling at me, but in an exasperated way. The way a

parent smiles at their toddler when they won't sit up to the table for lunch.

'I'm not worried at all,' I say, defensively. 'Just realistic. We don't want to over-promise and under-deliver. We have to build our reputation – we don't have one yet, just a lot of goodwill in the industry . . .'

'If it comes to it, I'll work every weekend to pull it off,' Ash says. 'I'll stand outside Farringdon station dressed as a giant lipstick and flyer everyone I see. I don't mind. You know I don't. This brand means everything to me.'

'It does, doesn't it?' I say. But it's not really a question, more a statement of exhaustion. I just want to go home now. I want to go home, put my pyjamas on and sit in front of Netflix with Jack and a giant mug of hot chocolate, like the old days. I want an empty week stretching ahead of me, just the two of us.

I want to not be pregnant.

'Oh, Helena,' Ash says, her face softening. 'You don't seem yourself. What's the matter? Is it your time of the month? Or has something happened with David?'

I open my mouth to reply, but there are no words ready, and so she continues.

'Don't worry,' she says. 'I'm not going to tell anyone. I saw you together ages ago – at the Christmas party. I don't blame you. He's a bit old for me, but he's handsome enough. Are you in love with him?'

'What?' I say, stunned not only by her cheek but by the fact she even thinks this. 'No . . . no . . . it was just . . .'

'You don't have to fib to me, Helena,' she says, putting her arm through mine and leaning towards me, her spicy perfume scratching my nostrils. 'I'm not going to tell Jack. I'm your friend – I'm on your side.'

'Ashley,' I say, firmly, 'I can't actually believe you're asking me this! It's really inappropriate! I'm just worried about Jack. We haven't been spending much time together lately, and it's been difficult. Work's been taking up all my time. I haven't been a very good wife.'

'Oh my God, please tell me you didn't say just say that . . . What does that even *mean*?'

'You're still very young,' I say, staring straight at her. My feet are aching from six hours of standing. Oh God, I want to go home so badly. 'You wouldn't understand.'

'No, I don't. Sorry, I thought you were a feminist.' She turns away from me, crossing her arms.

'Listen,' I say, pulling her back round to face me again. She's crossed a line, but the last thing we need is a massive fight at our launch party. 'I just don't want him to get pissed off with me because I'm spending all my time at work.'

'He doesn't look very pissed off,' Ashley says, nudging me.

I look up, and there he is, red-faced and panting slightly. What is he doing here?

'Did I miss it?' he says, breathless. 'Oh God, I'm so sorry if I missed it. Ashley said your speech was at ten p.m., right? There's . . .' he looks down at his watch, 'three minutes and thirty-two seconds to spare.'

'You haven't missed anything,' Ash says, smiling at him. 'In fact, I had just come over to tell Helena that we needed to get a move on. I'll meet you at the front – give you two a couple of minutes together.'

'How come you're here?' I say, throwing my arms around his neck. 'I told you not to worry.'

He smells amazing, a mixture of washing powder and after-shave with a tiny hint of sweat. It's so familiar, so comforting, so exactly what I need. It's like burying my face in my pillow after a long day.

'Thank you for coming,' I say. 'I'm so pleased to see you. I can't tell you . . .' I feel tears stinging the back of my eyes, which is utterly ridiculous.

'Ashley sent me an email. Said she wanted to surprise you, insisted I come down. I guess she thought you could do with the moral support,' he says. 'Wow, darling. Look at all these people. Here for you! It's incredible. I'm so proud of you. I really am.'

I don't say anything, just continue resting my head on his shoulder, breathing him in but thinking of her. Surprise me? By inviting my own husband to our launch night? What's she playing at?

'Listen,' Jack says, pulling away from me. 'Can we go some-where, after? Somewhere just you and me? Spend some time together? Or do you have to . . . carry on mingling?'

'No,' I say. 'No! I've done enough mingling tonight to last me a lifetime. Let's go home, shall we? It's all I want.'

'Great,' he replies. 'I'll just grab a drink, then – and make sure I've got a prime seat. Good luck!' He kisses me on the forehead and disappears to the bar.

I stand for a few minutes, smoothing down my dress, taking deep breaths and flicking my eyes over the crowd. Our team is bunched together in one corner, definitely not networking as instructed, but at least they're all smiling. I spot Joel leaning by the bar, gazing at Ashley as he swigs beer from a bottle. They are a funny couple; he seems the opposite of her, still the opposite of who I'd expect her to go for. And then my eyes fall on someone else. Someone who is weaving past people he recognizes in his determination to get somewhere.

David, in a suit jacket, a slim scarf hanging around his neck, is heading straight for Jack.

THEN

Ash

I can't believe David's so late. But at least Jack turned up. He's late, too. But still, he's here. The evening is working out perfectly.

Helena was all white-faced during her speech, and stumbled over some words, so clearly having Jack and David in the same room has got to her, after all. It's interesting to see that David's messed with her head, despite her telling me he means nothing to her. I *knew* there was something between them.

They're all chatting, anyway, in a nervous little huddle. Helena, with her arm awkwardly around Jack's waist. David, looking completely unbothered, king of business networking. I walk towards them.

'Not bad, huh? Hope you're impressed!' I say to David, and for a split second there's a look on his face that says he's forgotten all about me, and I'm tempted to throw my drink over him. But he recovers well.

'Of course,' he says, taking my hand. 'What a party. Great work, by the way.'

It's all so superficial, but I'm learning to play the game. This is what you have to do, this is how you get ahead in life. Nothing to do with brains or skills, but everything to do with whether or not people like you, how you make them feel, how you network. It's the same whether you're a drug dealer or President of the United States. Life is just one giant popularity contest.

I tell David how excited I am that we're opening a division in Australia. He listens to me, accepts my compliments, and gives nothing away. But it's fine. He's been looking around, he understands the vibe in the room, can see that we're doing well.

Jack and David are discussing the rugby. This is how it works, you see: a little bit of shop talk and a lot of small talk. Helena pulls me to one side and starts whispering at me.

'I told you not to invite Jack.' Her voice is nearly a hiss.

'Did you?' I say. 'I'm so sorry! I thought you told me *to* invite him. Why wouldn't you want him here?'

She looks back over her shoulder. 'I get nervous when I know he's watching me.'

'I'm so sorry!' I say, enjoying the moment, allowing my voice to take on a slightly patronizing edge. I think of all the times she's patronized me, and I can't help but relish the opportunity to get my own back. 'I didn't think you got nervous. I thought you'd find it supportive.'

She screws her face up, and for a second she looks unattractive. But she changes her mind. She can't be bothered to confront me here, and the Helena smile returns.

'Well, it doesn't matter,' she says. 'The speech went well, that's the main thing.'

'Oh God,' I say, and I touch her arm, to show I'm genuinely concerned. 'I didn't think! Of course, having David and Jack in the same room . . . stupid me. I didn't mean to upset you. But don't worry, you said it was nothing . . .'

'Christ!' she hisses, grabbing my arm and pulling me away from Jack and David. 'Keep your voice down!'

'Sorry, sorry!' I gesture at my champagne glass. 'Too many of these. I got overexcited.'

'I thought you weren't drinking. Listen,' she says, and I don't know if she believes me, if she even cares any longer, 'I've got a thumping headache. I'm going to go – no one will mind if I slip off.' She gestures around at the packed room. 'Everyone's having a great time. Party's a success, we did it.'

I did it.

'Oh, of course!' I say, doing my concerned face again. 'You get off home.'

'Thanks,' she says, and she tugs at Jack's sleeve.

He turns to look at her, an unspoken message passes between them, and he sets down his glass on the table behind us and marches off in the direction of the cloakroom.

'We're off,' Helena says, eyeing David. He has a first-class poker face. 'Jack has an early meeting tomorrow, and I'm feeling a bit under the weather.'

'Of course,' David says.

'Don't you worry, boss,' I say to Helena, putting my arm around her and pulling her towards me. 'I'll take it from here.'

THEN

Helena

In the taxi on the way home, I try to pluck up the courage to tell Jack my news, but he beats me to it the second we're in the door.

'Listen,' he says, rubbing his eyes with his fingertips as we sit on the sofa together. 'There's something I have to tell you. You're not going to like it.'

I picture his ex-girlfriend, Darcey, her large brown eyes, her neat pointed chin, her crazy ringlet hair. She doesn't look like me. She isn't childlike; she's glamorous. Tall and chic. Thinks it's your right to stay in touch with your ex, even if he's married, no matter who it upsets, or how stalkerish it makes you. She must be back again. After all that drama last year: the constant texting, requests for lunch dates, claiming to be 'just around the corner from his work' . . . I blame her entirely for my stupid insecurity, the situation with David. Why the hell can't she leave Jack alone?

'Oh, Jack . . . please,' I say, even though I know whatever's going on, it won't be his fault. I feel dizzy and light-headed, that dreadful churning feeling getting worse as the evening draws on. 'Not Darcey again?'

'No! God, no.' He won't meet my eye. He scratches his forehead. 'Nothing like that. It's just . . .'

'Tell me,' I say, after some time. 'Whatever it is, I'm sure it's not that bad.'

He takes a deep intake of breath, as though he's preparing to shout, and the words follow.

'I lost my job.'

'What?'

'Two months ago.'

'Two months ago?!'

'I was fired under the pretence of being made redundant. One of the guys had an epic fuck-up, and I refused to go along with the cover-up. It's a long story . . . I was talking to a lawyer about it, but they convinced me to take the money and slink off. But . . . it's going to be hard for me to find another job in the City. I've been trying – that's where I've been going every day – meetings with recruitment agents, lunches with old colleagues, interviews . . . But no one wants to know. Word gets around. You know I never fitted in there—' His words have tumbled out in a rush, and he stops suddenly and breathes deeply again, as though he's run out of air. 'I've thought about it long and hard, and I'm trying to see it as a blessing.'

'You lost your job,' I say, repeating the words in an attempt to assimilate them. Of all the things I could have pictured him saying, this is the least likely.

'I'm sorry,' he says, reaching forward and taking my hand. 'You know I hated it, anyway. I've been struggling for a long time. I'm sorry I didn't tell you. I just thought . . . what with everything that was going on with your work – you've been so busy, so much going on. I didn't want to stress you out.'

Pieces start slotting into place. The day he turned up at the office, all agitated. The subject line of that email on his phone – *Termination of Contract* – and me assuming it was him letting someone go, not the other way round. His sudden interest in escaping to the country, the times he's surprised me by being at home when he'd usually be in the office, the not-so-subtle hints that there's more to life than work.

'Is this why you've been talking about moving out of London?'

'You know I've always wanted to set up my furniture business,' he says, looking down at his lap, suddenly shy. 'I thought if we cashed in the money we'd made on this place, we could actually get something quite decent, and I could give it a go, use my pay-off to get started. I know you and my mum think it's a stupid idea, but my dad made a good living out of it. I'm so tired of everything being about other people's money. I want to do something myself, create something of my own.'

'I don't know what to say.' I have so many questions, but so little energy. 'I . . . the thing is, Jack, I'm knackered. It's been a long day. It's been a long . . . week.'

'I'm sorry I didn't tell you before,' he says again, scratching at his bottom lip. 'I just didn't know how you'd react. I was hoping I could find something else . . . I didn't want to have to rely on you, but seeing as you're doing so well, the pressure's off a bit. I know I should have told you straight away but . . .'

'It's fine,' I say, and I realize I genuinely don't mind. In fact, part of me is relieved. I always felt guilty about how hard he worked at a job he despised. 'Honestly. I just want you to be happy.'

I stand up, and as I turn to walk towards the kitchen, Jack grabs my arm.

There is something fierce inside both of us, something that has been missing for months now. I kiss him hard, biting into the skin around his mouth, wanting to be lost in it completely. We half stumble through to my bedroom, and I am completely consumed with a strange aggression. It has been so long since we made love like this, with passion rather than familiarity. It's different from before; it's a new, raw feeling that somehow tells me we'll be all right.

Afterwards, I lie there and watch him as he drifts off to sleep. My whole body feels alive and sparkling, as though I am plugged into the mains, lit up like a string of Christmas lights. I want to wake him up and make him do it all over again. In the half-light I watch his chest rise and fall, listening to the softness of his breath. As he sleeps he looks as though he is smiling.

I lean over and kiss him softly on the mouth. As I do so, my hand rests on my stomach as I imagine the baby. Our baby. Him as a dad, throwing him or her up in the air. The smiles on both their faces. Maybe it's all working out the way it's meant to. Maybe it won't be so bad. Maybe David will understand. Maybe I'll be able to go back to work after three months, like they do in America. The KAMU maternity policy is rubbish, anyway. All I need is some decent childcare. Women all over the world do it, every day, don't they? This is the twenty-first century, after all.

It will make Jack happy, so happy, and he's right, I don't want to be an old mum. Perhaps it's better now – to get it over with, and get back to the job – before KAMU Boutique grows too much and I feel I can't tear myself away. At least if Jack is doing his own thing, he'll be around more to help out, he'll be flexible. We could even share the childcare – he could do the nursery pickup, so I wouldn't have to leave early. It doesn't have to mean the end of everything I love and enjoy. Not if we work as a team.

I put my arm loosely around him, and whisper in his ear. He mumbles slightly, rolls towards me, then opens one eye, sleepily.

'What did you say?' he says, his voice foggy.

'I'm pregnant,' I say, again.

His eyes, and then his smile, widen fully.

'Helena!' he gasps.

I bury my face against his shoulder, breathing in his shock. For the first time, I'm filled with excitement rather than fear.

THEN

Ash

My desk phone rings and I snatch it up, jamming it against my ear.

'He won't leave,' Karen says. 'He's now insisting he knows you. He's becoming quite unpleasant.'

'I told you,' I hiss into the mouthpiece. 'I have no idea who he is.'

'He says he wants to check that the gift he left for you arrived?' Karen's voice sounds less frightened and more nosey, suddenly. 'Is he . . . an ex?'

It was only a matter of time before he turned up here again. Just like when I was nineteen, when he lost me my job at the Co-op. When I refused to steal cigarettes for him, he turned up every day with his meathead friends and hung around outside, scaring off the punters. He was there for three days until the snotty-nosed manager told me my services were no longer required.

He knows how to get to me, how to really hit me where it hurts. The bottle of vodka keeps looking at me from the corner of the desk. His idea of a little joke, probably nicked from the nearest off-licence. Must get rid of it. The note it came with is long gone. I pushed it through our shredding machine, but the vodka isn't so easy to deal with. Guess I'll have to take a lunch break and throw it away then. Or give it to the nearest homeless person, perhaps.

'No,' I say, fingering the label on the bottle. 'I promise you, I have no idea who he is. He sounds like some nutcase.'

'In that case,' Karen says, disappointed, 'I'll have to call the police.'

'No!' I say, again, raising my voice. I lower it, keeping my head down. The last thing I need is the rest of the office earwigging on this conversation. Thank God Helena's upstairs in a budget meeting. 'I'll . . . don't do that. If he really insists he wants to speak to me, then tell him I'll come down in five. I've no idea who he is, but just in case it's a client I've forgotten about. Leave it with me.'

I lean forward and rest my forehead on my palms, but there's a noise behind me, making me jump. I look up to see Jess, offering me the bag of crisps she's holding. Her fingers are covered in crumbs.

'Jesus!' I say, glaring at her. 'Don't creep up on me like that. What do you want?'

'Nothing,' she says, pulling the crisp packet back. 'Just wondered if you were going to come out for lunch. We're all going to the new café on the corner.'

As she speaks I realize that the rest of the team are standing by their desks, coats on, staring at me. Toby looks away as I meet his eyes. I don't care if they like me or not, of course, I never have. Helena might be the boss, but she's far more popular than me – she's so soft, so concerned with their feelings all the time.

She fusses over them when they call in sick, rather than telling them to man up. But here they are, inviting me to lunch.

'I'll be staying in today,' I say – even though, for once, I am actually going to go out. 'Too much to do.'

'Sure,' Jess replies, and her body relaxes slightly. They were just inviting me to be polite. I swallow away the brief sting of hurt. 'Don't work too hard!'

And with that, she practically skips towards the rest of them, and they filter out of the room, one by one, small talk filling the air.

I grab the bottle of vodka, stuffing it into my bag, then linger in the stairwell until I hear the team's inane chatter evaporate. And then I walk slowly down the stairs myself.

I spot him as soon as I enter the reception area. He's sitting at the same table I sat at on my first day here, right in the far corner. The best vantage point. *Like brother like sister.* Mum's needling voice in my head. *Always ganging up on poor Mummy.* Karen sees me come in and points towards him, giving me an encouraging smile. Nodding my thanks, I take a deep breath and stride up to him, wondering how best to get him back out on the street where he belongs.

'Well, hello,' Jason says. 'Nice place. Again.'

He gestures around the reception area, with its velvet button-back sofas and spherical vases full of lilies.

'And were they your *colleagues*?' His voice is full of sarcasm as he says the word. 'I think I counted . . . eight worker bees trotting out just then. Impressive. Must be quite a big operation.'

'Jason . . .' I begin, but I have no idea what to say to him at all. I can feel Karen's eyes watching me. Nosey cow.

'So,' he says, 'I need your help . . .'

There's no big black holdall today, and he looks worse than the last time I saw him, his denim jacket stained with what looks like drops of blood down the front, combat trousers spattered with mud. There's no way Karen will believe he's a client. He reaches into his pocket and pulls out a bag of tobacco and begins to roll a fag.

'You can't smoke in here,' I say. 'Do you *want* to get me in trouble again?'

'Look,' he says, 'I'm sorry about the other day. About the . . . mug. It's just . . . I've got myself into a situation. And I need your help. I need enough money to put down a deposit on a flat.'

'What situation?'

'It doesn't matter. I just need to get my shit together.'

We're agreed on one thing, at least. If I can just get him outside the building and to somewhere where people won't see us . . . I stand up straight, imagining I'm talking to a complete stranger. Karen mustn't suspect I know him – she's got the biggest mouth in the whole building.

'Come outside,' I say. 'And we can talk.'

He stands up grumpily, but follows me out on to the square in front of the office.

I stop walking once we're behind the double-storey cycle rack round the side of our office. In the distance, I hear the sound of glass bottles falling into the giant recycling bin outside one of the restaurants on Granary Square. All those people out there, living their lives in the sunshine, drinking their lattes, not having to deal with *this*.

'Why are you staring at me like that?' he says, his eyes widening.

'It's not too much to ask, is it? Some help from my own sister? Or do you want the whole world to know exactly what Miss Ash-L-E-Y Thompson did when she was fifteen. What's that website that seems *so* impressed with you? Bet they'd love some gossip on you.'

'You're trying to blackmail me?' I say, attempting a different tactic. 'For one thing, I didn't do *anything* when I was fifteen. For another, I hardly have any money.'

'Not what I heard,' he says. 'Apparently, you're really making waves.'

'Don't be so stupid, Jason,' I say, sounding like his big sister all over again. 'You want to talk? Let's talk. Tell me what the problem is. Do you owe someone money?'

To my surprise he listens. He leans back against a bike rack, grabbing the roll-up from his pocket.

'I told you!' he says, lighting it. 'It's nothing like that. I just need some help. I need to find a place. It's all right for you, all set up in your happy new world, with your posh office and your fancy events. I just want to get myself a roof. Not much to ask, is it?'

'There's more to it,' I say. 'Tell me what it is, or I won't help you.'

He won't meet my eye.

'You'll probably find out eventually, anyway,' he says, after a pause. 'It's Lisa. I want to make a go of things, but she's not interested until I've got myself sorted.'

'Jesus, Jason,' I say, exhaling. 'You put her in hospital last year! Seriously? You think she'd have you back?'

'It wasn't like that,' he says, looking down. 'It was an accident. They forced her to testify. Anyway, it's none of your business! You should want to help me. I'm trying to get my shit together.

That's what you *want*, isn't it? I'm gonna get straight. Lisa said if I can get a place, we can be a family . . .'

I nearly laugh out loud, but then I see something rare in his eyes. He's telling the truth, and part of me wants to cry. He wants what we all want, even though he does himself no favours. He just wants to be loved, wants someone to give a shit. Underneath all the bravado I can see my little brother, the one who asked if he could call me Mum, because I was a better mother than his real one. On the surface he appears to have gone, but he's still in there somewhere. I just need to look hard, and then I'll find him.

'I'm sure I can help you out, somehow,' I say, warily. 'But I can't just hand over loads of cash. You must understand that. I've got my own bills to pay. And turning up like this . . . at my work, it's not going to help either of us. Trust me.'

'You owe me,' he says, beginning to scowl. The smoke from his cigarette billows in my face, making me cough.

'You're being very short-sighted,' I say. It's like playing a game of chess with a grand master. I have to find the moves to outsmart him but the truth is, he's always been brighter than me, with less to lose. And I can tell his threat isn't empty. 'Me handing over money isn't going to sort your life out. If you really want to do that, you need to get help. I dunno, see a careers advisor or something. What happened to the dusters and tea towels?'

'Got fed up of the abuse,' he says. 'Anyway, I don't want a *career*. I told you, I just need to get a place. To show her I'm serious.'

I give a loud sigh, rubbing my forehead. And then I feel his fingers suddenly tighten around my right wrist, squeezing it until my palm begins to go numb.

'Listen,' he says, his pupils wide as he stares at me. 'Please. I'm asking you nicely. I need money. I need it now. If you don't get it for me, I'll tell everyone what happened with Mum.'

'You sound about six years old,' I say, but I've misjudged it again, forgotten how easy it is to turn on his anger, like flicking a switch.

'Fucking hell. I'm your brother!' he roars.

I brace myself, squeezing my eyes shut and protecting my face with my hands. But all I hear is a thump and the clang of metal as he kicks one of the bikes, and when I finally look up I'm alone on the side street, Jason's cigarette lying crushed at my feet.

THEN

Helena

I never used to be the sort of person who overslept, but here I am, late for work again. There was no time to even shower this morning, so I'm bare-faced and stressed as I race into the office, only to see a copy of *Style and Beauty* on my desk, open to reveal a double-page spread all about the pop-up. I take in the headline, the photos of shiny happy people having fun, the highlighted quotes declaring that KAMU B are 'shaking up beauty like never before' and then I close the magazine and push it to the corner of my desk.

'There's no link at the end of this,' I say to Ash. I know I sound petty, but I don't care.

She looks up from her desk opposite me and I notice she's wearing winged eyeliner for the first time. The effect is a little startling. Some people just don't suit make-up; how ironic that she's one of them.

'But did you see the headline?' Ash says. 'It's amazing coverage! And the editor wants to take me ... um, us out for lunch next week. She's considering running some kind of partnership or sponsorship programme for the next event. Ticket giveaways for the readers – that kind of thing. I'm now thinking about running a programme of talks from beauty insiders—'

'But there's no link to the website,' I interrupt her. 'In fact, there's no mention of the website at all.'

Ash looks down, gives a little sigh.

'Yeah,' she says. 'That is a bit poor. Sure it's just a mistake at their end.'

'Did you even mention it when they interviewed you? I've told you before,' I say, the words rushing out before I have the chance to stop them, 'that we're a digital business first and foremost. That's where the real money is. It's fundamental that people are aware of KAMU B online as well as the pop-up events. It's not just some London-centric throwaway children's party we're trying to build here.'

Her face melts into one of her fake smiles. Her teeth seem whiter than I remember. As I grow weaker, she seems to grow stronger, more attractive, more confident. *You're not in competition with her*, I have to remind myself. *The opposite, in fact. You're not rivals, you're meant to be a team.*

'I'm sorry,' she says, fixing her blue eyes on me. 'It was an honest mistake.'

'Is this article going online?'

'I think so.'

'Can we please make sure the website is properly linked to from that. And while we're at it, ask them for multiple mentions on social, with trackable links. Let's make sure we know exactly how useful this PR hype is to the bottom line.'

'Of course,' Ash replies. 'Consider it done! By the way, I've finished my final budget report for the pop-up. Would you like to see it? We can go through it together? The main thing to know is that we . . . tripled our profit target! I'm over the moon. Hope you're impressed.'

'I can't look now,' I say, logging into my computer. 'How about . . . three p.m. this afternoon instead?'

'Oh,' Ash says. 'I've got a meeting with David then.'

I raise my eyebrows at her, my heart pounding in my chest.

'Can I ask what about?' I say.

Ash glances around at the team and lowers her voice.

'Just an HR thing,' she replies. 'Shall we do four p.m.?'

'Fine.'

My emails swim before my eyes. There's no way I can concentrate now, so I get up and make my way to the bathrooms. Inside, I stand in front of the mirror above the basin and pull out my make-up bag. It's time for war paint, because this is war.

When I finish, I look back at myself and want to scrub it all off. I look too tarty, too done up, too bothered. I sigh again. I'm always tired, these days, but today feels like climbing a great big hill against gale force winds.

I can't believe Ashley is now arranging meetings alone with David. I logged on to Facebook earlier, and was surprised to see that she had become friends with almost my entire social circle – every single person that had turned up at the launch party had been added as her 'friend', even the ones she barely spoke to. It feels like she's trying to steal my life, piece by piece.

I shake the thoughts away; tell myself I'm being ridiculous. She's just trying to better herself, and after all, people aren't possessions. I don't own my friends. But still, she needs to understand her place. I take a deep breath and march up the stairs to David's office.

The KAMU team all look up and smile as I weave my way through their desks. David spots me approaching from inside his glass cube and waves me in. I push the door open. I've tried to avoid being alone with him recently, but this is important.

'Helena,' he says, giving me his broad smile. I can never tell exactly what he's thinking – it's both unnerving and impressive. 'I've been meaning to come down and congratulate you on the *Style and Beauty* piece. Impressive coverage. Well done.'

'It's only a trade mag. But . . . thanks,' I say, standing in front of his desk. He gestures for me to sit down, but I ignore him. 'I'm not stopping. I just wanted to ask . . .'

I pause. If I didn't know David as well as I do, would I have the nerve to ask this? I've lost all sense of what's appropriate.

'Ashley mentioned she had a meeting booked in with you later. And I was wondering if you needed me there?'

'Have we?' he says, frowning and clicking his mouse. 'Oh, at three. I'd forgotten.'

'So do you need me?' I say, a little more forcefully. 'I mean, if it's an HR thing, I think as her line manager I should probably sit in.'

David gives a loud sniff, his eyes flicking back and forth.

'Um,' he says. 'I'll be honest. I've got no idea what it's about. But if it is an HR thing, perhaps best I see her alone. I'll feed back to you afterwards?'

'Sure,' I say, defeated. 'Whatever you think.'

'Best you're not there – just in case she's making a formal complaint about you!' he says. Despite knowing this is a misfired attempt at a joke, my heart pounds as I consider it. 'I'm sure you've got more important things to do.'

'Fine. But . . . if it's about Toby,' I say, 'he has my full support. So I'd appreciate it if you'd let me know. The two of them have had difficulties working together, and from my impartial perspective, it's Ash who's the cause of most of the issues.'

Even as I say the words, I feel a conflicted stab of guilt. She's worked herself into the ground for KAMU B, while Toby's always the first to leave in the afternoons. But still, she's definitely not a team player, and that's important on a small team like ours.

David nods and I turn to leave.

'Oh,' he says, calling me back. 'While I've got you . . .'

'Yes?'

'I've just had a call from Brian in the New York office. They're very excited about the concept. I don't want to get your hopes up yet but I have a feeling they'll be calling on you to roll it out over there . . . It's a different market, of course, entirely – but the commercial model ought to hold up in NYC, at least . . .' He pauses, watching my face as the news sinks in. 'How do you think Jack would feel about relocating?'

There's an edge to his voice that makes my skin prickle.

'Wow,' I say, knowing that Jack would find the idea intolerable. 'That's . . . brilliant. Certainly very exciting. I'm glad they're so impressed.'

'You get all the credit – it's all down to you, kiddo,' he says, and as if on cue, his phone starts ringing.

I murmur a goodbye and escape through the heavy glass door.

Back downstairs, I find Ash already in her coat, lingering by my desk and thumbing through that bloody issue of *Style and Beauty*, her new Kate Spade handbag tucked under one arm.

'Ready?' she says, beaming at me.

'Ready?' I reply, confused.

'Yes, the follow-up meeting with Rose & Blue? It's in your calendar.'

'Shit,' I say, then give myself a little shake. Perhaps baby brain is a thing, after all. I feel Toby's presence as he appears behind me, hovering just out of view, trying to catch my attention. 'Yes, of course. I thought it was at eleven.'

'Nope,' Ash says. 'Shall I meet you by the lifts?'

I nod, pushing a smile to my lips and grabbing my iPad from the drawer.

'Sorry, Toby,' I say. 'Not now. Can we chat when I'm back?'

He smiles but his eyes tell me how frustrated he is as he nods politely and slinks away.

We catch a cab to the private members' club – my idea, not hers. I can't face the idea of getting the Tube. It's incredibly warm and I am wearing too many layers, my skin itchy and hot underneath them. Thankfully the taxi is quick, and we are early, meaning we arrive before the Rose & Blue team. We take a seat in one of the leather booths, and Ash's mobile rings. She picks it up, a flicker of anger passing across her face as she mutes the call. I watch her, wondering who it was, and realize that I barely know her. No one really does.

'Was that Joel?' I say. 'You've got time to talk to him, if you need to. They'll be another ten minutes.'

'No,' she says, her voice emotionless as she tucks her phone back into her handbag. 'It's fine.'

I give a little shrug and turn back to my iPad, desperately scanning the figures for the Rose & Blue landing page. As suspected, they're less than superb. Outright disappointing might be a more accurate way of describing them. Yet I know their stand at the pop-up was one of the busiest. I search my brain, trying to think of reasons – no, excuses – that I can give them, and then I swallow a wave of nausea as I see them approach our table.

'It could have been worse,' Ash says, as we leave the club afterwards. 'They're pleased with how the pop-up went at least.'

'Yes,' I say, their words bouncing around my mind.

Don't see why we need to sign up to coverage on the site. Can't we just do the pop-up?

It's becoming an all-too-familiar refrain.

We pass one of my favourite coffee shops. I need to eat something, I'm beginning to feel light-headed again.

'Listen, let's not go back to the office just yet. It's a little bit early, but we could call it brunch?'

She looks up at the café sign.

'OK, why not?'

Inside, I order a peppermint tea and a flapjack, while she chooses a fruit salad. We settle at a table in the corner of the café, lit overhead by a huge skylight. The June sun is bright and warms my skin through the glass.

'It's amazing, you know. What we've achieved,' she says, stirring her almond-milk hot chocolate. The colour of it – a kind of off-putting beige – swilling around in a mini tornado makes me gag a little, and I have to turn away and wipe my mouth with a tissue. I sip my peppermint tea. 'No caffeine for you today?'

I look down at the peppermint tea.

'No . . . I don't know, I just didn't fancy it.'

She raises her eyebrows and pierces a neatly sliced grape with her fork.

'Rose & Blue were so happy with how the event went.'

'Yes, I'm aware,' I say. 'But we really need to start focusing on the site. That's where the recurring revenue lies.'

'I know, I know . . .' she says, fixing her eyes on a spot on the wall behind my head. 'But technically speaking, building traffic for the site isn't *my* job, is it?'

She's right and I hate it.

'David mentioned the Americans were pleased.'

'Really?' she replies, smoothly. 'That's exciting. Forgive me, Helena, but you . . . you don't seem yourself lately. Aren't you enjoying working together? Because . . . well, I'm loving working with you. You've taught me so much.'

'Have I?' I say, giving a half-hearted smile. 'Hope some of it was useful.'

'Of course!' she says, and then she beams at me again. 'But you've achieved so much in such a short time . . . this can't be your only dream?' She sounds a bit shy then, the way I remember her when I first interviewed her. Less than a year ago, but so much has changed since then.

'What do you mean?'

'Don't you have other dreams? Ideas? Things you want to do with your life. Things you wanted to do when you were young?' She picks a tiny bit of dirt off one of her strawberries with her finger.

I think of Jack; his furniture business.

'I don't know, really,' I say. 'When I was a child all I wanted to be was a mother. But then I grew up and having a career seemed a lot more appealing.'

'I always wanted to sew.'

'Really?'

'Yes,' she says, staring at the strawberry. 'I wanted to be a seamstress. When I was a kid . . . I used to make things for me and my little brother, Jason. Cushions, naff bags made from scraps of fabric, that sort of thing. My gran taught me to use a sewing machine when I was ten. I thought doing that for a living would be the ultimate dream.' She laughs. 'Then I found out how much they get paid. And I woke up.'

'Life's not all about money, though, is it?' I say. 'There's more to life than money.'

'Spoken like someone who's never been without it.'

What can I say to that? It's true; I've never had to worry about money. But I only saw my mother twice a year up till the age of ten, and no amount of money can compensate for that.

Then again, the two things aren't mutually exclusive. Maybe Ash had neither.

'You never talk about your family,' I say, steering the subject away. 'I mean, I know your mother passed away but . . .'

She shrugs, and hides her face behind her hot chocolate. A habit of hers when she doesn't want to show you how she really feels about something.

'Nothing much to tell,' she says, putting down her mug and pushing her remaining blueberries around with her fork.

'Well, you've got a brother, right? You've just told me that. Any other siblings?'

'Nope, just Jason.'

'How old is he?'

'Four years younger than me,' she says. 'So, he's twenty-one now.'

'Is he at university?' I ask.

She shakes her head.

'No,' she says. 'He . . . er . . . he's taking a gap year. Gone travelling around America. I hardly hear from him. Just a few emails, every now and then. We're not that close any more.'

I know she's lying, because, for all her faults, Ash is an open book. Nothing stops her from saying exactly what she really thinks at any moment. There's no pausing to consider whether a response is appropriate, no dumbing down her message to make it more palatable to the audience. And everything that just came out of her mouth sounded false, stilted, under-rehearsed and just . . . wrong. I wonder why she's lying, and what her brother is really like. I make a mental note to google him later.

'And your dad?' I ask, even though I know I'm pushing my luck.

'Yeah, we're not that close, either,' she says. 'He didn't cope well with my mum dying. I didn't have a great time, growing up. But my gran's always been there for me. Can we talk about something else?'

'Of course,' I say, eyeing my flapjack. Even though I have to, to stop the nausea, I don't actually want to eat it. Pregnancy is so strange – these are the flapjacks that I used to dream about late at night, yet now it looks completely unappetizing. 'I don't want to upset you. Listen—'

'Oh no, oh no, you're not upsetting me,' she interrupts, and this time she is telling the truth. She looks at her phone as she

speaks, scrolling through her emails. 'I just don't find it construc-
tive to talk about my family, that's all. Not when we have more
important things to discuss like . . . shit.'

'What?'

'Oh, she makes me so cross!'

'What? Who?'

'Jess! Sorry, Helena, but she is useless. Useless. How hard is
it . . . ? I mean, come on . . .'

'What's happened?'

'I asked her to send over a sample product brief to MollyMoo.
And copy me in. But not only has she not cc'd me, she's sent a
live mock-up, with all their details on . . . the MD has just emailed
me to complain. *Worried about how seriously you take NDAs in light
of this.* You're on it, too.' She nods at my iPhone, which is sitting
next to me. I pick it up and open my emails, finding the message
she is referring to.

'Oh . . . oh,' I say. 'Well, easy mistake to make, I suppose.'

'No, it's not. It's just careless. Makes us look like idiots. And
MollyMoo is a nightmare. If the Americans found out about this,
they wouldn't be excited about us *at all*. Seriously. Every day it's
something. Every day.'

'I'll talk to her when we get back to the office,' I say. 'I promise.'

'Make sure you do,' she says, and there's something in her eyes
I haven't seen before.

THEN

Ash

God knows how he got back into the office last night, but there was a note on my desk waiting for me when I got in this morning. He's resorted to begging, which is a new twist. I ignored it at first, but now I screw it up into the smallest ball possible, and drop it into my waste-paper basket. I've been thinking of the way his voice quietened when he talked about Lisa, and wondering if he really does want to make a go of it with her. Perhaps she'd be good for him.

I turn back to my computer screen, trying to focus on my work. I'm still waiting for a response from David after our meeting and I'm back to checking my emails every thirty seconds, like I did in the days after my first interview with KAMU. I even woke up at 3 a.m. this morning and checked them on my phone, just in case. David's in New York this week and I'm wondering if he might be running it all past the big shots while he's there. But still no updates. In the meeting he seemed surprised by my nerve, asking for a promotion outright, but there was definitely part of him that was impressed, too. How could he not be, with the results I've achieved? But still, I know it all hinges on Helena. She's the key to everything, the one who holds all the power.

She's not even here yet. No wonder Toby resigned. They say you don't leave your job, you leave your manager. Helena seemed genuinely upset when he told her he was off to work on the Beauty Trade Show, the biggest and most boring competitor in our market. But he's no great loss.

And anyway, what does she expect? She's not inspiring anyone any more. How can she, when it's half past nine and she's still not here? She'll be busy with her mortgage advisor or solicitor. She's been all excited lately, banging on about her and Jack buying a new place in the sticks. Spending her weekends driving around gawping at village pubs and Instagramming the shit out of them. Apparently, Jack's decided to 'part ways with the City' and is going to spend the rest of his life making chairs. Or something. Her decision to move out of London amazes me, despite her insistence they'll be moving to somewhere commutable. After all, she struggles to make it in on time as it is.

She hasn't replied to any of my emails since 4 p.m. yesterday afternoon. I feel like phoning her and asking her where she is. A few months ago I might have done, but I'm beginning to realize I don't actually *need* her most of the time. In fact, I'm not entirely sure what she does all day long, apart from suck up to David. I'm amazed how much power she still seems to have over him. I know she's attractive, but I can't believe men are so pathetic, really.

There's a noise from the other end of the office, and I look up. Helena is racing towards me, her hand clutching a Caffè Nero cup, her hair scraped back in a bun that's too severe for her small features. Probably never heard of a Croydon facelift. Her mouth is opening but I have to force myself to listen to what she's saying.

'Morning!'

She pants slightly as she sits down at her desk, her top lip sparkling with sweat.

'Missed the bus?' I find myself saying, trying to make a joke of it.

'Something like that,' she replies. 'Listen, can we have a chat – go for a coffee in a bit?'

'You've already got one,' I say, nodding towards the cup. 'But sure.'

Suddenly, I feel cheered up. I open up the spreadsheet I was working on – analysis of KAMU B at the end of Q1, something else that Helena should really be doing, but she might not think of it – and my brain finally starts working again.

Every now and then I think of the note that was left on my desk, wondering how on earth he got into the building. I think of David's radio silence. At 10 a.m. exactly, I look up and Helena is already standing, a silk scarf tied around her neck in a bow, like an old woman.

'Let me just save this . . . cool, ready,' I say, getting up and following her out of the building. We walk to the coffee shop in silence and I wonder whether now would be a good time to bring up what I discussed with David. Probably not. Don't want to jinx it.

'What do you want to drink?' I ask, as she stares up at the blackboard behind the counter. 'Flat white?'

'Er, no . . .' she says, frowning. 'Just water for me, please.'

'So,' I say, because she's suddenly gone all quiet, and is staring at her drink as though she wishes she'd got something else instead. I'm reminded of that time at Ted's, when she first told me her plans for KAMU B. 'What's up?'

'Something strange has happened,' she says, rolling a packet of sugar between her fingers. 'It wasn't expected, but . . . I'm just going to come right out and tell you, before I tell the rest of the team, because you're my second-in-command, after all.'

Second best, always second best. I flinch slightly. *Don't I know it.*

'The thing is . . . I'm pregnant.'

I sit back in my chair.

'Is this a wind-up?' I pause, breathing out. 'I don't know what to say.'

'I think the customary response is "congratulations", but I understand your surprise,' she says, smiling – actually *smiling*. 'It wasn't planned . . . it's been a shock to both of us . . .'

It wasn't planned. We don't live in the dark ages. How can a pregnancy not be planned?

'. . . but we've decided to keep it,' she is saying.

My ears begin to ring.

'I know the timing isn't brilliant, but seeing as KAMU's maternity policy is so shocking, anyway, I was thinking I'd only have three months off, then come back part-time, and then full-time after six months. We'd get cover in, and I'd still be online all the time, I'd still be available . . . the baby's not due till the end of December, anyway, which is ages away. Who knows what might happen before then? But I wanted to tell you first, just so you're not worried . . .' She tails off.

'You mean . . .' I begin, although I can't even believe what I'm about to say, 'you're keeping it?'

Her eyes are saucers.

'I just said,' she says, after a pause. 'Of course I'm keeping it.'

'But . . .' I say. This doesn't make any sense. 'What about our team? The Americans are actually impressed with us! The timing couldn't be worse. You're the only reason David even let us do this in the first place. If you leave, they'll just shut down the whole thing!'

'I don't think that's true,' she says. 'Listen, I know it's probably a big shock – it was a big shock for me, too – but it doesn't have to be a catastrophe. KAMU are invested in this project, it won't go under just because I'm not around for a few months. And it's not like I'll be disappearing tomorrow – I'll still be working for months. It's all manageable.'

She sounds like she's trying to convince herself.

'Jesus, Helena,' I say.

'I know it's a shock . . .' Her eyes begin to fill with tears. 'But . . . please, try to be supportive. I'd appreciate it.'

'I'm sorry,' I lie. 'It's just a lot to wrap my head around. I really wasn't expecting it.'

'You and me both,' she says.

'How far along are you?' I ask. Perhaps it's all a storm in a teacup. Perhaps her period is just a bit late.

Must. Stay. Calm.

She's just taken an entirely selfish course of action, no remorse about what it means for me, no concept of how much more difficult it makes my life. In fact, it's worse than that. She doesn't even care. What if David decides to pull the plug on the whole idea? Where does that leave me? Jobless, and marked as part of a failed, very public experiment. But she couldn't care less. She doesn't care how frightened I am, she doesn't care that I'm twenty-five and I already feel like I'm carrying a ton of weight on my shoulders, she doesn't care that I've never done anything like this before, that I'm learning as quickly as I can. She thinks she can swan off and play happy families – and who gives a shit if I lose my job because of it?

'Nearly four months,' she says. 'I wanted to tell you sooner but . . .'

The question lingers on the tip of my tongue, but I know I can't ask it. She's watching me and she knows what I'm thinking. She knows, because she's thinking it, too.

Who is the father?

THEN

Helena

'Helena Brenton,' David says, drumming his fingers on his desk. 'Well, well, well. You are certainly full of surprises.'

'I'm . . .' I begin, but then I stop myself. No, I am not going to apologize for being pregnant. 'I appreciate that the timing is not ideal, but as you've always told me, everything is workable.'

'Hmmm.' David stands up and paces towards the window. 'What did I tell everyone when we first started working on this shiny new ship? No getting pregnant until our IPO! There's no denying that you like to keep me on my toes. Always one step ahead of me, eh? In all seriousness, though, and just to make sure I stay on the right side of legal action, many congratulations.'

I give a tight smile, grinding my fingers into the sides of my thighs and wondering what I ever saw in him.

'Thank you, David.'

'I expect you've seen how meagre the maternity policy here is?' he asks. 'Nothing I can do about that, I'm afraid.'

'Yes,' I say, determined to stay professional. 'I've read my contract and seen it's just the minimum statutory amount.'

'Better than the US team get, though,' he replies, as though I should be grateful.

I nod, unsure what his point is. I just want to get out of this office as soon as possible.

'I expect Jack's thrilled?' he says, his voice softening as he meets my eyes.

'Yes,' I reply, like a parrot. 'He's very happy and excited about becoming a father.'

David gives a deep sigh and fiddles with the blinds, straightening out the wonky slats.

'Having children was the best thing I ever did,' he says. 'But I'm not sure Elizabeth would agree. Did you know she was a lawyer? Before?'

'No.'

'She was good at it, too. Shame. I think she prefers what she does now . . . helps out at a local charity. Can't really call it a *job*, I suppose. But I guess she can go back to law one day, if she likes. Although Penny needs a lot of support, she's a challenging child.'

He's talking more to himself than to me. I glance over at the immaculate silver photo frame on his desk. The three of them on a pristine white beach, tangled blonde hair blowing across their eyes, smiles in perfect coordination.

'They're beautiful children,' I say, pointlessly.

'Yes,' David says, sitting back down again. 'They are. Well, then. Given your news, I suppose it would be pertinent for me to make a decision about your protégée?'

'Ashley?'

'Yes. She's been in my Inbox for weeks. She told you, did she, about her little plan for promotion?'

I swallow.

'I suspected something was on her mind,' I say.

'What do you think, then?' David asks. 'Let me see if I can find her email. Sixteen-page proposal, indeed – she's certainly thorough. Here we are. All the reasons why she should be made Events Director. She's even detailed her proposed new salary bracket, set against the specific ROI she's brought to the brand. I'll give her one thing, she's a better salesman than most of that team sitting out there.'

'She's a hard worker,' I say, but it feels like the words are going to choke me, and a tiny voice in my head is telling me to be careful, that I'm shooting myself in the foot. 'Has a tendency to act before thinking at times, but she's tenacious and she gets results. Not much of a team player, though. And she behaves like a man. Whether or not that's a good thing is down to your perspective.'

'Reckon she could cover your maternity?' David says, scrolling through her PowerPoint presentation as though he's choosing what takeaway to order.

'I don't think she'd want to,' I say, then stop myself. I have to fight for this. 'I mean, she's shown very clearly that her focus is on the pop-ups, not the website. She likes all the fuss, the kudos, the buzz of live events. I don't think she's actively contributed to the site at all. Which is strange, given that we hired her initially for her enthusiasm for digital.' The last sentence comes out a little more cutting than I intended.

'Hmm,' David says. 'Right. Agreed. We'll think carefully about who covers you when you're off. But in the meantime, let's reward her for her hard work. I keep hearing from people about the pop-up, everyone's excited about the next one and it's what's got Brian and the rest of them all a-flutter over the pond, after all. Don't want her getting tempted to go elsewhere.'

'Fine.' I don't care about Ash's job title, or her salary. But one thing I do know is that I don't want her covering me while I'm away. 'But I've thought about my maternity leave,' I say, my breath coming more quickly as I speak. 'And I'm going to take the minimum three months. I'm passionate about this job, about this role, and we're at a really critical time. I don't want to be away for longer than I need to be. Like I say, I'll be back here before you know it.'

'I'm glad you're so eager to return,' David says, his eyes wrinkling as he smiles at me. 'But you haven't even gone yet. Don't make decisions about the future before you've lived it. You may feel quite differently once the baby arrives. And there's no need to rush back. We can survive without you. Right, I'll speak to HR about bunging your Ashley some extra cash. You can tell her the good news.'

I smile, nod again, and leave the office.

I know his words about not rushing back were meant to be comforting, but somehow, deep down, they feel like a threat.

There was some mix-up at the hospital, and I'm four months pregnant by the time I have my first NHS scan. We had a private one at eight weeks – Jack had insisted – but there wasn't much to see then, really, just a blob on the screen, with a reassuring heartbeat, meaning my risk of miscarriage was low. I'm excited to be here, in the hospital waiting room, about to see my baby looking like an actual human being.

Jack is playing a game on his phone, seemingly carefree, but I can tell by the way his leg is twitching up and down that he's nervous. I stroke my stomach. There's nothing much there yet, of course, nothing but a bit of water retention. I try to imagine something inside, moving around, but it's difficult. I've nothing much to show for this pregnancy, so far – other than sore breasts and an all-consuming desire to eat carbs. I reach in my bag for another cereal bar. Eating constantly is the only way to stop myself from feeling as though I'm stuck on a dinghy in the middle of a huge thunderstorm.

'Helena Brenton?'

I look up at the sound of my name. The sonographer smiles and Jack and I both follow her into a room opposite the waiting room.

'Hello,' she says. 'I'm Frederica. If you just lie down on the couch there, and lift your top for me. Right . . .' She looks down at my notes. 'It's your first pregnancy?'

I nod.

'Okaaay, then, let's have a look.'

It's just like in the television programmes. She squirts gel on to my stomach and then places the probe on top of it.

'Excellent,' she says, moving it around. Within seconds I can see a fluttering grey blur on the screen. 'There's baby.'

I look over at Jack.

'Is it OK?' I say, staring at the screen, trying to make sense of what I'm looking at.

'Everything looks absolutely fine,' she replies, pressing some buttons on the machine. 'Let's have a listen to the heartbeat . . .'

The room is suddenly filled with an alien-like sound, loud and pulsating.

'Lovely,' she says.

I start to cry again, just like last time. Jack looks at me.

'Hey,' he says, reaching out and taking my hand. 'It's OK! Look. It's amazing, darling, it's amazing.'

I nod, swallowing. For some reason I can't speak.

'All looking great,' Frederica says. She looks as though she loves her job, but what on earth must it be like when she has to give people bad news? I can't even imagine it. 'I'll just take some measurements, and then we're all done.'

She continues pressing buttons and clicking on various areas of the screen. Then she takes the probe away from my stomach and hands me a huge wodge of paper towelling.

I sit up and wipe my stomach clean.

'So, everything is looking perfect. Your risk for chromosome abnormalities is very low, lower than the average for your age, so we won't be suggesting you have any invasive tests. The heartbeat is great; it's growing right on track. Now, here's your picture . . .'

She pulls out a grainy black-and-white photograph from the bottom of the machine and places it into a cardboard frame, handing it to me with a beam.

'Thank you,' I say, looking at the strange seahorse-shaped creature in the picture. I stroke it with my finger.

'And we'll see you back here again for your anomaly scan at twenty weeks, or thereabouts. Now, do you have any questions?'

I shake my head, my eyes fixed on the image of the baby.

'So everything's OK?' I hear a voice behind me. I've momentarily forgotten that Jack is even in the room. 'The baby's healthy?' His voice is strangely high-pitched.

'Yes, everything looks absolutely perfect,' she says, smiling at him. 'You just take good care of mum.'

He nods and stands up, handing me my coat.

'Thanks,' I say, taking my notes back from her. 'Thanks so much.'

We leave the hospital and, without speaking, start to walk towards the high street, Jack gripping my hand. With the other, I hold the picture tightly, trying to connect it with my body, my stomach, my womb.

'It feels . . . more real now,' Jack says.

I nod.

'I can't quite believe it's an actual baby,' I say, stupidly. 'Thank God everything's all right.'

He laughs and puts his arm around me, kissing the top of my head.

'Now, how do we celebrate?' he asks. 'Where shall we go?'

I look around. We're in a particularly unlovely part of North London, but I can see a park a little further ahead.

'Let's just go and sit in the park for a bit.'

The park is little more than a patch of scrubland, but there are a few benches along each side, and we find one and sit down. I still have the scan picture in my hand. Jack takes it from me and sighs.

'I never believed people when they said they had accidents,' he says. 'Not like this. What are the chances? One in a million or something?'

'One in a million,' I whisper, taking the picture back from him.

'Fate,' Jack replies.

I think of Ash again, the sheer balls of her, asking David for a promotion. I think of all the new clients, the way they signed up to our ethos, to what we believed in. I think of the staff, most of whom have only been working with us for a few weeks. I think of my finances. I think of David, and KAMU's derisory maternity leave.

'I don't know what I'll do about work,' I say. 'We're struggling to get the site off the ground as it is. I think we need a bigger marketing budget. There's something that's just not gelling, and the brands are picking up on it. If they find out I'm off on maternity leave, I'm scared they'll lose all faith. And I can tell Ashley isn't impressed.'

'What does it matter what she thinks? She works for you, remember. Don't let her upset you.'

I smile, and squeeze Jack's hand. Easier said than done. Every time I tell her I'm not feeling great, every time I rush off to the toilet to be sick, she pulls a face.

'She's been promoted, you know,' I say. 'Events Director. Imagine that! With absolutely no experience in events before. It's almost a joke.'

'Job titles mean nothing, you know that. David's just trying to keep her sweet. You're still in charge, you're still her boss. Listen,' he continues, 'you know the Pembury house? The one we saw two weeks ago. They've reduced it again. It's ridiculously cheap, Helena. Maybe, maybe it's a sign . . . We could try. It'd be good to be nearer your family, wouldn't it?'

He's wary, his voice shakier than usual, but with a steady determination that somehow reassures me that everything is happening for a reason, that it's all intended, that the universe knows what it's doing, and I just have to relax and stop fighting it.

'Yes,' I say, 'it would.'

Jack straightens up, his body tensing next to mine.

'That's great,' he says. 'I'll call the agent back in a bit, say we're interested . . . and listen . . . I don't like to interfere in your work – I know you know what you're doing – but remember, this site was your idea. *Your* idea. You had all the contacts, you got the ball rolling, you plucked Ashley from her internship, or whatever it was she was doing, and gave her the opportunity. You were at KAMU first, and you have all the experience. Don't let her push you around. Promise me, darling. Promise me you won't.'

THEN

Ash

Something must be wrong, because Gran never phones me.

'Are you OK?' I say, slowing my pace to a quick stroll as I press the remote on my headphones and answer the call. I'm out of breath, and she notices straight away.

'Oh, duck, are you busy?' she replies. 'I shouldn't have interrupted you, with all your important work.'

'No, Gran, it's fine,' I say, impatient for her to get to the point. 'I'm just out running, it doesn't matter. What's wrong?'

'I can call back later,' she says, ever self-sacrificing. 'Or how about you give me a call when you're done? I know you have a lot on your plate.'

'Gran,' I say, holding my temper back, but only just. She's right, I don't like being interrupted when I'm in the middle of something, but being interrupted by someone who just wants to tell you they're going to interrupt you again later is even more annoying. 'I just told you, it's fine. What's the matter?'

'It's your brother,' she says, her voice faltering. 'I don't know what to do with him, Ashy dear, I really don't . . .'

I listen as she gives me all the details. Him turning up drunk, trying to climb in the kitchen window. 'We only leave it open for the cat to do his business, you know that, but stupid, wasn't it? Like Grandad says, I'm always so stupid, dear . . .' Then getting frustrated and smashing it with a brick, before grabbing Grandad's keys and trying to steal his car. Of course, the racket 'woke Grandad, who went downstairs with his cricket bat'. A scuffle broke out during which Grandad pushed my brother against the dining-room wall, meaning 'four of my lovely plates ended up broken, one of which was the Princess Diana . . .'

'Grandad's gone to see if next door have any superglue,' she says, forlornly, at the end of her speech. 'But I don't think there's much hope for them.'

'Jesus, Gran,' I say, but I'm not cross with her, not really. And she already sounds better just for telling me the whole saga. Most of the time I think she's just lonely. 'What did he want?'

'Your brother? Just money, I think, duck. Well, the car, but like I said—'

'Did you give him any?'

'He took my housekeeping from the jar in the kitchen, but there was nothing in my purse, so he went away rather frustrated, I'm afraid. Grandad wanted me to call the police, but I talked him out of it. He's still family, after all.'

I take a deep breath. Without realizing it, I've walked home. So much for today's 15km.

'I'll have a word with him,' I say. 'He's been on at me lately, too. I think he needs some money for a deposit on somewhere to stay.'

'You know, Grandad won't have him in the house, not with his temper as it is,' Gran says, her voice shaking again. I don't know whose temper she's talking about – Grandad's or Jason's. They're both as bad as each other. 'If it was up to me . . .'

'I know,' I reply, furious. 'It's fine. Don't you worry about it. I'll try and get hold of him, tell him to steer clear. I'm sorry you had to deal with this, Gran.'

I end the call, telling her I'll be down to visit her at the weekend. I don't want to go, and I have no idea what I'll tell Joel. If he knows I'm going home, he'll certainly want to come along, and meet the family. But it's been ages since I saw her – and I'm all she's got, these days. She's the only person who sees the good in me, who understands the way I struggle, who knows I'm just trying – just fighting – to make something of myself in a world that deals you a bad hand for the fun of it.

No time like the present.

I rummage about in my bag, find the note that Jason left me last, dialling the number on it, checking I've got the digits right. But when I hold it to my ear, it doesn't ring; instead, it goes straight to a pre-recorded message.

The number you have dialled is no longer in service.

I hang up. Jason's not going to make it easy for me, then. I roll my eyes at my own naivety. Of course he's not.

I'm pacing now, turning back and forth on the street outside my block of flats, looking like a crazy person. I hear a noise, and I turn to see the skinhead, standing right behind me, lighting up. The dog has gone. At least that's one thing dealt with. At least he's not in pain any longer. Before the owner has a chance to speak to me, I push my headphones firmly back in my ears, turn on my music and head back towards the park.

THEN

Helena

I keep thinking back to last night, to the dream I had. I was in a lift, and it kept going up, higher and higher, gaining speed as it went, but I wanted to go down. I needed to go down. There was something waiting for me on a lower level, but no matter how many times I pressed the buttons for the ground floor, it kept rising. Up and up, quicker and quicker, digital numbers scrolling to impossible levels, as though the building I was in had no top. In the end, I was cowering in the corner, curled up with my arms wrapped around my knees, begging and whimpering, but still it wouldn't stop. I knew it was going to hit the roof and explode out of the top, and that I would die as it did so, along with my unborn baby. Before it had the chance, however, my alarm woke me up and I wrenched myself groggily back from oblivion.

Unlike most dreams, this one stayed with me throughout my journey on the Tube. And here I am, at 10 a.m., still mulling it over in my mind.

The GP is running forty minutes late for my check-up. Which means I will be forty minutes late – at least – for our first meeting with MollyMoo since the mess-up with Jess. *Come on, come on!* As I twitch anxiously on the plastic chair, scrolling through Twitter to distract my addled brain, I see a tweet advertising a new position at KAMU B. *Events Assistant. Minimum one year's experience in a client-facing role.* I am about to phone Ash and ask what on earth she thinks she's doing, advertising a job we had not only not discussed, but one that David hasn't signed off. But I don't get the chance, because just as my shaking hands start to press the buttons, my name is called, and I have to follow the GP down a sterile corridor into her room.

'How are you feeling?' she says, briskly, one eye on the clock.

'Fine,' I say, my heart still pounding with fury. I'm as disinterested in this appointment as she is, now. Then I remember what Jack told me to say. 'I've been having a few headaches, now and then. Probably work stress.'

'Headaches can be normal,' she replies, taking my urine sample from me. I had forgotten I was clutching it. 'Let's do your blood pressure.'

I sit there as she wraps the cuff around my arm, trying to relax, trying not to think of Ash, and what her behaviour means. Has she decided that I'm no longer worth discussing things with? Is this what it's going to be like when I'm on leave – her just doing what the hell she likes all the time, without even giving me a second thought? How did I lose control of this situation?

'Hmm,' the GP replies. I know from the name plate on her door that she's Dr Barisha, but I have no idea what her first name is. I've never even met her before. I assumed, when you were pregnant, you'd get one person looking after you through the whole process, but I've never seen the same doctor twice.

She loosens the cuff on my arm, pulls it off, turning back to my notes.

'Your blood pressure is raised,' she says.

'I'm quite stressed today,' I say, as if to give her an escape clause. 'I just . . . I've had a disagreement with a colleague.'

She nods, regards me thoughtfully.

'Let's have a look at the baby,' she says. 'Then I'll test your urine. Just hop up on the bed and raise your top for me.'

She takes out a tape measure and busies herself with measuring my stomach. It amazes me how basic this procedure is, but I suppose it's worked for years, so there's no need to change things.

'Hmm,' she says again, looking back at my notes. 'I'm just going to listen to the heartbeat.'

It takes her a few seconds but then that glorious sound fills the room. I'm not sure I'll ever get tired of hearing those pulsating thumps, and I feel myself relax as I lie there, suddenly wishing I didn't have to get up.

'Movements been OK?' she says. 'Feeling at least ten a day?'

Instant shame pierces me as I realize I keep forgetting to count. I'm a terrible mother already, and I haven't even had the baby yet.

There's just been so much going on – five new clients on board this month alone, and we attended six pitch meetings for the next pop-up last week. Rather than winding things down before my maternity leave, Ash seems intent on packing in as much as possible. Thankfully, the website revenue has started to pick up – as I knew it would, eventually. It's still nothing to write home about, but thanks to some favours from my most influential blogger friends, we've had a record few weeks of sales.

'I . . .' I say, ashamed. 'I think so. She seems very active in the evenings . . .'

Dr Barisha nods and takes the probe away, handing me some tissues to wipe my stomach. I lurch myself back on to my elbows and swing my legs off the side of the bed. She has her back to me now, and is fiddling with my urine sample.

'Is this your first urine of the day?' she says, staring at the little test stick that looks like something you'd use to work out if your pool has enough chlorine in it.

'Um, yes,' I say, feeling embarrassed and wondering what else I've done wrong. 'I'm a bit dehydrated.'

'It has a little protein in it,' she says, matter-of-factly. 'Try to always wee for a few seconds first, then put the pot under the stream. Are you able to do another sample for me?'

'Now?'

'Please.' She hands me another screw-top container. 'Toilet's just on the left, down the hall.'

'Is something wrong?' I say, standing there, all rotund belly and swollen neck.

'Let's hope not,' she says, smiling. 'Try not to worry. Baby seems fine. If you could just do me another sample . . .'

While I'm on the loo, I feel the baby thump my ribcage, as if to reassure me that she's on my side. I want to cry. The past few weeks, all I've thought about is work. It feels as though I've betrayed my own child.

I hand Dr Barisha my sample, apologetically, but she doesn't seem bothered by its pitiful quantity.

There's a tense few seconds while she tests again, then she pours my sample down the sink, rips off her gloves and bins everything in a large metal container, before washing her hands. I wonder how many times a day she has to do that.

'How are you feeling?' she says, taking a seat next to me at her desk and scrawling on my notes. 'You mentioned headaches?'

'Yes,' I say, suddenly wishing I hadn't. 'But they're not terrible. I sometimes think I'm just not drinking enough. Was my second sample OK?'

'Yes,' she says, still writing. 'NAD. Sorry . . . no abnormalities detected. But your blood pressure is very high, for you, and you're measuring slightly behind. I'd like you to go to the hospital for a scan. They're open till five p.m. today.'

'Measuring behind?'

'Yes,' she says, putting down her pen. 'As far as I can tell, the baby hasn't grown since your last appointment, so I'd like them to check that there's nothing untoward occurring.'

'But . . .' I say. 'I'm so much bigger – how is that possible?'

She looks at my bump, then down at my feet, wedged into the only pair of shoes that still fit me.

'Your feet are swollen,' she says, as if this is something else I should have told her.

'They've been like that since I was about twenty-four weeks. The midwives said it was normal.'

'I'm sure there's nothing to worry about,' she says, closing my folder and pushing it towards me. 'I've written a note for the hospital. If you go along to the scanning department, they'll see you as a priority.' She smiles again, giving my arm a little squeeze, and I wonder if this is why they do it, why they mess around with people's piss every day. The chance to reassure someone, to be kind and calming. 'I'm sure everything's fine. Try not to worry.'

THEN

Ash

I've called her five times, but all I get is her voicemail.

Hi, this is Helena, sorry I can't take your call . . .

I hang up.

'I'm so sorry,' I say to Paula, who's glaring at me. 'She must have got held up. Why don't we just start? I'm sure she'll be along shortly.'

'Pregnant, isn't she?' Paula says, and her voice, with its hint of transatlantic accent, is cold as metal.

'Yes,' I reply, because actually, it's not my job to defend her. 'She had a doctor's appointment this morning. You know what it's like . . .'

Paula rolls her eyes. She looks like she's in her mid-forties, and unmarried, if her ring finger is anything to go by. There's a touch of bitterness that feels familiar – I *understand* her – and then I realize: she reminds me of my mother.

'Never understood why they have to see the doctor so often,' she says, one side of her lip curling up to meet her nose in distaste. 'It's not as though they're ill.'

I smile and take out my iPad.

'Let's go through last month's report,' I say, as pleasantly as I can manage, but as I call it up I notice I have a new email. Just a few lines from Helena.

I have to go to hospital for a scan. May be late for meeting. See you when I see you. Sorry.

The apology feels tacked on, insincere, and I feel myself burn with rage as I realize she's dumped this shit on me, that I'm going to have to deal with Paula and her fury alone. Couldn't she have gone to the scan after the meeting? Priorities, Helena. I'm receiving you loud and clear.

'Last month's report,' Paula says, her voice a sarcastic hiss. 'Indeed. Can you tell me why I'm paying you so much money for these sales figures? Do you think I'm a moron, is that it?'

I take a deep breath, look her squarely in the eye.

'We explained in our first ever pitch that these things take time to build. And we've explained on the phone since,' I say, reminding myself of Jason, and Mum and all the other arseholes I've had to deal with in my life. *I won't be intimidated by you, bitch.* 'As our activity increases, the whole thing snowballs, you'll see the results start to increase—'

'The quality of your work is appalling,' she says, interrupting me, and it's then that I accept I'm on a road to nowhere. Nothing I can do or say now will be enough for this witch; she wants out. How can Helena have left me to face this alone? It's not fair, it's really not fair. 'The pop-up shop worked all right for us, yes, but this website . . .'

'Our writers are highly trained professionals,' I say. 'They—'

'Pfft!' she says, snorting. 'I could write better English than that, and I'm dyslexic!'

In the corner of the room, her assistant shrinks behind square-framed glasses, glancing at me in sympathy. What a place to work. Mixing up organic skincare in one corner of someone's kitchen.

'I don't think . . .' I begin.

'I'm not interested any more,' Paula says, tossing the printout of the report I gave her into the bin by her side. So much anger. 'You're what? Twenty? Your boss is pregnant and can't even be bothered to show up to the meeting, despite the fact I've told her how unimpressed I've been with your . . . service. The people you have working for you just aren't good enough. I haven't forgotten that breach of my non-disclosure agreement, either. All your digital this and digital that. Just nonsense. No evidence, no results, and numbers that mean nothing. I won't be paying your invoice, and I don't expect to receive any more from you.'

I stand up, before she has the chance to do so.

'I can see we're getting nowhere,' I say, and although my voice is calm, inside my heart is thundering. Thank God I checked out her contract before I came today. 'I accept you wish to terminate our agreement. However, you have signed a contract with us, and I'm afraid it includes a three-month notice period. We expect to receive payment for contracted work, whether that work is still required or not. You'll see it in the terms you signed. We will be sending you future invoices for the duration of your notice period, and we will be expecting payment for them.'

I turn and leave, before she has the chance to say anything else. but once I'm safely out on the street, surrounded by picture-perfect Hampstead houses, I feel the tears start to come in big fat splashes, and I don't try to stop them.

THEN

Helena

They let me go home with promises to rest more, minimize stress, keep my feet up and keep an eye on any headaches, swellings or tummy pain, but they don't seem to be very happy about it.

'Try to take it easy,' the midwife says to me, but her voice doesn't sound sympathetic. Instead, it feels as if she's telling me off – reminding me what a failure I have been at this mothering thing, so far. 'Remember, it's not just you that you have to think about now.'

I want to tell her that I never think about me, that I think of nothing but other people. I want to tell her that I made promises to David, that I love my career – or at least, I used to – but my incessant working isn't about that, that of course it's all about the baby, because I'm worried about our finances now Jack's not working. I have to work hard to make sure the baby has everything she needs. But I don't have the courage, so instead I just nod and tell her I'll do my best. Even though that's never enough.

I try to call Ashley on the way back from the hospital, but it just rings out. The meeting would have ended an hour ago, and I know she's just avoiding me or punishing me. Since her promotion she's treated me as though we're on the same level, sometimes as though she thinks I'm her subordinate. She goes to David over my head all the time now, with no apologies or indication that she thinks she's doing anything wrong.

I leave her a message, telling her the GP was worried about the baby's growth but the hospital said everything was fine, even though part of me worries that that makes it sound worse. Like I was making the whole thing up, or overreacting.

I take my time making my way to the office. The pavements are coated with leaves, past their sell-by date, like me. I can't believe it's October already. I'm dreading it. I'm dreading seeing everyone. The staff no longer feel like allies. The other day, I ended up swearing out loud as Ash left the office, slamming the door behind her, as she always does, without regard for anyone else's concentration levels or eardrums. Amy, once seemingly mute, stunned me by defending Ash's behaviour, explaining that she was 'a busy lady', as though that made it OK, but more significantly, as though *I am not*. That's when I realized: they think I'm lazy. She's got them all on her side now. She's the burning martyr, picking up the slack while I sit and line my pregnant pockets with the proceeds.

Most of them did a terrible job of hiding their surprise at finding out I was pregnant, and Jess actually asked me if it was planned. I lied, of course, and then kicked myself for it as I felt Ash smirking behind me. I shouldn't have even answered the question – it was none of her business. But being pregnant has made me feel like a great big lump of a burden on everyone around me, and I feel I owe them all something.

Ash is on the phone as I come into the office, chatting away in what sounds, bizarrely, like French. Then I remember; she's been teaching herself in the evenings. She's always teaching herself something, taking classes on the quiet. Her new passion for languages comes from her deciding we need to go international, get some foreign clients on board. She wants a dedicated area at the next pop-up and we've had to move the event to a bigger venue to accommodate all the brands that want to be involved. Her newest idea is to create a special feature area, showing off global brands. She's beaming as she laughs away, charming the pants off whoever she's speaking to, and again I feel like she has sucked out all the energy for life I once had: I'm the dying flower and she's the one about to come into bloom.

Is this what happens to women as we get older? Is it really this obvious?

She hangs up and smiles at me as I sit at my desk, wedging myself awkwardly into my office chair. I actually feel jealous of her.

'Hi!' she says, her voice bright, and whatever happened with Paula has been forgotten. This is what she's like: one minute furious, the next euphoric. 'How was your appointment?'

'Fine,' I say, because she doesn't care, anyway – and I've already spent twenty minutes on the phone reassuring both Jack and my mother in minute detail. 'How did the meeting with MollyMoo go? Listen, I'm so sorry . . .'

She waves my speech away.

'Oh, she dumped us, but don't worry, we'll make her pay. I've spoken to David, the contract's watertight. But anyway, listen, that was Aimez-Moi – they love what we're doing, want us to go out there and meet them. How exciting is that!'

I smile weakly, her once-infectious enthusiasm no longer enough to lift me out of my sense of displacement. I'm a sweaty lump between two stools – no longer the high-flyer.

'That's great,' I say. 'When?'

'A week Tuesday – I was looking at the flights when I was talking to him – he *loves* me, by the way. I think my attempts to speak French might have scored us a few more brownie points. Anyway, there's a flight that leaves at five twenty in the morning. Yes, I know, *ouch*, but then we could be there for the whole day, and come back in the evening. It'd be fun to stay over, but on the Wednesday I'm chocka, so . . .'

I screw my nose up, filled with a powerful and overwhelming urge to sob. The tears are always right behind me, these days.

'What's the matter?' Ash asks.

'Nothing,' I say. 'I have to have another scan on the Tuesday, that's all. I'm sure I can rearrange it.'

'Oh, if you could,' she says, smiling stiffly. 'I think it's important you're there for this one.'

For this one?

There's a pause and she swallows. 'He says he knows your dad. I think he'd like to meet you.'

'Of course,' I say, looking down at my phone. Jack has messaged me.

Take it easy! Are you taking it easy?!

A *Fawlty Towers* quote. He always knows exactly how to make me smile.

But then I remember the thing that's been niggling at the back of my mind, the way the day started, even though it already feels as though it was a hundred hours ago.

'Ash?' I say, and that rush of anger returns as she looks at me, her face blank and unfeeling, the waxwork mask back. I'm so relieved that I still have some guts somewhere. 'I saw you advertise for an Events Assistant. I thought we discussed this. Guy can help you out, if you're struggling. But at the moment, we can't afford to have someone just assisting the events, given that they're only happening every quarter.'

'Oh that,' she says, and if she thinks that she's going to be able to charm me like she did the Frenchman on the phone, she's wrong. 'Don't worry. I spoke to David about it and he signed it off without even a murmur. Said we can have the budget for a grad-level position. I think I'm learning how to wrap him around my little finger, like you do!'

I think of all the times I've asked David for a marketing assistant, or just more budget for marketing in general, and the fury rises in me. I stand up, jerking my chair back and thumping my phone down on the desk hard. A voice in my head tells me that this is *not* taking it easy, but it's too late, the anger has exploded.

'For Christ's sake!' I say, and I don't care that I'm shouting, that everyone in the office is staring at me, amused and amazed at the sudden sideshow. 'I told you not to go over my head to David! You need to include me in these discussions, and you can't make decisions like that without consulting me first! Stop trying to take over everything!'

And with that, I storm out of the office as quickly as a heavily pregnant woman can, slamming the door behind me.

THEN

Ash

'Trust you're both well?' David says, gazing at both of us. Is it just me, or is there a little smirk in his eyes as he looks at Helena? Pregnancy hasn't been kind to her. I noticed this week she now has two distinctive rings running around her neck – must be something to do with the water retention. It would explain her burgeoning double chin, too.

'As well as can be expected at seven and a half months pregnant,' she replies. There's a slight scowl on her face, as though she thinks it's our problem she's in this situation, but it's almost as though she notices herself doing it and so she rearranges it into an unconvincing smile. 'But can't complain.'

'Well,' David says. 'Let's hope I can cheer you up. I've got some exciting news for you both. You can probably guess what I'm about to say ... I know it's been a long time coming but Brian has asked for both of you to fly over next week to present KAMU B to the team there. As an initial start, they want to go ahead with the Easter pop-up in New York – as you proposed, Ashley.'

I see Helena glance at me out of the corner of her eye. Shit. I forgot to cc her in my proposal. Oh well, never mind. She'll be on maternity leave in a few weeks, anyway, and she knew this was on the cards.

'That's brilliant!' I say. 'Wow. I've never been to New York.'

'Helena got married there, didn't you?' David says.

'Not married, just honeymooned,' she replies, her voice as dull as her complexion. 'That's great news. What exactly will they be expecting?'

'If you can put together a presentation, that'd be great,' David replies. 'Although, to be honest, I think what Ashley's already pulled together will stand up – we might just need to flesh out some more of the details, put some meat on the bones of the marketing and PR sections, tighten up some of the action points . . .'

'Definitely,' I say, nodding. 'I can ask Jodie to run me through what she did; she was brilliant. I think she'd be keen to help out on the next one, in fact. I was wondering if you might consider seconding her for a while? I think she really enjoyed it . . .'

'Really?' David asks, looking directly at me. How things have changed from the times when it was as though I wasn't even in the room. 'I'll speak to her, see what she thinks. Carly will sort your flights. I think the easiest thing is to go out Monday and return Thursday; that'll give you both two full days in the office. I'd come with you but, unfortunately, I've got rather a lot on helping out with the Australian launch. I'm sure you'll be just fine without me, and we can put some time in the diary for Friday afternoon to go through everything, just to give you a bit of reassurance.'

New York. New Bloody York! And they're going to pay for me to actually go. Gran will be stunned when she finds out. I can't wait to tell Lauren. Poor Lauren, stuck behind a counter checking people in and checking people out, while I'm swanning off to New

York to present my project to the board of directors of a global corporation. Men twice my age with half my potential. I wonder if we'll be flying business class. It is a business trip, after all . . .

'I . . . I don't want to rain on anyone's parade here,' Helena says, butting into my daydreams. 'But I think I'll need a doctor's certificate to fly as I'm over twenty-eight weeks. I'm sure it's fine but . . .'

David bites his lip.

'Right,' he says, and there's no hiding the hint of irritation in his voice. 'I don't want you putting yourself at any risk.'

'No, no, it's fine, absolutely fine,' Helena says, and we all know she's protesting too much – that it's not fine, and she knows it. 'It won't be a problem, I'm in perfect health. Well, apart from my blood pressure, but that's been all right the last two times it's been checked. I just need to make sure. Let me confirm before Carly books anything.'

'Sure,' David says, but he's barely looking at her, and then he turns back to me. 'But planning ahead . . . if the worst comes to the worst, Ashley, would you be prepared to go alone?'

There's a moment's hesitation. I can't bring myself to look at her, because if I do I might not hold my nerve, might think I owe her something, like those idiots on *X Factor* who refuse to go through to the next round without their less talented singing partners. I think of all the times I've had to cope alone over the last few months, all the meetings she's missed, thanks to her condition. *What goes around comes around.* I think of Jason, still needling me for cash, my promise that I'll help him as soon as I get my Christmas bonus.

'Of course,' I say, squinting slightly so that I can no longer see Helena. I fix my eyes on David, and it's as if she's not in the room at all. 'If that's what's needed, then of course I would.'

THEN

Helena

I was determined not to cry. But like everything else I've attempted lately, I've failed.

I'm in the toilets, trying to muster up the courage to go into the office. But when I came out of the lift this morning and hobbled towards the door, I looked through to see them all crowded around Ash's desk, laughing and smiling. Someone's brought in a Statue of Liberty headband and hung it sideways from Ash's computer. Since when did they actually start to like her? Jess is the only one who doesn't seem to have firmly signed up to the Ash is Great Club, and that's only because she likes attention as much as Ash does.

I sit on the toilet, sniffing into a tissue. I feel like I'm gradually fading away, despite there being literally more and more of me as each day passes. My swollen feet are killing me, the water floating around under the skin like some kind of hideous heavy jelly that wobbles when I walk, making every step uncomfortable. My back aches, my neck folds over on itself if I look down, my entire body feels swollen and bloated. I want to go home. I don't want to go into the office and tell Ashley that the doctor has strongly advised I don't travel. I don't want to have to watch her pretend to feel sorry for me, watch her portray herself as the hero of the hour, saving KAMU B from the curse that is my pregnancy. But I have no choice.

But first, I have to see David.

He's not there when I arrive, and so I sit in his office, sipping the glass of water Carly brought me. It came accompanied by a sympathetic look and a pat on the shoulder – she can clearly tell what a mess I'm in. It's such a different experience, being pitied. Just awful. And Carly's about twenty-one, she has no idea. Lizzy announced she wasn't coming back from maternity leave this week, and so Carly's keeping the job. Lizzy is the only other person at KAMU to have got pregnant since we launched. I so wish she was here.

David eventually arrives fifteen minutes after the meeting was scheduled to begin, rushing in full of apologies, enquiring after my health in an exhausted voice that tells me he doesn't really want to know. Maybe I'm just paranoid, but when he finally sits down behind his desk, he looks at me as though I'm a problem he needs to solve, something in his way.

Once upon a time, he wanted to sleep with me. Now, I'm just a nuisance. A fat, pregnant nuisance. I think about Jodie, the new object of his desire, the way she looked away as she saw me pass just now. How many women have there been? Men like him never change.

'I've brought the figures you asked for,' I say, trying to rouse some of the old Helena. 'They're improving, month on month, but I agree, they're not where we'd like them to be.'

He takes the pages of paper from me and glances through them, sighing, for several seconds, and then places them neatly on his desk, leaning back in his chair.

'I'm not sure what's going wrong here,' he says. 'But perhaps the problem is that people are unwilling to buy products online from a brand they're not familiar with. At the pop-ups, they get to try them, speak to the people behind them. Perhaps what we need is more social proof on the site itself.'

'Yes,' I say, sighing. 'I agree. It's been something I've wanted to focus on, but we've not had enough marketing support, really. Jodie's been helping out a lot, but we really need some more investment in the PR to get the brand out there.'

'Hmmm,' David says. 'Yes. Right. Leave it with me. I'm going to have a good think about it all. Perhaps . . . perhaps we were a little ambitious going with a dedicated site and team from the get-go . . .'

My eyes widen.

'But . . .' I begin, but he holds his hand up to stop me.

'Try not to worry,' he says. 'It'll all come out in the wash. Now about New York . . .'

'I'm afraid I've not been given permission to fly,' I say, my voice beginning to tremble. 'My feet are quite swollen, and the doctor's worried about the risks of DVT on a long-haul flight. I won't be able to go.'

As the words come out, I feel tears rush to my eyes again.

'Oh God,' I say, but it's too late as a sob escapes. 'Sorry. I'm . . . sorry. I'm tired. Shit.' I scrabble in my pocket for a tissue.

David reaches over and hands me one from his desk. I bury my bloated face in it gratefully.

'You're very hard on yourself, Helena,' he says. 'I know you like to think you're superwoman, but you're just human, you know. And no job is worth killing yourself over. You know that.'

'But . . .' I say, as another sob engulfs me. It's even harder to fight them now he's being nice. 'She . . . Ash . . .' I take a large gulp of air. 'She manages it . . . she's a machine . . .'

'She's also a lot younger than you, and makes a hell of a lot more mistakes,' David replies. 'And she's not heavily pregnant. Listen. You know how much I value you. How much I fight your corner. And not just because . . . well, that's water under the bridge now.'

He looks away briefly, and I wonder if he's thinking of Jodie, and I wonder what exactly is going on between them. She was my friend once – a good friend, at that – but we've drifted apart, recently. Thanks to him, and my pregnancy.

'I've always been so impressed with you, Helena,' he says. 'You're a shrewd and hard-working woman, with more than a touch of humanity. A wonderful manager. You've got so much to give. Not just now but in the future, too.'

'But I love my job,' I say, wiping away the teardrops as they fall on to my skirt. 'And you haven't even bothered to recruit any maternity cover for me! Don't think I haven't noticed. If you value me so much, how come you don't think I'm worth covering?'

David looks away.

'I didn't get the sign-off from the US,' he replies, but even in this state I can tell that he's holding something back. 'You know how different things are over there. They didn't see a business case for it, I'm afraid.'

I look up at him, sniffing loudly again. He meets my eyes, and then I know. I see it all: the future that's coming. The Americans who won't be impressed when I don't show up next week. The website that didn't take off, that's no longer viable. The crucial role that I naively handed over to someone else.

The job that isn't worth covering, and that won't be here for me when I get back.

I see something else, too.

The upstart who's made a success of herself, who charms them all like she once charmed me. The upstart who's played the game, had the vision and gone for it.

The upstart who's here to stay.

Four weeks later, I am alone in the office, packing up my desk. Ash and the others have all gone to the team's Christmas dinner, and I've decided to use this opportunity to leave without any big goodbyes. Jess has been making noises about having a lunch later this week to wave me off on maternity leave. I can't think of anything worse, but I don't want to offend anyone, so here I am, sneaking off into the gloomy December evening. Thankfully, they accepted my excuse of agonizing heartburn as the reason I'm missing the Christmas dinner.

After I've finished packing all my possessions into a small holdall, I sit for a minute, enjoying the peace and quiet. It's the first time I've been alone in this office for months. I look over at the whiteboard behind Ash's desk, her sales figures for the Christmas pop-up gleefully scrawled across it, and in a petty but satisfying move, waddle towards it and erase her spidery boasts with the sleeve of my coat.

As I turn back to my desk, there in the entrance to the office is

David. The motion-sensitive lights come on as he walks towards me, flooding the whole floor with a harsh fluorescent glare. He looks out of breath, panicked, like he's rushed to get here.

'Oh good,' he says. 'You're still here.'

'Only just,' I reply. 'Thanks for coming to say goodbye. I didn't tell the others that today's my last day. Couldn't face a big fuss. I saw Jess browsing nappy cakes online earlier this week . . . I know it's ungrateful, but it's just not me.'

'No,' he says, but he's not really listening. 'Um, have you . . . have you got a minute?'

I nod.

'Shall we sit down?' David says, gesturing to my chair. He pulls Ash's chair round from behind her desk and wheels it towards me.

'Are you OK?' I ask, suddenly worried that Elizabeth's found out about Jodie, or worse still . . .

'I don't know how to tell you this, Helena,' he says, and he looks genuinely remorseful, something I've never seen before.

As I meet his sharp brown eyes with mine, I suddenly know what's coming. How could I have been so stupid as to think it was something to do with Elizabeth? I have a childish urge to push my fingers in my ears and start shouting 'la, la, la'. But instead, I sit there, like a great dumb elephant, waiting for my execution.

'I'm just glad I caught you, so I could tell you face-to-face . . . I've just got off the phone to Brian and, as you know, he was very impressed with Ashley when she was in New York, with the pop-up, with the whole concept. But I'm afraid he can't be convinced of the value of having a standalone site. I've tried, I really have. But as we feared, he wants to absorb KAMU B into the main site, but keep the pop-ups. I'm afraid it means that the team will be restructured, and I'm afraid it means . . .'

'That she's stolen my job,' I spit, even though I know that's not it, not really. But who cares? That's how it feels. She's stolen my friends, my ambition, my confidence and now my job. And it feels like I always knew she would.

'Listen, it's not about Ashley,' he says, shaking his head. 'Not at all. It's your role, that's all, and some of the editorial staff . . . Jess will be going too, it's not just you. I'm sorry.'

'You do know I'm eight months pregnant?' My voice is nearly a shout, but it cracks and then the sobs come. 'I'm weeks away from giving birth, and you're sacking me! What is this? Revenge for what happened after the Christmas party?'

David reaches forward and grabs my hands, but I push him away.

'Listen, it's not my decision, and you're not being sacked,' he says. He swallows awkwardly as his phone bleeps in his pocket. 'It's just a restructure, they'll try to find something else for you . . .'

'Something else!' my voice is nearly a scream, the tears choking me. 'What else, exactly? Working for her? You already replaced my job upstairs . . . what exactly will you do with me? Where are you going to slot me in?'

He looks away. Enough of the histrionics, I've crossed a line. Even he doesn't get paid enough to deal with this.

'I'm sorry,' he continues, but the warmth has gone from his voice. 'It won't be official till next week, but I knew you were leaving today and I didn't want you to just get a letter in the post in a fortnight, I wanted to tell you face-to-face . . .'

'How big of you.'

'I can see you're upset,' David says. He stands and pushes Ash's chair back. 'Like I say, it's a regrettable situation. Please . . . please feel free to call me when you've had time to calm down. I only want to help you, Helena, I promise.'

'Help me? I've had enough of your kind of help! Get out . . . just get out!' I shout, and as I watch him retreat I collapse into sobs, burying my face in my hands. When I look back up, I'm alone in the office, just me and my unborn child sitting on our own in the dark.

THEN

Ash

Gran has bought special biscuits. A tin of them, sitting in front of me in all their insipid glory, failing to entice me despite their fancy packaging.

'Pound shop!' she says, pushing them towards me. 'Wouldn't believe it, would you? And they're Fox's, you know. Proper ones. Wanted to get you something special, to celebrate your news.'

'Awesome,' Joel says, with uncharacteristic enthusiasm. He takes two, winking at me as I glance over at him.

I smile at her and reach forward, picking up the smallest biscuit and placing it next to the weak cup of tea I've just been given. Bless Gran. She'll never get it.

'I bought you something, too,' I say. I reach into my handbag and take out a small paper bag, my fingers tracing the outline of the firm object inside as I pass it to her. 'It took me a long time to find.'

I don't tell her how I had to trawl the freezing people-clogged streets around Times Square to find something suitable, how I hated every moment, how New York frightened and overwhelmed me in many ways. I don't tell her about the absolute nausea that came with presenting to the board of directors, feeling their eyes bore into me as they over-analysed every word that came out of my mouth.

I'm determined to rewrite that narrative.

Her eyes light up as she takes the package from me.

'Oh, look,' she says, pushing her glasses up her nose. 'Grand Slam New York. Well then, what have we here . . . ?'

She turns the bag over and opens it, pulling out the garish painted plate, with its almost comically inaccurate depiction of the Statue of Liberty floating in front of the New York skyline.

'Oh, Ashy,' she says, beaming. 'How wonderful.'

'Not quite the same as Princess Di,' I say, smiling. 'But hopefully it'll do. It's the best one they had, you know. Gold-edged, and there's a little stand for it, too. Although I guess you'd prefer to hang it.'

I glance over at the wall behind her, infected with an outbreak of tacky souvenir plates. It's like a shrine to the most depressing seaside towns across the UK.

'I'll get Grandad on to it once he's back from the pub. Well, Marjorie will be impressed,' she says, clutching the plate to her, fingering the illustrations. 'All the way from New York!'

'Glad you like it,' I say, squeezing my nostrils together as I take a sip of the tea. It's no good, the smell catches the back of my throat, making me gag. 'I'm just going to put a bit more water in my tea. Back in a sec.'

In the tiny kitchen, I empty the mug into the sink as quietly as possible, and refill it with water from the tap. I can hear Joel asking Gran about the story behind each of her plates and I linger for a while, letting them chat. Behind the plastic splashback by the cooker is a photograph, faded with age and spattered with cooking fat, of Jason and me when we were kids, dressed up for the school nativity play. I know the only reason it's still there is because Grandad can't be bothered to unscrew the Perspex and take it out. I remember that day well. My mum didn't bother to show up, of course, and Jason howled with disappointment the entire walk home.

'And tell me now about your new job,' Gran says, when I'm back in the living room. I manage a nibble of the biscuit. 'You said on the phone it's quite a step up?'

'There was a restructure,' I say, smiling at her. 'The woman I was working for . . . well, unfortunately, her job became redundant, but you know, that's business.'

Gran nods, smiling as though I've told her something groundbreakingly impressive. Is it just my imagination, or do I feel Joel stiffen slightly beside me?

'So . . . do you remember, I told you, I was working on these events, and she was working on a website?' I continue. 'Well, they decided that they didn't need the separate website, after all. But as the events were so successful, they're going to continue, and I'm going to head them up. Have my own little team.'

At the end of this speech, my heart is fluttering with excitement again. The residual guilt that nags at me from time to time disappears whenever I tell the story out loud. At the end of the day, I did my job, and I was rewarded.

I did nothing wrong.

Don't turn down your ambition because someone else is uncomfortable with the volume.

'And it's a lot more money?' Gran says, encouragingly, even

though money has never been her thing. She's so used to not having it, she wouldn't cope if she did. It would frighten her, take her away from all that she's comfortable with.

'Yes,' I say. 'Enough to make a difference.'

'Well, then,' Gran says, reaching over and patting me on the leg. 'You ought to be very proud of yourself.'

'I am,' I say, squeezing the handle of the mug just a little bit too hard.

I leave Joel in the car. Jason is waiting for me by the swings; the grass is littered with cigarette butts and a broken bottle. Nothing changes in this awful place. I pull my coat around myself more tightly, feeling the bitter December wind from the sea burn my cheeks.

'Hi,' he says, as I approach. 'Nice new car. Christmas present to yourself?'

He looks better than before, and then I spot someone else in the background, hovering by the entrance to the park. Lisa, her mobile phone pressed to her ear, watching us curiously. I haven't seen her for at least five years. She's prettier than I remember, hiding her figure under a giant Puffa jacket. Shame about the gelled corkscrew curls, but at least it's a statement, I suppose.

'It's not a new car,' I say. 'It's ten years old. I got it so I can come and see Gran more often.'

'Nice,' Jason says, but he's not angry this time. There's colour in his cheeks, and he's cleanly shaven for once.

'Eleven years ago today,' I say, watching him closely.

'Yeah.'

'Wonder what she would have made of us now.'

'She would have wanted your money,' Jason replies.

'Hmm.'

'I don't blame you for what you did, you know,' he says. 'You didn't have a choice. Mum was . . . out of control that day. I know you were just trying to protect yourself. Weren't you?'

'Yes,' I say, looking him squarely in the eye. 'She was. And . . . you know, I never meant to push her, not really. At least, not that hard. I was just scared. You know how violent she could be when she was drunk . . .'

'Yeah, I know,' he says, looking down at his feet. 'It's just hard to get away from it all. You know. The shit in my head. I don't know how you manage it.'

Neither do I.

'Don't believe the things you tell yourself when you're sad and alone,' I murmur, and he looks up at me, confused. I take a deep breath. 'Just something someone once told me, when I was struggling. With Mum, the accident, our childhood. It's helpful . . .' I pause. 'And work. Work is helpful. Work is the most helpful.'

He doesn't reply, but gives me an unconvinced look.

'Anyway,' I say, reaching into my bag and pulling out a brown envelope. 'Enough of the philosophy. This is for you. Although, to be sensible, I should really give it to Lisa.' I look over at her. As I do so, she puts her phone in the pocket of her jacket, and it's only then I notice it; the round belly that protrudes above her jeans as her coat falls open.

Finally, it all makes sense. All his talk of getting himself into a 'situation', his desperation to get a home of his own, to win her back.

I hand him the envelope, making sure she can see what's in it.

'It's a grand,' I say, wondering why he never told me. Probably knew I wouldn't have approved. 'Enough for the deposit, like you asked. You'd better not waste it.'

He nods, his eyes widening.

'You don't know what it cost to get that. Make it count.'

I look away, and bite my lip. I reach out and take his hand, squeezing it tightly.

As I meet his eyes again, I focus on the gratitude in them, and try to force the other feelings away. To be dealt with some other time, when the world is a fairer place.

PART THREE

NOW

Helena

Controlled seizure. There's something quite oxymoronic about it.

It's too late, now, I suppose, to tell them that there's something jabbing in my back. I can't tell what it is: perhaps part of my jumper has folded over on itself, creating a little lump. But it's annoying me. I want to reach up with my hand and rummage about, find what it is and pull it flat, but of course, I can't. Not now.

The anaesthetist is telling me something, but I'm not listening. I know what I have to do. Breathe deeply into the oxygen mask, count down from ten in my head. Then everything will go black, and I'll wake fifteen minutes later, to a glass of water and sympathetic monitoring.

There's a problem, though; someone's missing or something's missing, and the anaesthetist has disappeared again, leaving me alone. Or maybe not alone, there's another body in the corner – a nurse, I think – but she's got her back turned away and from this angle I can't make out much more than her arms, moving about purposefully. Instead, I fix my eyes on the most comfortable available surface: the ceiling. It's mottled, some kind of grey-and-white paint effect. I think of the dentist, when I was a kid, how you looked up and there was a hanging mobile or plastic stars or something stuck up there to focus your attention, to keep you still.

But there's nothing on the ceiling here. Just this grey-and-white paint, speckled together, someone's attempt at aesthetics in a room that doesn't need any. I imagine the decorator being told by an NHS honcho to, 'Dulux Trade White the whole room, mate,' and him (or her – maybe it was a woman – wouldn't it be great if it had been a woman?) thinking, *No, fuck them, there's an art to what I do, too. They won't notice.* And they're right, the only people who will notice are people like me, the people who lie flat on their backs covered in stickers, the broken toys waiting to be fixed. The rest of the walls are white, but they're dirty now, they've suffered years of abuse, years of trolleys and instruments being knocked into them, scraped past them. Years of patients' rebellious bodily fluids not quite missing them.

But what does it matter how the room looks? I'll spend most of my time in here unconscious.

I'm lying on a kind of slab on wheels, black plastic-topped foam underneath me the only attempt to make it comfortable, raised metal bars either side, ostensibly for wheeling me about with, but maybe they're there to stop me rolling off. There's a white pillow under my head; the sharp chemical scent of industrial laundries burns my nostrils. A length of blue paper towel has been placed along the middle of the black plastic, to offer some sense of per-sonalization. Or maybe it's there to soak up the mess. Do people wet themselves during this procedure? So many questions, so many leaflets, but it's something I have never thought to ask.

The cannula in my hand is aching. I feel like a woman on death row, waiting for her injection. My vein is throbbing, impatient. There will be two injections for me, the second a muscle relaxant, to come after the anaesthesia. 'To stop you from hurting yourself,' the nurse had told me, with an apologetic downturn of her mouth.

But that's what I do best.

The anaesthetist returns, accompanied by the consultant, both smiling down at me.

'All ready, now,' the consultant says.

Just another day at work, another poor lost soul to microwave.

'Shall we start, then, Helena?'

The knot of fabric is still digging into my back. I am not afraid. I am suddenly thankful for that uncomfortable lump under my skin, something to focus on, a welcome distraction. I nod, give him a brief smile of acquiescence. And then the oxygen mask is placed over my face. He tells me to relax, and I start my countdown from ten, a countdown I won't finish.

I get to seven before the world disappears.

This wasn't how I imagined motherhood.

THEN

Helena

This wasn't how I imagined motherhood.

I am barely conscious by the time my daughter rips her way out of my insides. As I lie there, one leg hoisted above the midwife's shoulder, the other completely numb, a bulging catheter resting on the inside of my thigh, and I feel her slimy body finally, finally, finally exit mine, it strikes me that what I had feared would happen all day, was finally happening.

I am dying.

Something I have known all along, but something I have been denying myself. Something they don't tell you. Something they hide, the darkest secret of all.

There can be only one outcome to this situation.

Her birth.

My death.

The second that my daughter gives her first howl – not a cry, not a delicate, fragile thing, but a visceral eruption of noise – I realize that Helena Brenton: wife, career woman, friend, daughter, girl-about-town has died. Gone. Never to be seen again.

They set her down on my chest. She is grey and sticky and

angry with me and she hates the world already. She smells strange, something sweet, unfamiliar, other-worldly. I kiss her head, the slime from her skin coating my lips.

I love her.

She terrifies me.

They tell me to go for a shower. I can understand why; I'm covered in blood. Not just my legs, but somehow it's all over my chest, too – even seeped into my bra strap, a dark smudge on the skin of my shoulder. Jack has the baby and is sitting on the plastic chair by my bed, his face bent over hers, mindless of me or the bossy midwife.

I just want to sleep.

The midwife starts rummaging through my hospital bag, awakening the memory of a different me two weeks ago, sitting on the floor of our bedroom packing it, naive with trust. Birthing playlist and portable speaker, artificial candles, aromatherapy spray, bags of sweets and cartons of apple juice to keep my strength up. As though that was all it would take.

'Do you have any maternity pads?' she barks, spilling the contents of my bag on to the stained blankets on the bed. 'Here. Clean knickers, shower gel. I'll get you some pads.'

'They're in there somewhere,' I say, my voice so hoarse it doesn't sound like me. I try to sit up, but can't manage it.

'Right, here you go,' she says, handing me a pile. 'We need your bed, I'm afraid. Shower is just across the hall. Once you're done, we'll wheel you up to the postnatal ward.'

I look over at Jack, willing him to rescue me, to fight my corner. But he's oblivious, distracted by the new love of his life, barely aware I'm even in the room. Can't I just stay here a little longer? They've only just finished putting me back together; an hour of intense pulling and threading and hushed conversation between my legs. And despite all the injections, I'm still sore from where the catheter was ripped out of me.

'Come on,' the midwife says, dragging me to my feet. 'Up you get.'

I hobble after her, my body doubled over, my stomach not lighter, as I'd hoped, but weighty with the damaged muscles that can't or won't do what they're meant to any more. She leaves me with two scratchy towels in a tile-lined room that brings to mind a cell. Just a showerhead, toilet and basin, and a small mildewed window hinting at the real world outside. The floor is still damp and grainy from its previous occupant and my toes, the only part of me that doesn't hurt, curl with disgust.

A clear plastic jug stands in the basin, filled with cloudy pink liquid. I frown at it, and then I realize; it's someone's urine.

Taking a step forward, I turn on the shower and am stunned by its force; hot, aggressive shards immediately attack my already pounded flesh. Blood swirls around the plughole as I stand there watching it continue to fall from the newly created hollow inside me. Blood, blood and more blood. So much blood.

I reach for the shower gel, nausea overtaking me, and then I feel it coming. There's a split second when I hope that actually, thank God, it's all going to end. This is it, I'm dying – it'll all be over soon – and the room goes black and I fall to the floor.

They won't let us leave without the car seat. Apparently, I can't be trusted to carry my own baby to the car, even though she only weighs six pounds. This rule seems nonsensical, given that once we are off the hospital premises, no one will see, know or presumably care what I will do with my baby.

Jack has gone to get it.

I touch the sore spot on my forehead, feeling the egg that formed when I crashed against the basin yesterday. Even after all it has been through, my body is still trying to fix itself, still refusing to give up.

It's stronger than me.

I am sitting in the family area and the baby is barely even there, just a speck of pink human under all her layers of clothing. She's content now, not wailing and vomiting as she did all night.

She is warm and small and comfortable, and happy with her life at this moment. We are opposites. She doesn't want what I want.

I feel a buzz from the bag on the chair next to me and I reach forward to retrieve my phone, that tangible reminder of a different life. It'll be another message from another distant friend, congratulating me on doing something that I had no choice in. I press the button and the screen lights up.

But it's not a message this time. It's an automated reminder of our weekly budget meeting, from a calendar I deleted from my phone more than a month ago, but which still persists despite this. Some glitch in my phone software that serves to haunt me, taunt me and remind me every week that life is going on without me.

My life is going on without me.

NOW

Helena

It's 4 a.m. and I'm standing by the side of the road in the rain, soaked through. The woman in the car is dead, but I'm holding on to her hand through the shattered windscreen, anyway. As usual, there's nothing much to see, just a line of blood coming from her nose. She has a locket around her neck, which has swung forward and is resting on the dashboard. I lean forward and open it. Inside, there are pictures of two tiny newborns; one on the left and one on the right. Rain drops on to their faces and I wipe it with my finger, trying to rub it off. Little bundles, faded and worn from stroking.

I look again at the woman. I can't tell how old she is. Maybe forty, maybe fifty? It's impossible to tell in this light. I reach for my phone to check the time. It's only been five minutes since I called the ambulance, but it feels like much longer. I wonder where they are, when they are going to get here. It's Monday night, they should be quiet, quick to attend. Perhaps they're not coming straight away because I told them I thought she was dead already, although surely they shouldn't take my word for it? It worries me when medical professionals listen to me. They should know better by now.

I look back at the house, still stroking the woman's hand. Our house. The light is on downstairs in the kitchen, where I'd left it when I came out. Our kitchen doesn't have any blinds and it creeps me out to see that from here, from the side of the road, you can see everything. Anyone could watch us, going about our normal life in the kitchen – like their own personal television show. Jack didn't hear the crash, of course. He was fast asleep, earplugs in, flat on his back, dreaming of . . . dreaming of what? I have no idea any more. I don't even know where he was last night.

But I heard it, heard the all-too-familiar screech of brakes, then the impact. Almost a bounce against the low brick wall, hitting once, loudly, and then again, more gently. I could imagine the motion inside the car, everything thrown forwards, including her, smacking her head on the steering wheel, then bouncing back to hit it again on the seat. The jerking movement her neck would have made, the stress on her spine – I can see it all, I can feel it all, I've experienced it so many times before.

The rain gets heavier and my arm grows numb from reaching through the windscreen. But I can't let go of this woman, whoever she is. No one deserves to die alone at 4 a.m., by the side of an empty road. I peer into the back of the car, using the torch on my phone to help me see. What was this woman doing, driving at this time of night? She's not even wearing a coat – just a grey, long-sleeved T-shirt and a pair of jeans. With my free hand I push the phone into the belly of the car. On the back seat there's a large holdall – the sort you might take to the gym if you were really dedicated and had a lot of stuff. I can't reach it from here, but I don't need to open it. I already know what this woman was doing. She was running away.

I look back at her and, mustering up the courage, hold the phone light right in her face. She's staring straight ahead, her eyes already a strange grey, her skin mottled and unnatural. The blood that's trickled from her nose and across her mouth and chin is the only colour on her face. Except for one other mark – a large bruise underneath her eye. I can't know for sure whether this was caused by the accident or by the man she was running from, but somehow I do. I see it all: this man, their fight, his fist.

I pull the phone away from her face. I can't look any more. I want to let go of her hand too, but I won't. I feel a rush of love for this woman, this poor woman, racing to escape her tormentor, only to die in the process.

The ambulance still hasn't arrived and my teeth begin to chatter as I stand by the car.

'Hurry up, hurry up, hurry up,' I say to myself, stepping from one foot to the other to try to keep myself warm. I look down and realize that I'm not wearing pyjama bottoms. I must have been hot in bed, and taken them off in my sleep. My pink sheepskin slippers are black with wetness, and my legs look grey in the light.

I hear a noise behind me, and I look up in surprise, dropping the woman's hand in the process.

'Shit!' I say, looking back at her, but it's too late, I've let her go now. I look back at the direction of the noise, and there he is.

Jack, in his dressing gown, with his wellington boots on, holding an umbrella and looking at me. There's something folded over one of his arms – one of his hoodies.

'Helena,' he says, and his voice sounds far away and tired, as though he's sleepwalking.

'I'm waiting for the ambulance,' I say, but he doesn't seem to be listening. 'They'll be here any minute. She's already dead, though, it's too late.' I look back at the woman, but all I can see now is the roof of the car, which has concertinaed during the impact.

'Come inside,' Jack says, sighing. 'You're soaking.'

'I have to wait for them,' I say. 'I promised.'

'You'll get ill,' he replies. 'Please. Just come inside.'

My teeth have begun to chatter and I look longingly at our kitchen, so warm and inviting, a beacon in the darkness of the night.

'But . . . I need to stay with her, until they come,' I say, but my willpower is fading.

'I'll take care of it,' Jack says. 'Please. Just go inside and get yourself dry.'

He knows what's best for me, he's the only one I can trust.

'OK,' I say, walking towards him.

My slippers are so wet that it's like walking through sand.

'Thank you,' I say, as I approach him. 'She was escaping her abusive husband. That's what I think, anyway. That explains why it's so late, why she's alone, why she has a bag on the back seat. She has a black eye, too. They'll realize in the post mortem, they'll work it out. But don't you think it's just heartbreaking?'

He looks down, then takes a deep breath and straightens himself up, as though drawing on some inner strength.

'Here,' he says, wrapping the hoodie around my shoulders. 'Go back inside.'

I make my way back to the house, leaving him by the car.

Inside, I leave Jack's hoodie on the hall bench and take my slippers off, standing in the kitchen in front of the Aga. Neither of us have quite got to grips with it for cooking, but it's brilliant for drying clothes and warming your hands.

When my hands have defrosted, I climb the stairs to our bedroom, going through to the en suite. I see myself in the full-length mirror and I'm shocked. It takes a while before I even accept that this grey, skinny woman, standing in just her pants and pyjama top, is me. My thighs have nearly disappeared. They're almost the same width as my calves now, and hang awkwardly from my hip bones, making me look like a puppet.

I decide to run a bath, and sit in it as it fills up. The warmth of the water on my ice-cold skin is a shock at first, but after a few minutes I realize my teeth have stopped chattering, and my skin is no longer grey.

It feels as though I've been in the bath for hours, but I can't have been, because Jack pops his head around the door and tells me to come to bed, and the water is still warm. I reach for my towel and wrap myself in it, padding through to the bedroom. Jack has laid out a fresh pair of pyjamas for me on the bed. But there are no knickers. I look at him, wondering if it's a sign that he wants something or if it's just that he's a man, and doesn't remember that I wear knickers in bed. I slip the pyjamas on over my naked body.

'Did they come?' I ask, as I climb into bed next to him. 'The ambulance?' I try to read his expression. He doesn't want sex, that can't be it. He looks tired, fed up, beaten.

'Yes, it's all sorted,' he says, kissing the top of my head. 'Don't worry about it. Just try to get some sleep.'

I smile as I lean my head against his arm. He switches off the bedside light and the room is dark. Dark but safe.

I feel a wetness on my forehead, just a trickle, that makes its way slowly but steadily across my eyelid, down my cheek and to my mouth. It settles on my lips and I taste it then, the sharp recognizable saltiness of a tear.

I put my arm around Jack and I realize I am crying, too.

NOW

Helena

The next morning I am sitting in the kitchen, drinking a cup of tea. I left the tea bag in for too long, so it's stewed and makes me feel sick. But I drink it, anyway. I need the caffeine.

The kitchen door swings open and Jack comes in. He's in his overalls. He looks handsome, but there are bags under his eyes, and I know they're my fault.

'I'm sorry about last night,' I say, but he waves my apology away with his hand as he walks towards the coffee machine. I watch as he pours himself a bowl of muesli and drowns it in milk.

'How are you feeling?'

'All right,' I say. 'I just can't believe it happened again.'

'The main thing is it's happening less often. What are you doing today?' he says, eating the cereal in great untidy gulps.

My eyes flick to the clock on the wall.

'Just some research,' I say, because it's not a lie. 'And I might go into the village, if you want anything from the shops. I could get us something for dinner?'

He laughs, but not unkindly.

'Don't worry,' he says. 'I've got dinner sorted. Although I've got a six p.m. meeting in town, annoyingly. Will you be OK? You could always . . . give your mum a ring.'

I screw up my face at his suggestion. I don't feel strong enough today.

'Have you taken your medication?' he says, cutting through my thoughts.

I look at the small bottle of pills on the kitchen counter, just casually hanging out next to the fruit bowl.

'Uh-huh,' I say, nodding slowly and taking a great gulp of tea. I look back up and beam at him.

Jack watches me, mistrustful.

He throws his bowl and mug into the sink and splashes water over them with the tap. This would normally annoy me but today I'm itchy, desperate for him to go. He looks at the bottle of pills and back over at me again, opens his mouth and then shuts it.

Before he leaves, he comes over and kisses me on the cheek. He smells of aftershave – too much aftershave. I can't remember the last time he put aftershave on. He never usually remembers. I feel a surge of desire, and I stand up and press myself against him. There's nothing sexy about me any more, nothing at all, but he's a man and he loves me. I push my hips against him, hoping for some response, but instead he twitches and gives an embarrassed laugh.

'Hey,' he says, pulling away and holding my wrists. 'What are you up to?'

I stare at him, straight in the eye.

'Who's your meeting with later?' I ask. There's no beat before he responds.

'Brett Lowe,' he says, 'I told you before . . . he's thinking of investing.'

I nod. He's not lying. Not this time, anyway. But one thing I will say about the treatment is that it's helped me see everything more clearly, recognize the strangeness of his behaviour lately. All these late nights, days when he hasn't been in the workshop all day, times he's 'popped out' somewhere without telling me where. There's something going on, I know it.

'Good luck with it,' I say, and I kiss him hard on the mouth. This time he relaxes, kissing me back and winding his arms around my waist. I want to take him upstairs to bed, to make another baby, but something has changed in him. He's kissing me out of duty, not with any sense of desire. The thought makes me want to cry.

'Bye, darling,' he says, stroking my hair away from my fore-head. 'Have a nice morning, I'll pop in at lunchtime.'

And then he is gone.

I stand there for a few seconds, acknowledging the unsatisfied throbbing between my legs. I think of Darcey, of her stupid pixie face, her coquettish giggle, her curves. I think of Jack's iPad, sitting innocuously on the coffee table in the living room.

Before I have time to talk myself out of it I am walking towards it. I wait until I hear Jack's car pulling out of the gravel driveway and off down the lane. In the living room, I sit on the sofa and pull the iPad towards me, flipping open its cover. It asks me for a passcode. I try his bank card PIN number, but it isn't that. I try my birthday, but it isn't that. I try her birthday, but it isn't that, either.

In a desperate move I try our anniversary, and am stunned when the iPad unlocks. Perhaps I have got everything wrong. I am so tired, so very tired.

I click on the browser app and wait for it to load. There are hundreds of tabs open and they swim in front of my eyes: sports news websites, online wine merchants, eBay, BBC News, BBC Weather . . . I flick through them all, bored. The final tab is about post-partum depression, and I scan the words with little interest. I have read a million pamphlets on it, and nothing any medical professional can say will help. I close the browser app, frustrated, and move on to his calendar.

It's a mass of coloured blocks: pinks and greens and blues and oranges. Neat little slots dividing up his life. Today he has a personal trainer session at twelve. I didn't even know he had a personal trainer. What kind of partner does that make me? I think back to the washing, one of my many chores as a stay-at-home-wife. I can't remember washing a single piece of gym kit, not for ages. But Jack is fastidiously clean.

I scan the rest of the day. Nothing of interest. I feel disappointed. All this snooping, and I've found nothing.

Before I close his iPad I click on one last app. Facebook. I don't want to do it, because I know that if I am going to find anything, I am going to find it here. But I'm committed now, I've done something terrible, and so I might as well go the whole hog. I know Jack hardly ever uses Facebook – it just isn't his kind of thing, getting in touch with people from his past. But I know that his only communication with her has been through it, and so I have to look.

I click on Messenger. Unsurprisingly, there she is, all doe eyes and pouty lips, second from bottom. I open the last message she sent him, feeling sick but perversely excited.

Keep the faith, my love. It must be so difficult for you – for you both.

Let me know if there's anything I can do – you know where I am. Love always xx

It's dated 3rd February. More than ten months ago. And he hasn't replied to it, from what I can tell. I scroll down the rest of the thread and read her first message.

Hi darling, Antonia just filled me in on your news. We are all heart-broken. I can't even imagine what you are going through right now, what unimaginable pain. I hope Helena recovers soon. My heart is breaking for you, for what should have been. Here if you need me – ALWAYS here if you need me, remember that. You don't have to be strong all the time, Dxx

He had replied, three days after the message was sent.

Hi D, thanks for getting in touch, kind of you to think of us. We are taking it one day at a time. It's been tough. I'm hopeful we will come out the other side eventually. Congratulations on all your success, it's wonderful to see you achieving your dreams. J x

What success? What dreams? Typical Jack – deflecting attention away from his problems and serving her ego instead. I should be cross, but I'm not. I'm too tired. I move my finger to close Messenger, but then my eyes spot something unexpected in among the messages. One from Joel. Joel Haydon.

I click on it. It's also dated February earlier this year. As far as I know, Joel has only met Jack once, at the launch party of the pop-up.

Hi mate, sorry it's taken me a while to get in touch, it's been a busy time – as I am sure it has been for you, too. Thanks for the flowers. It's a shame that Helena couldn't have been there – Ash would have liked that. Hope you are doing all right. Joel.

I scroll upwards and down again but it doesn't seem as though Jack has replied to this message. I frown at the words, wondering what I am missing. Flowers? Why would Jack send Joel flowers? The only explanation is that Joel and Ash have got married. I snort to myself at the irony of it. I remember her insisting once that she'd never get married, that it was a mug's game.

I hadn't imagined that Ash was the sort of woman to put on a big white dress and float down an aisle, but I was wrong. I was wrong about everything.

And now, it seems, I was wrong about Jack. Why would Jack send them anything? He holds her responsible for the stress, for my skyrocketing blood pressure, for it all . . . It doesn't make any sense. He's all for being polite, he often preaches to me about water under the bridge, but when I mention her (which I rarely do, these days) he changes the subject immediately.

The humming begins in my ears again, familiar and unwanted all at once. It grows louder, until I have to put my hands against the sides of my head and press, trying to dull the sound. But it doesn't work. It never works. I know what's coming next.

I stand, walking shakily to the kitchen, my eyes roaming, wondering where my drugs are. And then, as I stand propped against the kitchen counter, leaning my forehead on the cool stone, I hear it. The unmistakable screech of brakes, the sound of metal hitting stone, glass breaking, a scream. Another one.

NOW

Helena

Monday, Wednesday and Friday. Three times a week, for two weeks. And it's over. I thought I might be able to get out of seeing my therapist on Tuesday afterwards, but apparently it would be *unwise* to make too many other drastic changes.

I eat my breakfast while watching a soap opera on catch-up, a new daily ritual, to help with my recovery. Something about the continuing storylines is meant to fuse connections in my newly fried brain, helping me to get it working properly again.

Jack comes into the living room, dressed smartly for a change. He smiles at me.

'You look well,' he says.

'Really?' He's not one for compliments – not during a normal day, anyway. Not just randomly.

'Yes,' he replies. 'There's more colour in your cheeks.'

'My appetite's got better,' I reply. 'They didn't mention that before . . . but I definitely feel hungrier.'

'That's great, darling.' His phone buzzes in his pocket, and he pulls it out. The message makes him smile, and I want to ask him who it's from and what they've said, but I don't dare. Perhaps it's from Ashley, his new best friend.

'Would you like me to cook dinner tonight?' I say instead, because I used to be a good cook, and last night I had the most sleep I've had in weeks, and I suddenly feel a rush of motivation and inspiration. 'I could do a Thai red curry?'

'That sounds great. If you think you're up to it.'

I'm fizzing now, and I realize I need to start breathing slowly or I'll make myself dizzy. But I feel so alive. I slept well last night for the first time in ages! My memory directly after each treatment is still pretty patchy, but at least I remember the treatments actually happening, which apparently some people don't. And best of all, there haven't been any more accidents.

'I think I'll go to the farmer's market in the village, get some proper chicken. How does that sound? Do you think they'll have coconut milk? Or will I have to go to Waitrose for that? Probably . . . I'm not sure, though . . . they used to have that herb stall, remember, coriander and stuff, maybe they'll do coconut milk . . .'

'Calm down,' Jack says, and he shoves his phone back in his pocket and comes closer to me. 'You're talking too fast. Don't worry, I am sure we have most of the ingredients in the cupboard, anyway – I did a huge shop at the weekend. But if you fancy getting out and getting the chicken, then that'd be great. Just drive carefully. Now listen, I have to go or I'll miss my appointment with the letting agent.'

He kisses me on the cheek and leaves the room. It's only when he's left that I realize he's left me a cup of tea on the coffee table, along with my pills. I stare at them, angry that I still need medication, despite all the sessions at the hospital. I think of today, the way I've woken up, full of hope and excitement, and yet I know that at the back of my mind I'm scared I'm starting to lose control, that my excitement will soon escalate into something else entirely. Something beyond my understanding, something that scares me. It can't be that easy to fix me surely? Just a few zaps with an electrical current and all my issues disappear? *Slowly, steadily.* That's what they all keep telling me. *One thing at a time.* I grab the pills, tiptoe through to the bathroom, stick my head under the tap in the basin and swallow them in one go.

Perhaps that will level me out.

After I've had a shower and got dressed, it's half past nine. The farmers' market opens at ten, and I want to be there early, to make sure I get the good stuff before it goes. I impress myself by going through the cupboards before I leave, checking what we have and don't have – we're out of rice – and making a list. A real list, on paper, not on my phone or my hand or in an unreliable crevice of my brain.

Pulling out of our driveway is always a challenge. I hate the noise my tyres make as they bulldoze through the gravel outside our house, stones flying up at all angles as they do so. One hit the back window once and scared me half to death. I've told Jack several times that I want to get rid of the gravel and replace it with paving slabs. Anything would be better than this resistance under the wheels, the feeling that I'm trying to drive through quicksand, constantly shifting from under me.

Eventually, I emerge, after creeping forwards and making sure there's nothing coming in either direction. And then I'm off, down the hill and round to where the lane narrows to a single track, with euphemistically described 'passing places', which are really just banks of earth, beaten and worn by their pummelling from 4x4s. It's only as I pull up at a set of traffic lights that I realize my hands are shaking, adrenalin rushing through my veins, the enormity of what I've just done gradually sinking in.

Parking isn't easy in the village. I thought that, coming from London, it would be a breeze, but it's often worse. There are no pavements, and people don't seem to do 'walking' in the same way they do in the city.

I find a spot in a bay along the high street, and say a silent prayer of thanks that I left early. Some of the stallholders are still setting up, lining up their chutneys and wheels of cheese and artisan loaves. I smile as I walk along the rows, recognizing a few of the stalls from the previous month. I find the butcher and ask him for two chicken breasts and some thighs, too.

'Ten pound ninety, please, love,' the butcher tells me, handing me a bag with the meat.

I pass over a £20 note, apologizing for not having any change. Such a mundane exchange, but it feels like a real achievement.

As I walk back to the car, I realize I am feeling the most normal I have felt in as long as I can remember. I want to phone my consultant, to thank him profusely. To tell him he's saved my life.

The market is filling up now, and I have to weave my way through the crowds of people to get back to the car. I pass the florist's stall, and stop. It's been so long since I bought myself flowers. Before KAMU B, before Ash, before everything . . . it had been a thing of mine, to stop off at the florist's right by West Hampstead Tube, and treat myself to a bunch every Friday. A celebration of the weekend, a celebration of myself. Something seasonal, I would say, asking the florist to choose for me. The only criterion was that the flowers had to smell. I couldn't be doing with non-fragrant flowers. What was the point?

It's November, and the flowers on offer seem incongruous, somehow – all bright pinks and mauves and yellows. Too many gerberas. I wrinkle my nose, searching for something more wintry in among the offerings. I wonder if it's too early to go for Christmas foliage, holly and ferns. My train of thought is interrupted by the sensation of someone tugging on my arm. I move aside, assuming they are desperate to get to the flowers, in a hurry, about to miss a train. These feelings are ingrained from years of living in London, where everyone is in a rush and everyone is more important than you. But then there's a voice behind me, and it's calling my name.

'Helena? It is you, isn't it?'

I turn and it takes a few seconds before I can place the girl standing in front of me. She's not a girl, of course, she's a woman, but she's younger than me and there's something else that makes me think of her as a child rather than an adult. A vision flashes through my brain, the sound of her laughter, thin and reedy, her mouth wide open. But she's not laughing now. She's staring at me, her mouth downturned a little, her eyes wide with affection.

'Jess,' I say, because I'm sure that's her name and I can't think of anything else.

'Oh my goodness! I thought it was you! Of all the places . . . what a coincidence! What are you doing here?'

'I live here. In the next village,' I say, and a middle-aged woman with a red face and a wax jacket steps in front of me, as if to persuade me to move back from the flowers. Jess grabs my arm and pulls me to the side.

'Oh yes!' she says. 'That's right. I remember now.' But I know she's lying, because no one from that life knows where we moved to.

'And you?' I say, and she frowns. 'I mean, er, how come you're here?' I glance back at the flowers, wishing I could escape into them. The bag with the chicken breasts is sweaty in my hand. I rest it on an upturned box to the side of the flower stall.

'My parents live here! Got a week off... always end up coming home. You know how it is. No boyfriend. Week off. What am I going to do in London? Sit around in my poxy room in my flat-share all week? Better to come up here and get waited on hand and foot. Plus, I get to see my cat, which is always a winner. She's nineteen now, on her last legs, but she's still feisty for a cat.' She holds up her hand, pulling back her glove to show me an angry red scratch. 'I got that for daring to stop stroking her last night! Little minx.'

I remember now why Ash didn't get on with her. She never stopped talking. The incessant chatter. She was well meaning enough, but she wasn't great at her job, either. And to get on in life, you really need to know when to shut the hell up.

'Well,' I say, desperate to get back to my car and to get home. The longer the chicken can marinate the better the curry will taste. 'I hope you have a great week off.'

'Thanks!' she says. 'And listen ... between you and me, I *saw* what Ashley was doing ... You know how she treated Toby. And then, well, the way she muscled in on your job, used your preg-nancy to get to where she wanted. David might have been too dumb to notice what she was doing, but I wasn't. Even so, I just wanted to say . . . I was so upset to hear about what happened to her. We all couldn't believe it when David told us.'

I stare at her then, and her edges start to look indistinct all of a sudden, as though she might vaporize, or fade into space.

'If I'm honest,' she is saying, and I find myself screwing up my eyes, trying to focus on her words and not the way she looks, 'we never got on. She didn't like me much. And she was so pleased when she found out I was being made redundant, too. But even so, no one deserves to die like that, do they?'

There is a moment of clarity, like a thunderbolt crashing through my brain, and then I remember. Ashley is dead. I knew this. I know this. But Jess is still speaking and I can't explain that I knew this already, that I knew it but that somehow I had forgotten it. That of course it didn't make sense; it didn't make sense to me, either.

'She only passed her test about a month before. Just after you left,' Jess says. 'Bought the car with her Christmas bonus. But those lanes round here . . . my mum always told me to be careful. You must know how lethal they can be, and especially in the ice. I heard . . .' and she lowers her voice, as though what she's about to say is somehow sensational, 'that she didn't die immediately. That she bled to death. That it was ages before anyone found her.'

She's wrong about that, but I am nodding now because, deep down, despite it all, despite my shattered mental state, I have an inbuilt mechanism to protect myself, as everyone does.

'There are accidents around here all the time,' I say, and my voice comes out robotic, like an artificial intelligence app on my phone, answering a question about road safety in the area. 'There were three outside my house last month.'

She is frowning at me, waiting for me to continue, wanting the details, but I find I can't speak any longer. I find that I am walking back to my car, without saying goodbye, that I have left the chicken by the florist's stall. I open the car door, climb into the passenger seat and stare at the road ahead. And I think of that night, of what I had blanked out for so long. I *have* blanked out for so long. Her face looking at me for help. My nightdress, the material waterlogged and translucent.

And finally, the memory unbearable, I think of the moment that I watched her die.

THEN

Helena

I am trying to make scrambled eggs, a simple enough procedure, something I've done hundreds of times before, yet my hands are shaking, fingertips still numb from all the squeezing they did while I was in labour, and even though I try to break the eggshell carefully I misjudge the pressure, and a large chunk of shell falls into the pan, sliding further and further away from me when I try to fish it out with my deadened fingers.

I haven't eaten since 7 p.m. last night – a supper interrupted five times, congealed and tepid by the time I shovelled it in – and my God, it's nearly four in the afternoon now and so I have to eat, I *have* to eat, if only I can manage to cook these eggs, and as people always say: 'I don't know where the hours have gone.' But in this case I know who's stolen them, and as I try again to fish the fragment of shell out I hear her start up once more; that piercing shriek, so perfectly pitched, an ear-split of sound that reminds me that my time is not my own any more, that it never will be again.

I push my hands to my ears, go to the fridge for the butter, try to ignore her, because after all, just a few minutes won't kill her, will it? And I have to eat, too – 'It's not all about you and your milk, you know, and if I don't get any food, then I won't have any milk for you, anyway' – and I am weak with hunger, with exhaustion, with a strange kind of misery that they told me would float by on day four, but it's not day four yet, and there's no floating, only drowning, which means I'm failing already.

I give up with the pan and decide to microwave the eggs instead – Jack would tell me it's sacrilege but he's not here, so his opinion means nothing – and as I think of him I am surprised by how angry I am with Jack for not being here, for leaving me all alone, because he's not the one who's had no time to eat or wash or . . .

In goes the butter now, then a splash of milk, even though I know aficionados would tell me I'm breaking the rules; sacrilege again, never doing things properly. Short cuts, half-measures. Tut, tut, tut. I whisk the sickly yellow mixture with a fork – shell and all – then shove it in the microwave, but her shrieks grow louder as I slam the door shut. *I'm coming,* I call to her in my head, *just wait a second!* My brain is sluggish as I press the buttons – is it two minutes or three for scrambled eggs? I go for three and rush upstairs, but as soon as she sees me she stops crying, gives a yawn and falls asleep, her lips twisting into a half-smile that makes her look evil, somehow, if such a thing were possible.

Just testing, her features seem to be saying. *You belong to me now. And you thought it was the other way round!*

The microwave pings, another sound so shrill and demanding I want to hit my head against the bedroom wall, but I don't, of course I don't, because I'm a mother now and that would be incredibly irresponsible and childish, and it's not all about you any more, Helena, and so instead I go back downstairs, answering the microwave's call like the compliant creature I am, and as I walk I feel the warm gloop sloshing about in my knickers, reminding me of another thing to attend to, another thing that Jack can't help with, even if he was here, but he's not – and anyway, who cares about the state of my knickers, about the state of *me*? First I must eat.

I yank open the microwave door to find a lump of bouncy rubber, inedible even to the ravenous, and I find myself mindlessly lifting the bowl above my head and smashing it on the floor because, like everything else right now, it feels like a test, a test of patience, a test of competence and I'm so angry at failing all these tests that I can't bear it.

So much to do.

So much.

I haven't slept now for eighty-five hours. I know this because I have been keeping track because some part of me is so amazed, so impressed with myself, that I'm pretty sure I'm going to write to the *Guinness Book of Records* when I get a minute and ask them to include me, because surely I'm the first new mother to survive on so little sleep, and I mean, who knew it was possible really, to still be alive when you haven't slept for three and a half days and that everything they ever told you about needing sleep was a lie, a strange lie, that you'd die without it, what nonsense, apart from babies, of course, babies need sleep, because they need to grow, but this baby doesn't seem to want to sleep, which is strange when she is so small, so very small . . .

She is small but she won't eat and when I put her against my nipple she just turns and squirms away and goes red with frustration and disgust, her fingernails so sharp for someone so small scratching and scraping at my vein-filled breasts until the skin is cracked and raw and it hurts both physically and emotionally to pull my T-shirt back down over them, to give up on the whole endeavour and to give her a bottle instead, which she slurps at greedily in her impatience to get to it, letting the milk run down over her chin where it settles in the folds of her neck.

I have made so much milk for the baby that I am now pumping it into a little bottle, just like the midwife told me – 'Freeze it for the future! Liquid gold!' – just like a cow, except I don't feel like a cow at all, instead I feel like a creature from outer space, a hideous creature that's bleeding heavily and passing clots as big as plums and leaking milk when I bend over and has a stomach like a stress ball – I can push it in and it holds its shape before slowly pushing back out.

Jack is talking to me right now but all I can see are his lips moving – there is no sound coming out of them – and I smile and tell him that everything's OK, that I've got a handle on it all, that he doesn't need to worry, that of course he can nip out again if he needs to, that the baby and I will be just fine because, like the midwife said, I am superhuman, because I survived a three-day labour, because I gave birth without any painkillers, without anything, and because my third-degree tear is healing already, I can tell it's healing because I can sit down now, and even though it smells, that's OK, it's to be expected, everyone says so.

Can't make an omelette without breaking eggs.

Or something.

Eggs, I was making eggs.

So much to do.

My mother is here too, I think, somewhere in the background, trying to stop the baby crying because that's the one thing that isn't going so well, the baby keeps crying, and especially when I pick her up, but that's because she was stuck for so long in my birth canal, I think, and she's recovering from the trauma of being born but it'll be fine eventually, I looked it up, and Dr Google said I just need to take her to a cranial osteopath, like they suggest on Mumsnet, and she just needs to drink some of this milk that I can't stop squirting, rather than vomiting it all up, and she needs to get some rest because, after all, she's a baby, and babies should sleep all the time, shouldn't they, they shouldn't be crying all the time like this.

Maybe it's my mother that the baby hates.

My mother thinks that it's absurd that the baby doesn't have a name yet but what she doesn't understand is that there's been no time at all to think of such things, because I've had so much to learn, not just the bleeding and the pain when I sit down and the bruising on my body and the never-ending milk but learning how to dress this tiny scrap of a thing and how often to feed her and how often to wind her and what to do about the smell coming from her tummy button, which doesn't seem to be healing despite what all the midwives say.

Jack is still talking to me and his face has changed expression so I squint to listen to him because I'm scared he might be angry with me, even though I am trying my best, whereas he has done nothing but sit by me and answer text messages from people congratulating him on the birth of his daughter when I was the one who did it, but anyway he's saying something now about the baby crying, and me having to go and pick it up or he'll call my mother again, which means that she's obviously not here, after all, and that I've got confused.

I tell him it's OK and that of course I'll go and get the baby, because I've got this, and he doesn't need to worry, and then I push past him and ignore the way he is looking at me as though he doesn't recognize me any more, even though I suppose he doesn't recognize me because I *do* look different, what with my stained pyjamas and the fact I haven't washed my hair since that horrible shower in that tiled cell, but how can I wash my hair when there's so much to do here with the baby?

I pick her up and I tell her to be quiet, that she is a lucky baby because she has a superhuman supermum who is never going to leave her, and I repeat this bit very carefully because I don't want to be like my mum, and so I tell my baby, 'I will never leave you,' and, 'I love you,' and, 'It's going to be OK,' but you have to stop crying now because your brain needs to grow because sleep is the most important thing for you – not for me, I am OK, I'm going to get in the *Guinness Book of Records*, but for you – and did you know that babies are born three months before they should be because humans' birth canals are too narrow and it means they have to be born before they're neurologically ready to cope with *life* and the only way they can get neurologically ready is if they *sleep*?

There must be something wrong with her, even though everyone keeps telling me she's beautiful and perfect and amazing, that's what they've all written in the cards cluttering the floor of the fireplace, which keep falling over in the draught when Jack opens the living-room door, and they make me itch with irritation but why am I worrying about them when the baby won't sleep?

I look back up at Jack and he is wearing his coat and he has his bag slung over his arm and then I remember the reason that he is so worried is because he's going out again – 'Just for the afternoon, I promise, just for an *essential meeting*' – and I was cross last time he left me alone with the baby, my lovely baby who is five days old now, or is it four, I can't remember, and doesn't have a name yet but it doesn't matter because I love her, and what do names mean anyway, they're just affectations and they're not feelings, and nothing will sum up the way I feel about her, unless I call her Loved, but that would be ridiculous and everyone would think I had lost my mind.

Jack is kissing me and then he kisses the baby and I notice in his eyes that he doesn't want to go at all, he doesn't want to leave her any more than I want him to leave. But what doesn't make sense is this ache in my ribcage that tells me that I want to go to work today and that I am envious of him because he has had a reason to get showered and dressed and put on aftershave and open his computer and check his emails but I don't have any reason to do any of these things. Not any more, because now my job is to be here with this tiny baby and try to keep her alive ... and until she sleeps and eats I'm not even doing that right.

The next thing I know, I am waking up and I am on the sofa, but I can't remember how I got here or how I fell asleep, and I'm cross with myself because goddammit I was going to get the Guinness World Record and now it looks as though I have scuppered my plan.

It takes a while for my thoughts to untangle themselves, but then it comes back to me in a rush: I am here, alone, except I'm not alone and I'll never be alone again because I have a baby now, and there's no taking her back even if I wanted to, which I kind of do, but that's not right, is it? *Not allowed to say things like that, Helena, how absolutely shocking.* And she has a birthmark in between her non-existent eyebrows, but other than that she is absolutely perfect, the most perfect baby you ever did see, as all the cards in the fireplace keep telling me, even though they're all messy because they keep falling over and people keep shoving them back up without any thought or care as to how they are arranged.

I turn the television on, wait for the screen to come to life, and when it does it is filled with pictures of David Bowie, and for a while I don't understand, and as I wonder what's going on and if it's his birthday or something, I listen to a woman with too much make-up on waving her arms around saying something about his eighteen-month battle with cancer, and it takes me a while before I understand what she means, that he has 'lost that battle', if indeed you can call it a battle when it's not your fault that you lose, it's not that you didn't fight hard enough or weren't strong enough but that it was simply your time to go, and if you get hit by a car, people don't say you lost your battle with the road, or walking, do they?

Either way, it doesn't matter, all that matters is that he has died, and this fills me with a hollow feeling that I can't explain, and I think back to my teenage years, to the time my dad brought out his records – 'Enough of your teeny-bopper pop nonsense, listen to something groundbreaking for a change' – and we tried to make sense of 'Starman', and my dad said not to read too much into it, but that Bowie was trying to tell me that I'd never be alone, that there'd always be someone up there, looking down, taking care of me.

I'm alone now, though.

No, that's not right. I'm not alone. I'll never be alone again.

I clamber off the sofa and go to find the baby because, the truth is, I can't remember where she is or where I put her before I fell asleep and there's something strange going on in the back of my mind, an instruction or something, from someone – the midwife, or my mother. But I haven't seen my mother so that can't be it, I must be confused, I must be getting muddled up, perhaps instead it is Jack who has asked me to do something with the baby, but I have failed him because I've already forgotten what it is.

I go through to the nursery and of course the baby is in there, in her cot, where she's supposed to be, because I am superhuman supermum – no pain relief for me! Except she's not supposed to be here in this cot on her own without me being in the room because the health visitor said she must be in the room with me at all times until she's six months old because she can't yet regulate her own breathing and she needs to be close to me in order not to die from cot death.

And then I remember that now it's not called cot death any more, it's called sudden infant death syndrome, and I have to poke my baby to make sure she hasn't succumbed but it's OK because she gives a mewing sound like a kitten and I pick her up and then it's there again, that voice, telling me that this baby is special, that she doesn't need a name because she is too important, that no name would ever be worthy of her and that scares me because it means that I, too, am inadequate and I, too, can't live up to her.

Later I am loading the washing machine with tiny Babygros and muslin cloths, all covered in vomit and milk that she has rejected, when I hear my phone buzz and I pick it up, thinking of course it's going to be Jack telling me what time he will be home, but instead it's not him, it's someone else entirely, someone I don't want to see, someone I never want to see again.

Someone who took my trust and obliterated it, someone who targeted me at my most vulnerable, someone who put profit before kindness, before everything.

I look again at her message and I don't understand what she's saying, or how she knows where I am, but apparently she has a gift for me, for me and the baby, and she wants to bring it over, and she thinks this afternoon would be a good time and she's on her way over and Jack has said it's OK.

And then I realize, I realize it all.

She thinks it's David's baby and she's going to tell Jack, and she's going to ruin everything and there's nothing I can do about it even though she's already taken my job and my self-esteem and my livelihood and chucked me on the stay-at-home-mum rubbish heap to rot because she doesn't want anything to do with me any more because she has used me, used me up, got what she wanted and got rid, and she's won, in the epic battle of good versus evil she's won, she's beaten me, she's the cancer and I'm David Bowie, and now I'm stuck here and I'm doubting myself and I'm wondering whose baby this is, and thinking perhaps I did sleep with him, after all, even though I was sure I didn't, and maybe that's why I can't name her, because she's not worthy, because she's the Devil's child and it's only a matter of time before Jack finds out and everything will be over once and for all.

I am calmer now. It has taken a while. I had to put the baby downstairs in the utility room, turn the washing machine on to drown out her noise and shut the door, and then I came upstairs and now I'm having a bath, finally washing my hair, and everything is OK because I can't hear her crying.

She can't get me in here. I'm safe.

I have been focusing on my breathing, counting to ten, deep breaths in and out, in and out, in and out. Someone told me to do that when I was upset a long time ago. I'm staring at the pictures on the ceiling of the bathroom. I never noticed them before, but they are swirling around in circles, mixing colours and drawing me in, like an abstract painting being completed before my eyes.

I know what I have to do now. It's simple. I should have thought of it before.

My phone is balanced on the side of the bath and I check the time. It's exactly six o'clock, and now I need to move. I push my phone into the water and watch it bob about before it sinks, leaving a trail of bubbles behind so delicate that looking at them hurts my eyes.

I climb out of the bath and pull on my nightdress. There is no time for shoes, and somehow shoes don't seem right for what is about to happen.

I count the steps down to the ground floor. It has bothered me since we moved in that there are eleven of them, such an odd number, *eleven*, both literally and figuratively. But now I am happy because I have realized that it's the 11th, and it's all meant to be, it's all working out perfectly. This is God's plan, except I don't believe in God, so it must be someone else's plan, and I know it sounds crazy but I'm sure David Bowie has something to do with it all, that he's watching and waiting, and he's going to make sure everything's OK.

It's darker than I expected it to be downstairs. I turned all the lights off earlier, and it's January, so of course it's dark outside already. I tiptoe to the utility room, and push the door open. It creaks and the light from upstairs filters down through the hallway, casting a glow on what's inside. The washing-machine light blinks at me. And there she is, the baby.

David's baby.

He is going to blow our minds.

She's not asleep, but for once she's not crying. She looks up at me with those foggy eyes – eyes that can't see anything and don't know anything. Her arms are twitching, her hands outstretched, fingers opening and closing in some kind of reflex, an unknowing experiment, trying to work out what they can do, who they can hurt. I know from my research on these reflexes that if I make a loud sound she will startle, her whole body will jerk and her arms will fling outwards and back in again, and then she'll cry.

So I don't make any sound because, even though I know she can't live, I don't want her to be in any distress.

I lean down and pick her up. She is so light that it is like picking up a piece of cloth.

She settles in my arms, turning her face towards me. She is wrapped in a bright yellow blanket. Underneath the blanket she is wearing a fleece Babygro, the colour of morning snow. Her hands are covered by little mitts and the only skin visible is on her face and the top of her head, peeking through patches of sandy hair.

She doesn't cry out as I walk through the kitchen, opening the patio door with one hand. She lies there in my arms, trusting, her cloudy eyes drifting around, trying and failing to focus on something. *Not yet, little one.* I feel the wind against my bare ankles and I realize that it's cold outside, but for some reason I am so hot I am burning up.

The grass is wet underneath my feet and I sink into it as I walk round the side of the house towards the road. The only light is coming from the bedroom upstairs but it's enough, it's all I need.

The baby begins to squawk as I tread slowly across our gravel driveway to the road. I can't tell if she's cold, or if she knows what's about to happen, but I visualize her cries being packaged up into a little box and sent away and I find that this time it's OK, they don't matter.

We are standing on the road now. I look up. It's a clear night and the sky is flecked with stars that swell as I run my eyes over them. The moon is a thin crescent somewhere to my left. I think of David Bowie again, the Starman, waiting in the sky. At last it all makes sense.

I stare down at my feet, which seem to be bleeding, even though I feel no pain. I watch them, the shredded skin around my toes falling away, as I carefully count the paces into the road. There must be eleven of them, no more, no less, to find the perfect spot. It takes me three goes to get it right but eventually it's done.

I lay the baby on the tarmac and look down at her. Like the stars, she is gleaming, there is light coming from her chest and her head, and there is no way they won't be able to see her here, no way she won't be taken to where she belongs.

Her little legs twitch and her arms quiver under the blanket but she's stopped mewling now. Slowly, her eyes begin to shut and she is ready. We are both ready.

NOW

Helena

The DJ is talking drivel on the radio, something about how we all used to love to create mixtapes, how it was once a way of wooing your beloved. And I want to shout at the radio for him to shut up, because how can he be talking about something so stupid when there is something so serious going on? But then he says something about number one on his ultimate mixtape being this song, and I hear the first few bars and I know instantly, I know with my whole body, what's coming next.

Goodbye love

Didn't know what time it was . . .

And I turn it off, because I can never listen to that song again. The song that killed my beautiful baby girl.

As I drive I am focused on my goal completely and utterly – which is liberating, at least. I just need to get home now, as quickly as possible.

Before long I am pulling into our driveway, my tyres scrunching against the gravel, as always. But I barely notice, this time, and I don't even care enough to leave the steering wheel straight. I am out of the car and into the house in seconds and I rush straight to

Jack's iPad, tapping in our anniversary and clicking immediately on the Find my iPhone app.

It takes a few seconds to work and I shake the iPad in frustration, flipping the screen into the other direction.

'Come on!' I shout at the screen, and as if it is listening to me, suddenly a map appears with a small pin on it. Telling me where Jack is.

I squint at the pin for a few seconds, my brain struggling to understand what I am seeing. But eventually there's no mistaking it.

Jack is at my mother's house.

THEN

Helena

The stars are still up there, still bright.

I saw the car coming. I saw it swerve, spinning in the road before bouncing off the low cobbled wall and turning over completely. It's her. Of course it's her.

For some reason, Ash has been thrown from the car and is lying by the side of the road, her body flung up against the wall like a discarded shop mannequin, limbs twisted and out of place. The headlights are still on and they provide the perfect stage illumination. Behind us, the car is making a strange hissing noise.

He is still watching.

I kneel down and crawl towards her, the glass on the tarmac cutting into my knees. I feel nothing but a strange tugging sensation on my skin. When I'm close enough, I look at her face. She's staring at me, her mouth opening and closing like a fish. There are bubbles coming from her nose as she tries to breathe – bubbles tinged with blood. I try to shush her, to stop her from talking, but her mouth keeps making that same O shape, over and over again.

'No,' I say to her, and her eyes widen suddenly. 'Don't speak.'

But she doesn't listen, she keeps trying to speak, snorting blood bubbles from her nose. There is saliva running down her chin and on to her coat. Black trousers, now ripped in places, her skin pierced, blooded patches of it peeking through the material. There's a faint smell of urine, mixed with that same masculine perfume I always hated.

'I can take care of the pop-ups,' I say, and her eyes tell me she doesn't like this idea at all. 'Don't worry. Now that David has taken the baby. I'll take care of work.'

Her mouth is still moving and, eventually, there's a sound, something like a word.

'What did you say?' I ask, and I can't help it because, despite myself, I am enjoying this, and part of me thinks it must be a dream, my subconscious acting out my fantasies. That's it, it's a dream, and I will go with it because in a dream no one can get hurt.

'H-el . . .'

There's a brief shake of her head that obviously causes her pain because it's followed by a groan, a long, low, guttural sound that comes from somewhere deep inside her stomach.

'He . . . lp,' she gasps and then collapses inwards, shutting her eyes.

'I am helping,' I say. 'What do you want from me? I didn't ask you to come. I didn't ask you to crash the car. I didn't even know you could drive. You come to a dangerous lane like this, in the middle of winter, and you take the corner too quickly. And what about your seat belt? Didn't bother to wear one? That's always been your problem, Ashley. Never taking care. Always running before you can walk. But you never listened. You never listened to me.'

I start to cry.

Her eyes spring open again, bloodshot and popping.

'I . . .' she begins, but there are no more sounds, just a trail of bubbles from her nose, a line of blood trailing from her mouth. Her eyes stop moving, and fix me with a stare.

I stand up, suddenly confused as to where I am, and what I'm doing here. And then I remember her, my baby. My beautiful baby. She's gone. David's taken her, and I have missed it. Thanks to Ashley, I have missed it all.

I run into the road, but behind the upturned car it's too dark to see more than a few inches in front of me. Can I hear a baby crying, or am I just imagining it? I spin on the spot, wondering how it's all gone so wrong, where I am and what I'm doing, and I look down and realize I am frozen to the bone, that my nightdress is soaking wet, that my knees are bleeding.

And nothing makes any sense.

And then I hear my own voice screaming at the stars and the universe to help me understand what's happening, to tell me where they have taken her.

And as if to answer me, I see something in the distance: two lights, growing larger, and then I know they are coming for me, and I don't mind. I don't even care.

THEN

Ash

All around me is blackness. I can't tell if my eyes are open or not.

I try to blink, but I don't know if it's working, whether my muscles are doing what I want them to. There's a burning wetness on one side of my face, and I can't feel anything below my waist. I try to lift my head, to make sense of it all, but nothing happens.

I was driving. The road was winding, there was black ice – I felt it under my wheels as I turned the corners. So many corners.

I was driving.

Cheap car. Seat belt broke this morning. Joel told me not to go.

I was driving and there was something in the way. Lit by my headlights, laid out in the middle of the road. A bundle, something in a blanket, a baby moving.

Where is it now?

The baby was in the way, and I swerved to miss it, but the car seemed to fly over the road and then there was a sound of scraping metal, so loud it hurt my ears. The last sound I remember before I flew through the air. And then nothing, just this blackness.

Helena. I was coming to see Helena. Why? To tell her about

Kayleigh, my new niece. How much I love her. To give her a present. To congratulate her on something . . .

Kayleigh. Perfect little mouth. Cheeks. A smudge above her eyebrow.

Pain in my shoulder. Where am I? The thoughts muddle, and suddenly I can hear her voice. Kayleigh's . . . no, Helena's. A voice close to my face, saying something, but I can't see who it's coming from.

Who is Helena?

David. Work.

The voice is telling me things, but I don't understand them. Am I moving my lips? Am I asking for help? I'm trying. I'm trying. Whoever you are, help me, I'm trying.

Why isn't she helping me?

The thoughts are coming too quickly now, crowding my mind and fighting for attention. The road. I had a feeling. I wanted to share. Forgiveness. Understanding. Kayleigh. Who's Kayleigh? She matters, but I don't know why. I need words. Must explain. The words, there are no words . . .

The thoughts spiral away from me, even though I'm reaching for them as hard as I can.

The steering wheel turned in time. This is all I know.

I feel a heaviness in my chest. A gust of wind across my forehead, cool and comforting, and then, the blackness suddenly all-consuming, I feel nothing more at all.

NOW

Helena

It is the second time today I have had to pull out of this driveway, but this time around I'm fearless and I don't try to take care. I don't try at all.

My mother's house is a twenty-minute drive from here. It was a conscious decision when I was pregnant, when I thought everything was going to be OK, that we would be a normal family like everyone else. Everyone told us to move closer to her, that when you have your first baby your mother is invaluable, that you need her by your side, that you can't do without her. But in the end, of course, there was no baby, and my mother was as devastated as I was and had no value at all.

When I speak to her on the phone now, she tiptoes around me, asking me how I am, if I'm feeling more like my old self, but she always breaks off the conversation in tears when I don't tell her what she wants to hear.

I have no idea why Jack is at my mother's house, but I feel betrayed. By both of them.

I turn the radio back on as I drive. The same DJ is still wittering on about mixtapes, and several carefree people are phoning in and regaling the world with their song choices. I think about Jess, about her story earlier about her cat, about the way she shared every inconsequential detail of her life with anyone and everyone, as though somehow her thoughts meant something to others.

The DJ is playing Aerosmith 'I Don't Want To Miss A Thing' and I remember the lyrics coming to me as I cradled my baby, minutes after she was born. I had always hated the song, dismissed it as cheesy. But now there are tears in my eyes as I listen to the words.

I pull into my mother's driveway and, sure enough, Jack's car is there already. Her house is not dissimilar to ours; an old farm-house off a single-track road with a large garden. Her pride and joy. The house is smaller than ours, though. Cosier, more friendly and less ostentatious.

I sit outside for a few seconds, gathering my thoughts. Even though I was so sure I needed to come here, now I am here, I can't remember why. But then it comes back to me. Ashley's death. The accident outside our house. Finally, I remember it. But there's something else, another piece of the jigsaw that's missing from this picture, a blank space in my memory. What happened after the accident? I need to talk to Jack. That's all I can think; I need him to help everything make sense again.

I walk up to the front door and push the brass doorbell. I hear it ring out inside, shrill and demanding. Through the pane of glass at the top of the door I watch my mother make her way towards me. She is throwing her head back, talking to someone else as she approaches. She isn't expecting me.

'Helena!' she says, and the expression on her face is something I can't place at all. She is wearing a tracksuit, as though she's just come back from the gym, and her short blonde hair is flattened on one side, her face make-up-less, reading glasses hanging on a chain around her neck. Despite all this, she is still beautiful, and she is glowing, her cheeks shiny, as though she's just been laughing.

'I need to speak to Jack,' I say.

Her eyes dart around nervously.

'Are you feeling all right?' she asks, putting her arm out and stroking my shoulder. 'How did you know he was here?'

'I just need to speak to him,' I reply.

'OK,' she says, her lips twisting. 'But, just wait here, will you? Just for one minute. I'll go and get him.'

And then she closes the door on me.

I stand on the doorstep, the cold wind whipping around my ears. I look down at her porch. There's a pumpkin here, precisely carved into a beaming smile. It's so incongruous, so out of place. Since when did my mother care about Halloween? Perhaps she has a new man on the go, someone younger, someone with a family. That would explain it. I give the pumpkin a little kick, and its lid falls in on itself, revealing the inside to be rotten.

The door opens again and my husband is there, standing in front of me.

'Darling,' he says, putting his arms around me and pulling me to him. 'You're freezing. What are you doing here?'

'Why didn't you tell me Ashley was dead?' I say. 'Why?'

'Darling,' he says, stroking my hair. 'I did. Many times. How did you remember? The treatment . . . they said it might. Let's go home. Let's go home now and we can talk all about it.'

We turn to leave but then there's a sound from the back of the house, from the large open-plan kitchen my mother had

316

completely remodelled when she bought this place, adding a huge glass extension that in no way fitted with the rest of the architecture, infuriating the villagers who insisted the farmhouse should have been listed.

'Wait,' I say, and I see Jack's eyes are wide with terror, and there's a movement, a shift, and he almost bundles me off the front step and into the driveway. But he's not quick enough and I hear it again, clear and unmistakable, calling me.

The sound of a baby's cry.

The sound of my baby's cry.

I push past Jack and run through to the extension. It's unrecognizable since the last time I was here. My mother's previously immaculate white kitchen is filled with an explosion of coloured plastic: a plastic high chair, plastic playpen, plastic toys scattered all over the floor and covering every surface possible. There's even a huge printed oilcloth covering the glass dining table. And there, in the furthest corner of the room, is my mother, crouching down over a small child. They both look up at me as I come in.

'Helena,' my mother says, snatching up the baby – except she's not a baby, not at all. She's almost a toddler, all long legs and wide eyes and curly blonde hair, pinned back with a pink hairclip. She's wearing striped leggings and a pink knitted jumper and she looks at me and hands me a small plastic brick.

'Dadadada,' she says, smiling. 'Deee!'

I walk towards her instinctively. There are no thoughts involved as I reach for her and take her from my mother. I kiss her head and smell her. She looks at me and gurgles, but then she glances back at my mother, checking that everything is OK. It's only then that I remember I saw her, a few months ago at the park. My mother was there then, too. I feel my body stiffen as I pull her closer to me. She's so heavy, so much heavier than the last time I held her. She moans a little and holds her arms out towards my mother.

'Helena,' Mum says, eyes wide with fear. 'Let me take her back, please.'

I stare at the baby. My baby. She doesn't even have a name. *Does she have a name?*

'Sophia,' I say, the name dropping into my brain like a coin in a slot machine. Jack has appeared behind me and I can feel his hands on my shoulders, trying to prise her away from me, but I cling on tightly, breathing in that smell; a combination of milk, baby skin and fabric conditioner. She smells so clean, so untainted, so perfect. 'Her name is Sophia.'

'Sophia,' Jack repeats, his hands now firmly on Sophia's small body. 'Helena, please, don't frighten her. Let me take her. Please, darling.'

'She's fine,' I say, looking at Sophia, but her eyes are wide with fear and I can see her bottom lip start to tremble. 'And if she's scared, whose fault is that?' My voice comes out harsher than I meant it to, and Sophia can sense the tension in my body. She lets out a long wail and starts wriggling, struggling to get away from me and back to my mother.

'Helena,' Mum says again. 'Let's talk about this. Give her to me, and we can talk.'

'You stole my baby!' I hiss, and I squeeze her even tighter. 'You told me she was dead!'

'That's not true,' Mum replies. 'You know that's not true. I've been looking after her while you've been unwell, since you came out of hospital. Now please, try to think what's best for her and give her back to me. She's tired, it's nearly time for her nap. Let me put her down for her sleep, and then we can talk. OK? Let's do this like the grown-ups we are. Please.'

My eyes flick to the large clock. It's huge and ugly and takes up the entire wall along one side. It's 11.45 a.m. Sophia's wails become more persistent. I think of the sound she made when she was a newborn, those five days when she seemed to do nothing but cry, no matter what I did. But that cry was nothing like this. How can she have changed so much? Yet when I look at her face I can see her eyes, the set of her cheeks, the shape of her head; these are all the same as I remember.

'You're fine,' I say, jiggling her up and down, smiling at her with all my might. She notices my necklace and, distracted, starts yanking it out from underneath my coat, her little forehead furrowed in concentration as she wrenches it free. When she finally has it in her podgy fist she beams with glee, and claps her little hands together. 'See, you're fine, aren't you? Do you like Mummy's necklace? Isn't it lovely? Daddy bought it for me for our anniversary . . . Daddy bought it for me just a few weeks ago.'

There are tears cascading down my face now, as I lean in again and kiss her head through her hair. I am overcome. I want to squeeze her until there's nothing left, eat her up, kiss her all over, never let her go. My teeth clench with an unexpected aggression.

'Why?' I say, looking back at my mother and Jack, who are standing watching us, their eyes also wide with alarm. 'Why have you been keeping her from me? Why did you tell me she was dead?'

I start sobbing. I have no idea what to do, where to go or what happens next.

'We didn't,' Jack says, softly. 'We didn't tell you she was dead.'

I frown at him. Nothing makes sense any more. Nothing. I need to be alone, I need to think. To sort out the truth from the fiction, the dreams from the reality. And I can't do that here. Not with them – the two liars, who have kept me from my baby for nearly a year. I have to get out of here.

Before I am even aware of doing it, I am walking towards the door.

Jack follows me.

'Helena . . .' he says, and I can hear the wariness in his voice. 'Helena! Where . . . what are you doing?'

I break into a run. As I approach it I am filled with gratitude for my stupid new car, a present for my birthday earlier this year from Jack, an attempt to cheer me up. It opens automatically if someone with the key comes near it. I am inside and have locked the doors before Jack or my mother have had time to catch up with me.

It has started to rain, and I listen as it pounds on the roof of the car. Sophia is gurgling gleefully at the steering wheel, trying to press the buttons for the radio. She thinks it's all a big game.

'That's right, sweetheart,' I say to her, whispering through her hair. 'It's all OK, you're safe here, safe with Mummy.'

It's only then that I realize I don't have a car seat. I don't have a car seat, or a plan.

I hear hammering on the driver's door and I realize it's not the rain, it's Jack. He's shouting something but I can barely hear him over the thumps from his fist. Sophia looks up at him, her innocent face confused but amused at the sight of her father banging to be let in. She points up at him.

'Oooh!' she says, laughing. 'Dada! Dada oooh!'

I want to scream at him to leave me alone, to leave me with my baby, my beautiful baby, but I can't scream because I don't want to scare her again. Instead, I sit her on my lap, facing outwards, zip my coat up around her and stretch the seat belt over us both. It's not ideal, but it will have to do. It's the only solution.

I look up at Jack, his face a watery blur through the car window. His mouth opens in horror as he realizes what I am about to do, but I don't care. I am not here to reassure him any more, to make him feel better.

I push the start button on the car and reverse out of the driveway.

NOW

Helena

I have no plan so I just drive, aimlessly, crossing over roundabouts and taking the path of least resistance at traffic lights, seeing where the roads will take me. It's only a few minutes before I notice Jack behind me. He's driving my mother's car. After I spot him, I refuse to look back. He can follow me all he likes. I'm not stopping yet.

Sophia begins to wriggle and wail on my lap, and I start to panic. I try to shush her, but she's frightened and unwieldy, and in the end I have to take one hand off the steering wheel and use the other to firmly restrain her. Before long, she is screaming, tears running down her fat cheeks. Her ears have turned bright red.

Of course, I am crying too. I am crying because my little girl shouldn't be sitting on my lap in the car, wailing with fright because she has no idea who this crazy woman is or why she has taken her. I am crying because I just want to be alone with my daughter, but I can't be, because Jack is following me, and there's no way I can escape him without doing something terribly dangerous that might kill us all. And now, after all these months, the last thing I want is to die. I want my baby. I want to be loved by my baby. I want to have known her and for the last year to be rewritten.

But it's not possible. I have come through the village and am back on the main road. My speed has dropped to a snail's pace, and Sophia seems to have worn herself out screaming and is now slumped against the side of my coat, using it as a makeshift pillow. I keep getting scared that she's stopped breathing, that the exertion of crying has somehow stopped her little heart, but every now and then she gives a heavy sigh, as though she's worldly-wise and already fed up of her useless mother. My tears continue to come and I kiss the top of her head. She's heavy, squished into her coat cocoon, pressing on my bladder.

At the next set of traffic lights the road splits into two lanes and I realize that the turning on the right, just ahead, will take me home. Jack pulls up next to me at the lights. The rain is finally starting to clear. I glance at him sideways, out of the corner of my eye, not daring to meet his gaze. But despite not looking at him directly I can see his animated gestures and imagine his frantic worry. I kiss Sophia's head again. She gives a soft murmur, like consent.

'Shall we go back to Daddy?' I say, and I am sobbing again, barely able to pull away when the lights turn green.

I take the turning towards our home, slowing to ten miles per hour, terrified that something will go wrong just before we get there. Wouldn't that be ironic? To crash at the very same place I once thought my baby had died.

I begin to wonder if I might be dreaming. If everything is a dream. I look in the rear-view mirror and watch Jack, his forehead furrowed with worry and concentration. His car is so very close to mine. He is leaning forward over the steering wheel, his lips aren't mouthing song lyrics as they usually are when he drives. Instead, his jaw is clenched, and I can imagine the tendon underneath his cheek pulsating as he focuses on one thing and one thing only: getting his daughter back alive.

In the end, I pull over at a passing place. I can't face that corner, can't take the risk. I put my hazard lights on and wait for him to come. Sophia has fallen asleep, and I bury my mouth and nose in her soft blonde hair, wiping my tears on my coat sleeve.

It's only seconds before Jack is at the side of my car. I look up at him, and I see that he is crying, too. His face is red with it, his eyes bloodshot and strained. I open the car door.

'Oh my God,' he says, and then he erupts, his whole body convulsing. 'Thank God . . . thank God . . .' he says in between his sobs.

'She's asleep,' I say, softly, my own tears suddenly stopping short.

He looks down at her, his eyes clouded with relief and love. He rubs his thumb across her hair, gives a short laugh.

'Of course she is,' he says, smiling with damp eyes. 'She loves the car. When she was tiny and wouldn't settle, I used to drive her around for miles . . .'

'I'm sorry,' I say, because I shouldn't have taken her, not like this, not without a proper seat. 'I . . .'

But he doesn't want my apologies.

'We need to get out of the road, to get home. Her car seat is in your mum's car. Let me take her.'

I look at him.

'Where will you take her? I want to see her. I want to be with her.'

He bites his top lip, his eyes unfocused as he decides my fate.

'OK, we can go back to ours. She's exhausted. Hopefully, she'll stay asleep and then we can talk.'

He leans down and gently, carefully, unclips my seat belt, guiding it back into position. I open my coat so that he can take her from me. As he lifts her out of the car my stomach suddenly feels cold. I miss the heat of her little body already. She was once there, inside me, and she belongs there still.

I watch as he carefully carries her back to my mother's car, opening the back door and sliding her into her seat. Her head flops forward and then back again, and her eyes flick open, but once she's in position she falls back to sleep without so much as a cry. She looks so peaceful, her head resting on the side of the car seat. Another memory rushes back to me: that first journey with her. Tucking her into her car seat in that waiting room, before we left for home. She looked so tiny, just a scrap of a thing coated in clothing. Now she fills it, her legs hanging over the edge, her head nearly reaching the top.

'You've changed so much,' I whisper.

'I'll see you at home,' Jack says, and I can't tell anything from his tone. At least he's stopped crying. As for me, as for my feelings, they have deserted me. I am comfortably numb.

It's only five minutes before I am back in the gravel driveway. I left here barely an hour and a half ago, but everything has changed. Everything I believed was wrong, back to front. Ashley is dead, my daughter is alive. How is it possible that I confused the two?

Jack brings the car seat with Sophia in it inside the house and puts it down in the hallway. She doesn't stir, doesn't move an inch, seemingly unaware of the drama of her momentary kidnap. I crouch down next to her. Her eyelids flicker as she sleeps, and I wonder what she's dreaming about, and I hope that it's comforting. I hope that she feels safe, that I haven't scared her.

'I'll make us some tea,' Jack says.

I follow him into the kitchen and watch, wondering what will happen next.

'Are you hungry?' he says as I sit on one of the bar stools, staring at the mug he places in front of me. The concept of drinking the tea right now, let alone eating something, feels bizarre, but this is Jack's way of bringing order to the chaos, normality to the insane.

'No,' I say. I have forgotten it's lunchtime.

'Me neither.'

There's a silence then, and I think that one of us should fill it with anger. That's what seems appropriate. I have every right to be angry with him for keeping my daughter from me, and he has every right to be angry with me for taking her and putting her life in danger. But neither of us has the energy for anger, it seems.

'Tell me what happened,' I say, instead, watching the surface of my tea still swirling as Jack stirs in the milk. 'Nothing makes sense.'

Jack gives a deep sigh but then, somehow, rights himself and sits down at the bar stool opposite me.

'You were very ill,' he says. 'Do you remember? You were very ill when Sophia was born.'

I search my memory but there's nothing. Only the grief, the absolute grief.

'I don't remember,' I say. 'I don't remember anything about the night of the crash.'

'We brought Sophia home the day after she was born. Do you remember your labour? You were in labour for three days. You didn't sleep. Your contractions stalled and Sophia got stuck, and in the end the doctor had to use forceps to get her out. You had a nasty tear. But you were fine. For those first twenty-four hours, you were fine. Exhausted, of course. But your blood pressure came down, everyone was happy.'

I shake my head at his words. I remember nothing of this. I blanked it all out afterwards, my way of protecting myself from the pain of remembering her.

'We took her home,' he continues. 'And that's when things started to change. You were worried, fussing continually, anxious that she didn't seem to be breastfeeding well. You didn't sleep that first night, because every time you put her down she would cry. She just wanted to be held. So you sat up with her and held her all night on the sofa. I came down in the morning and found you there. There was something different about you, even then. Your eyes seemed bigger, you were staring a lot, and you started talking fast. So fast. I could barely keep up.

'At first, I thought it was normal. Just your excitement and having Sophia, the relief of the labour and your stressful pregnancy being over. But it got worse. Your behaviour started to change even more. At some point, I told you to go upstairs and have a nap while I took over, and you went upstairs. But when I came to find you, you hadn't slept at all. You hadn't even laid down. You were in Sophia's nursery, going through all her clothes. You said they were all too big, you were sorting them out and throwing them away. I told you not to be silly, that she would grow, that we would still use them, but you insisted. Said something about it being a bad omen, that you'd bought the wrong size clothes. You ordered a whole load more online and paid extra to have them delivered that day. And then you spent the whole evening washing and ironing them, folding them neatly and putting them away in the drawers underneath her changing table. I remember . . . they were all white. Plain white Babygros. I asked you why and you said she was an angel, and she could only wear white. It was so unlike you. I couldn't tell if you were joking, or what. I didn't know what to do. I had no idea. I had no idea how sick you were.'

'I was just tired . . . I hadn't slept . . .'

'The midwives came to check on you the next day. You hadn't slept again. They were concerned, they wrote it down in their notes, they told you that you needed to rest. But you were in a flap about the breastfeeding. Sophia was a little small when she was born, and you were convinced she wasn't getting enough food. You'd started pumping, even though the midwives said there was no need, that Sophia was perfectly healthy. They told you to rest, and told me to keep an eye on you, and to get back in touch if you carried on behaving strangely. They were quite bossy – and when they left, you said they were idiots, which was also so unlike you.

'The next morning, I woke to find you downstairs again, in the utility room. You were washing everything again. You'd read something online about the chemicals they use to protect clothes from getting damp in factories, and you were paranoid that you hadn't got them all out, that Sophia might get sick. The irony was, Sophia was fine. She was fine, and you weren't.'

'But . . .' I say, 'the crying . . . I remember the crying. She was always crying. There was something wrong with her . . .' My voice fades to a whisper.

Jack ignores me.

'The next day I called the midwives again. The one who had visited us was on annual leave, and I had to speak to someone else. She tried to dismiss it all as baby blues. Said it was normal, that there were massive hormonal changes that happen a few days after you give birth. But I knew it was more than that. I was so frustrated. They weren't listening to me. They told me to ring again the next day, but by then it was too late . . .'

'I don't understand.'

'You had a fever by then. From the infection. Your stitches were infected. But there was more than that. You were ill. There's this thing . . . they don't talk about it much, it's very rare.' He gives a rueful laugh. 'Lucky us! It's called post-partum . . .'

He pauses then, and I know what he is going to say.

'Depression. I know,' I finish his sentence. My voice is flat, like my emotions. I remember promising never to succumb to the illness that stole my mother from me. I remember vowing never to let myself become a victim, vowing always to be strong.

'No,' he says, and his eyes flick heavenwards, as if calling for strength. 'Not post-partum depression. It was much more serious than that. You had post-partum psychosis.'

THEN

Helena

I am standing in the middle of the road, watching the headlights approach. Not caring if they hit me.

They don't. They stop short a few metres away, and then the driver's door opens and Jack steps out.

'Helena!' he shouts, but I don't move. 'What are you doing? Where's the baby?'

The baby.

I don't know.

'What's happened?'

He is next to me now, pulling on my shoulders, shaking me, trying to get answers. I can't speak. I just watch him as his face distorts and reddens. At one point I think he's going to slap me, but he doesn't. Instead, he shoves me to one side and runs past me. I turn round. Ashley's car – *I didn't even know she had a car* – is turned upside down, one wheel wrenched off. There's a strange hissing noise coming from beneath the bonnet. The smoke has faded now. From my position in the middle of the road I can see Ash, still slumped against the low cobblestone wall. But my baby. Where is she?

'It's OK,' I call out after him, but I'm confused, and I don't know if what I'm saying is true. I'm only saying it to calm him down. 'I think David took her.'

Seconds later, I hear Jack's voice again. He is shouting something. I turn round and see him, his phone against his ear, the baby cradled in one arm. He slumps to his knees and begins to sob.

'Come quickly!' he is saying into his phone. 'I can't tell if she's still breathing . . . please . . . please! She's so cold.'

He's taken her, then. She'll be up there, in the sky, with him. I have done what I was meant to do, and Ashley was there to witness it all. It's strange, how these things work out.

Finally, my mind is still. It is over. I can rest. She is safe, and so am I.

I walk towards the house, feeling lighter, liberated, at peace. Everything is going to be OK. I can never fail her again.

Inside, I climb the stairs to our bedroom as a free woman. I take off my soaked nightdress and step into the shower. The feeling of the warm water running all over my skin is incomparable. A rebirth. My rebirth. I watch as the blood and mucus run down the insides of my legs, mixing with the soapsuds and disappearing down the plughole. Afterwards, I dry myself carefully with a towel and pull on a pair of clean knickers and pyjamas.

There's a blue light outside the bedroom window, flickering. I have no idea what it is, but it's comforting. I climb into bed. And then, finally, I sleep.

NOW

Helena

I am back in the kitchen again. Back with Jack, sitting at our kitchen counter. The cup of tea is cold now.

'What happened?' I say, because there's nothing in my memory but a huge black hole. I have no idea. 'After the crash?'

'You were taken to hospital. Both of you,' he replies. 'You were in hospital for a month. They transferred you to a specialist psychiatric unit in the end, and you stayed there for ten weeks before they let you come home. Sophia was in hospital for three weeks.'

'But she had a . . .' My brain is crackling, like an old radio trying to tune itself. A single word forms, pushing itself forward from the noisy backdrop, '. . . seizure.'

'She developed hypothermia from lying in the road, out in the cold. When the ambulance arrived, she was unconscious. They took her to hospital, and in the ambulance she had a seizure. There were complications after . . . she was sedated, and put on a ventilator for a while, in intensive care for a week. But she's a tough thing, and she made a full recovery. While you were in the psychiatric hospital, and once she was well enough, we brought her to visit you, but you didn't want to know. You weren't yourself. You said she wasn't your

332

baby, you pushed her away from you, told us how sick we were to be trying to replace her with this other baby. We tried so many times, and then the final time you lost control, screaming at us all: your mother, me, the nurses. Saying we were lying, that your baby was dead. Asking us why we were tormenting you, how we could be so cruel. You were so sick. The doctors tried everything, all the usual drugs, but nothing seemed to work. You were convinced that Sophia had died. If we talked about anything else you were almost your normal self, but the second we tried to talk about her you would scream and cry and lash out.'

'It must have been the guilt,' I say, suddenly no longer scared. 'I bottled it all up. There's something I haven't told you . . .'

Jack smiles gently.

'About David? The night you nearly went home with him? You did tell me. You told me that Sophia was his baby, that she'd been taken away because you cheated . . . you were so ill, you were so confused. I spoke to him about it. He explained nothing had ever happened. He was quite honest with me, said he'd tried it on but that you'd rebuffed him. And look at her.' He smiles again. 'No doubt about it, she's one hundred per cent mine. But you wouldn't accept it. Kept telling me that the doctors were conspiring against you, that it was all a trick. At one point you were so angry you hit a nurse across the face. Eventually, we gave up. We stopped taking Sophia to see you. We stopped talking about her, and gradually you seemed to get better.'

'But I knew she was dead . . .' I say, even though I don't know anything now, and wonder how I could ever have been so sure. 'I felt it, when she left. I was so sure. How could I be so confused? How is it even possible?'

'Darling,' Jack says, 'you were ill.'

'And you've known about David? All this time? Why didn't you tell me?'

'Believe me, there were nights when I wanted to, when I just wished you were back to your old self and we could have a blazing row about it. But it wasn't important in the grand scheme of things. I just wanted you to get better. And after all, you changed your mind in the cab, made him drop you home. There was nothing to tell.'

'But what about my job? He – they – they stole it from me. And Ashley, she was so horrible to me . . .'

'I never trusted her. But it was just bad luck, you handing over such a valuable role to Ashley . . . Ashley worked the system all right. I'll never forgive KAMU for making you redundant when you were at your most vulnerable. It ought to be illegal. I know David felt guilty about it, thought he'd let you down. Well, he did. I wondered if it might have been revenge for you rejecting his advances, but I spoke to him afterwards, and he was as cut up about it all as I was.'

I look over at Sophia sleeping and wonder how I could ever have not known she was mine.

'When I heard her earlier,' I continue, 'I knew even from her cry that she was my baby. It doesn't make any sense. Why didn't I believe you?'

'The doctors thought it was your way of coping with what had happened, a side effect of the psychosis, the stress you felt during pregnancy, the infection you got . . . it was all linked. The perfect storm. It's called dissociative amnesia. Your brain just shut down. You were coping the only way you could, by forgetting the

334

parts that were too painful. We've been waiting so long for you to have a breakthrough. We've even taken you to see Sophia – several times, in fact – and for a while, you've understood what's happened, but you never remember it afterwards. We've tried everything to make the memories stick, and finally, we tried the one thing we haven't tried before. Your mum and I have been fighting for months about it. She didn't want you to have ECT, said it was barbaric. But I realized nothing else was working. It was the last resort.'

His voice breaks and he stops speaking. I reach out and take his hand, squeezing it, but he doesn't meet my eyes.

'It's been so hard,' he says, croakily. 'The hardest period of my life. Watching you lying on that trolley, knowing what they were going to do to your brain . . . wondering if you'd ever be back to normal again. Or if I'd lost you forever.'

The room with the speckled ceiling, the injection in my hand, the consultant with the oxygen mask, telling me the treatment would last only a few minutes. The headache afterwards. Going to bed and sleeping for fourteen hours.

'I thought that was for my depression . . .'

'It's an effective treatment for many things. It didn't work for your mother, that's why she was so against it. But it's been working for you. Except for the hallucinations. They're still there, but you're having them so much less often.'

I look out of the window, out at the road beyond, where the cobblestone wall once was.

'The accidents,' I say, and finally the clouds are clearing.

Jack stands up and pulls me towards him.

'There's only ever been one accident,' he says. 'The rest . . .

they were all just side effects of your illness. Replaying it all in your mind, trying to fix what can't be fixed. Confusing what's real with what isn't. Your brain's way of coping with the trauma.'

'The trauma of leaving Sophia in the road?'

'No,' Jack says, and there's a tenderness to his voice that I have only heard once before, when he first held Sophia, that afternoon in hospital when my life changed irrevocably. 'The trauma of watching Ashley die.'

NOW

Helena

Jack has just taken Sophia away from me again.

He has taken her back to my mother's. He said it's for the best, that it will take time for us to rebuild things, to make everything right again. He said he's worried I'll wake up tomorrow and I won't remember any of today. That I've had lucid moments before in the past, but that they've been snatched away as quickly as they've come.

I try to imagine ever not knowing her again, and the thought is too painful to bear.

I spoke to my mother briefly on the phone before Jack left, and thanked her for what she's done for me, for us. How I have misjudged her – all those years, thinking she'd failed me, when she was actually suffering, ill, just like me these past ten months. I think of the way Sophia gazed at her in the kitchen earlier, with love and, most importantly of all, *trust*, and wonder how I can ever make it up to her, how I can ever thank her enough for loving my little girl as much as I do.

I am sitting on the sofa, my pink blanket over my legs, cradling my phone. There is a photo on there now. A new one. Me and my baby. Except she's almost a toddler now; a giant, smiling thing, who threw her arms around my neck when she woke up, as though she loved me, despite everything I had done. They say babies always recognize their mother's smell. I hope it's not too late for us. I hope that I remember her tomorrow, and that she remembers me, too.

I keep pressing the main button on my phone, making the screen light up, looking at us, smiling together as a mother and daughter should. I am aching that she is no longer in the same house, that she has had to go back, but I know that I must put her first, and she needs stability, the familiar.

I press the button again.

I must remember her.

My phone lights up but then a warning screen flashes across it and it switches itself off. My battery is dead. I sigh and lay the phone down on the table. In my lap lies one of Sophia's muslin cloths. I pick it up and sniff it. That same scent, so unmistakably hers.

Before Jack left, he went upstairs, then came down several minutes later with a small present. I recognized the cursive handwriting on the card attached to it immediately. Curly, with looped letters, *pretty* almost, nothing like the bullish character she tried so hard to be all the time.

'I never opened it,' he said, as he handed it to me. 'It was addressed to you.'

The box is sitting in front of me now, on the coffee table. She was coming to see me that day, but what for? Just to give me this gift? How had we left things? I wish I could speak to her again, but I know I can't. I accept that now. I will never know what she wanted to say to me, so I can only hope. Hope that she still cared for me, despite all the times we disagreed.

I open the card. My fingers are shaking as I pull it stiffly from the envelope. On the front is a pencil drawing of a baby, all round cheeks and curly hair.

I open the card. Inside, there's just one word.

Congratulations.

And underneath; her name, spelled differently – *Ashleigh* – and a small, single kiss.

No great apologies. But I suppose she had done nothing wrong.

I open the box. Inside is a small silver photo frame. So plain and unremarkable that at first I don't notice there's something inscribed around the edges. The letters are tiny, and they feel bumpy as I run my fingers over them.

Here's to strong women. May we know them. May we be them. May we raise them.

That's it, then. Her final message to me: to raise my daughter to be strong. That's all Ash ever wanted to be. A strong woman. She just went about it all the wrong way, didn't realize you could be strong and kind at the same time.

I walk to the sideboard and reach into the bottom drawer, right at the back. I pull out my old work laptop, then scrabble about for the power cable. I haven't switched this on since I went into labour, and I'm not sure if it still works. I plug it in and open the lid. It takes a few minutes, but eventually the screen flickers into life.

I open Google. I don't have any pictures of Ashley. She wasn't the sort to take selfies – she was strangely shy about it, didn't seem to want to leave any evidence of her existence in the world.

But there are a few pictures out there of the two of us. One I remember in particular, from the pop-up party, taken before David arrived, before I went to pieces. It takes a few seconds of searching, but then I find it. We are standing on that little stage, our arms around each other's waists, our hair perfectly shiny and falling in sync, as though someone has styled it that way deliberately.

Our eyes are bright, wide, expectant, hopeful. And we are smiling at each other.

I run my finger over her face, think of what could have been.

And then I smile at what we were, if only for a short time. Two women, ready to take on the world.

AUTHOR'S NOTE

This book is a work of fiction. However, the seed of the idea came from my own experience of new motherhood. One of my friends once told me that giving birth was like being in a car crash, both physically and mentally. It stuck with me before I gave birth, and it proved to be surprisingly accurate.

I was 33 when I got pregnant, and although my daughter was very much longed for, I was shockingly naive and had no idea what to expect. I'd been a wholly selfish 'career woman' up to that point – I was a successful journalist and PR consultant and knew nothing about babies, or how to care for them. Once the first few months as a new mum were behind me, I was amazed not to be able to find any novels on this subject, given all the women I knew who were also struggling to forge a new identity as a mum after so long in the world of work. And so I decided to write this story – a story for women who have struggled with this transition, in the face of a working world that is still so stacked against us.

I was lucky and am grateful that I didn't suffer from post-natal depression, or, for that matter, postpartum psychosis. However, like many women, my sleep deprivation in those early days reached the point where I started hallucinating at night, imagining the baby was in bed with me when she was actually asleep in her cot, and my moods swung from euphoric to desperate with exhausting frequency.

To add to my stress, I unexpectedly found myself on maternity leave without a job to return to. Sadly, this is an all-too-common situation. It was utterly terrifying: this open-ended new 'life' that was completely alien to everything I had ever known, and that I was woefully underprepared for. And when I did secure some freelance work when my baby was only four months old, I was averaging three hours' sleep a night, none of my 'work' clothes fitted me, and I felt exactly as Helena does in the book: a misplaced lump between two stools. Not yet confident as a mother, no longer a career woman.

It was the strangest time of my life. I had been the old me for 34 years by then, but a mother for only a handful of months, and despite my ferocious love for my baby, I felt bewildered by who I had become. I'd never really realized how much my identity was tied up in my work and independence.

Not working was very strange, and in the middle of the night I'd panic that I should be doing something with this time 'off'. I read on someone's blog that when you have a baby, it's OK for you *just* to be looking after the baby. You don't have to be trying to hold down a part-time job too, or finishing a long-neglected novel (!), or doing charity work, or whatever it is that you think is necessary to justify your existence as a stay-at-home-mum. That helped, a little. But it was still hard to give myself permission to do 'nothing'. Even though I was exhausted and probably working harder than I had done in ages – just in a very different way.

I feel like I really lost myself in those early months. In fact, I would say it took a year for my confidence to return. Thankfully, I have a very supportive partner, who, due to the nature of his career, is around a lot more than most fathers. I genuinely believe my situation might have been very different were it not for the fact that I had my partner by my side every day during those life-changing early months as a new mother.

Because this is what it boils down to, in my opinion. Support. New mothers need support. They deserve support. It can make a crucial difference – can truly determine whether they sink or swim.

Post-partum psychosis is thankfully rare, but not so rare that we shouldn't be aware of it, or the signs, which include: mania, depression, hallucinations, delusions, confusion, muddled thinking and a lack of insight in understanding that their behaviour is strange. It is classed as a psychiatric emergency, and should be treated as such. It can occur out of the blue, in otherwise healthy women with no previous psychiatric problems, although it's thought there's a genetic link. In Helena's case, her mother had also suffered from it, and this not only defined their relationship, but was also the reason she didn't have any more children. What's important to remember is that with the right treatment, most women make a full recovery and go on to be fantastic mums, as I truly believe Helena will do!

I wanted to share some organizations that provide support to women going through what's often the most difficult period of their adult lives, whether or not they develop a clinical illness. Please support them, if you can, and share their details with anyone you think may benefit. Thank you, and thank you for reading.

Pregnant Then Screwed – campaigning for better rights for
working mothers:
http://pregnantthenscrewed.com/

Maternity Action – offering practical advice on maternal rights
and all things work-related in pregnancy:
https://www.maternityaction.org.uk/

Action on Postpartum Psychosis – providing information and peer
support specifically to sufferers of postpartum psychosis:
https://www.app-network.org/

ACKNOWLEDGEMENTS

I found out this book was going to be published when my agent, Caroline Hardman, rang me to say we'd had an offer. I was in the playground at the time with my toddler. Meanwhile, she was at home with a baby, technically on maternity leave, but working like a trooper to help me realize my dream. Given the novel's themes, I love the fact that we were both looking after children when the deal came through. It just proves that motherhood really doesn't need to mean the end of your career.

So, on that note, first and foremost I would like to thank Caroline, for all her support and enthusiasm for this story, and for working with me to get it in the best possible shape. I'd also like to thank her for answering all my Annoying Author Emails with the patience of a saint, for telling it to me straight, and for never giving up on me.

The team at Quercus have exceeded my expectations, and I would like to say a massive thanks to them too. My editor Cassie Browne's guidance and insight has improved my writing immeasurably – not just in this book but for the future too. I'd also like to thank Rachel Neely, for her painstaking work editorially, and for picking up on my cringeworthy inconsistencies! It has been an utter joy working with you both and I keep having to pinch myself. Thank you too Andrew Smith, for a cover that gave me goosebumps when I saw it.

There are lots of other people who had a hand in this book somewhere. My tutor at the Faber Academy, Joanna Briscoe, really renewed my faith in my writing with her encouragement and interest. Thank you for believing in me. And then of course, there's my whole Faber Academy gang – you have all been a constant support and the best cheerleading team I could have asked for.

My friend and fellow author Becky Fleet, who has held my hand through my entire writing 'career' to date and was the first reader of this book – thank you for everything! I'd also like to thank my superstar unicorns, Vicky Harrison and Susie Ewart-James, for all the Whatsapp chats and general angst dilution you provide.

On a more serious note, thank you to Alice Marlow and Claire Emerson for your help with the medical research for the book, and for answering all my macabre questions. I promise I won't write too many more books with sick/dead children in.

Finally (I'm trying my best not to write 'last but not least' but it's a challenge . . .) my family. Mum, Dad and Poph, thank you for being so proud. And then of course, my own little team, Daphne and Oli. You're what it's all about. Thank you Daphne for napping (sometimes) enough that I could get my face back in front of my laptop. But most of all, thank you Ol for uncomplainingly taking on more than your fair share of the domestic load so that I could write this. If more men were like you, the world would be a much better place.